SHATTERED

DI KATE FLETCHER BOOK 5

HELEYNE HAMMERSLEY

BLOODHOUND
— BOOKS —

ALSO BY HELEYNE HAMMERSLEY

DI KATE **F**LETCHER **S**ERIES:

Closer to Home (Book 1)

Merciless (Book 2)

Bad Seed (Book 3)

Reunion (Book 4)

Suspense thrillers:

Forgotten

Fracture

Don't Breathe

...for 'The Gals'

1982

The cold is like a person: a big man with a lot of power who rules and controls all our movements and won't let us rest. He gets into my sleeping bag with me, under all my layers of clothes, and keeps me awake for a long time. He's everywhere, under everybody's blankets, in everybody's eyes. I hate him but I can't escape him because there's nowhere to go. We *have* to be here. That's what Mum says; that's what all the women say. Mum made me hold up a sign yesterday in front of three policemen who'd come to take some of the women away. It said: *when I grow up I want to be alive.* Huge letters, black on a white background like a headline in a newspaper but much bigger. The policemen were nice. They smiled a lot and made some of the women laugh but their eyes were hard because they have to do their job and their job is to stop us.

Mum says that what we're doing here is important; more important than staying at home and cooking and looking after me and Dad. She says that we're going to change the world but I'm not sure how freezing and trying to not let the policemen see us is going to do that. Some days it feels like a big game but sometimes it's scary and the women cry and make that funny high-pitched noise called keening. I thought keen meant that you like something, but this sound is more like pain.

We came here because of a letter that Mum got in the post a few days ago. She didn't let me read it, she just put lots of our clothes in a suitcase, rolled up our old sleeping bags and dragged me out to the main street where we waited for ages. I thought we were waiting for a bus, but we weren't at the stop and I tried to tell Mum this, but she just ignored me. Her lips were set in a straight line and her eyes stared in front of her, but she didn't seem to be seeing what was there on the street. She was lost in her own mind, I think, like something had taken over her body and was working the arms and legs like a puppet.

A van turned up after a long time and the back doors opened like arms reaching out to give us a hug. Mum lifted me up and somebody grabbed me and sat me down on a wooden bench then she followed me in and the doors closed behind us with a big clang like prison gates. The back of the van was gloomy and it was hard to see who was there but I eventually saw that there were four women, all smoking and staring at nothing, like Mum had been.

We put up a tatty red tent that one of the van women had given us right next to another two tents that were even tattier. Even though we were camping on the grass there wasn't much green. Instead, there was a lot of red and orange and dingy white canvas completely swamping the ground. The only space was right next to the huge fence where a strip had been left as though there was a force field around the wire that nobody could get close to. But we did get close to it – the very next day.

I didn't really understand what was happening, but Mum made me stand up against the fence and hold her hand, then

2

she held hands with the woman to her left and I put my gloved fingers up for the woman on my right to hold. I leaned back, looking along the length of the fence and all I could see was a line of women stretching into the distance until they disappeared round a corner. It was the same the other way – just heads and faces, all peering at whatever was inside the fence, all silent.

That was the first day. There have been a lot of days since then.

1

'Christ, I'm glad I'm not on call anymore,' a deep voice muttered as DI Kate Fletcher rolled over and groped around the surface of the bedside table for her mobile phone. It was his usual comment whenever she got an early-morning call and, while not an objection, it was always delivered as a grumble. As an oncology consultant at Doncaster Royal Infirmary, Nick Tsappis's hours were predictable and sociable, but he'd put up with Kate's career for the two years they'd been seeing each other without much complaint. Now though, they'd agreed to try living together and Kate was worried that he might not be as tolerant if he had to live with the unpredictability of her job all the time.

He'd done all the groundwork: found a house that suited them both when she'd refused to move into his and he'd just laughed when she'd suggested they share her flat; he'd put both their properties on the market when she'd finally agreed to buy a new place and he'd made himself available to prospective buyers. The big move was scheduled for later in the summer and Nick had offered to help Kate with her packing, but it felt like a step too far. She needed time to sift and sort.

'Dan,' she said, as DC Dan Hollis's number flashed on the screen. 'What's up? It's half past bloody six.'

'I know. Sorry. Barratt called – he's on the early shift – a body turned up in a house in Bessacarr. Looks very much like a suicide. There's a note, no sign of forced entry. The body's female. Wrists slashed in a bath full of water.'

'But?' She knew her team wouldn't be involved in a straightforward suicide.

'But the woman also cut her own throat, deeply.'

'Sounds a bit odd,' Kate agreed, trying to imagine the scene.

'It gets better. She smashed the mirror in her hallway and used a sharp piece to do the damage.'

Kate tucked the phone between her shoulder and neck and slid out of bed, mouthing an apology to Nick, before stumbling to the bathroom. 'Not the most obvious choice of weapon.'

'No. And, according to Barratt, there are no signs on her hands that she handled the glass. It's very sharp and there should have been cuts to her fingers if she'd applied any pressure.'

'Who found her?'

'The daughter, Sadie Sullivan. The mother's name is Julia. They were supposed to have met for a drink last night, but the mother didn't turn up. The daughter tried the house phone and the mobile but got no reply. She couldn't sleep so tried again this morning and then went round.'

'The daughter had a key?'

'Sounds like it. This is all second-hand from Matt. I'll text you the address.'

Hollis got out of his car as Kate pulled up in her Mini. The street was wide and tree-lined, located well away from the main road that ran from Doncaster to Bawtry. There were hardly any cars parked on the street itself, instead each driveway housed at least one vehicle, most of them expensive-looking. It wasn't an area that Kate knew well – regarded as one of Doncaster's more affluent suburbs, home to head teachers, solicitors and at least one former chief constable of South Yorkshire Police. It was also where Nick had wanted them to buy a house until Kate had pointed out her own lack of middle-class credentials.

She nodded a greeting to Hollis who looked uncomfortable in a dark suit, white shirt and a deep blue tie – his blond hair already beginning to spike with sweat. It was too hot to be dressed so formally but she knew that Dan wouldn't let appearances slip if he could help it. Being well over six feet tall, his height drew attention and he definitely wanted to be looked at for the right reasons.

'Number seven,' he said, pointing to a compact detached house behind a recently trimmed leylandii hedge. Kate would have known which house it was without Hollis's direction. There was a plain white van in the driveway and two liveried police cars parked opposite.

'Kailisa's here already?' she asked, nodding towards the van and referring to the pathologist who she'd clashed with on a number of occasions.

'Looks like it,' Dan said as they passed the van.

Kate flashed her ID at the PCSO standing next to the front door and stepped into a wide hallway, her footsteps echoing on the hardwood floor as she approached the stairway. A door opened to her right and DC Matt Barratt appeared looking flustered. He was a trusted member of her team and she knew that, if he was agitated, there was something odd about the case. Barratt liked the detail of his work, poring over statements and diagrams and positing theories that were usually perceptive.

'In here,' he said. She gave the stairs one last longing glance before following his direction – she'd hoped to see the body *in situ* and have a chat with Kailisa before dealing with any grieving relatives.

The cool green of the hallway was continued on the walls of the sitting room creating a feeling of calm that was echoed in the cream sofa and hearth rug. Whoever had decorated had good taste. A woman was perched on the edge of the sofa, one hand clasped round the remains of a tissue, the other, clutching the cushion next to her. She looked to be in her mid-forties although the lack of make-up could have been ageing and the streaks of grey in her dark hair may have been a fashion choice. Dressed in grey tracksuit bottoms and a pale-blue T-shirt, she looked like she'd just been for a run, or just got out of bed.

'Sadie Sullivan,' Barratt said. 'Julia's daughter.'

Kate offered the woman a thin smile before sitting on one of the two armchairs that faced the window, her synapses tingling. *Julia Sullivan.* The name was familiar.

'I'm sorry for your loss,' Kate began. 'I can only imagine how awful–'

Sadie lifted her head, skewering Kate with cat-like amber eyes. 'You don't have to imagine. She's still upstairs in the bath. Why don't you go up and have a look? Everybody else has.'

Kate shifted in her seat, uncomfortably aware that her first thought had been to view the body and that Hollis was probably up there now.

'I appreciate this is difficult,' Kate said. 'But I need to ask you some questions.'

'About who might kill my mother? I could write you a list, but it'd take all bloody day.' The woman's belligerence was disconcerting, as was her certainty that this was murder.

'Can you talk me through what happened,' Kate prompted. 'You were supposed to meet your mother last night?'

Sadie sat back, dropped the cushion and crossed her hands

in her lap. 'We were meant to be having a drink. I'd been over earlier in the day, but she'd been busy – church stuff I suppose. She'd fallen out with Dad again and I'm usually the mediator. I'd got Dad's side of the story on the phone a few days ago and Mum wanted to give me hers but she didn't have the time, so we agreed to meet later. I should have known something was wrong as soon as I realised she wasn't going to turn up. She never misses a chance to twist the knife where *he's* concerned.'

'Your parents have split up?' Kate asked.

'Not exactly,' Sadie said. 'They've always had a volatile relationship, so they've been living apart for the past few months. Dad moved out in April and lives in his studio now. I think Mum wanted to buy him out of this place. To be frank, I don't know what's going on between them and I was hoping to piece it all together last night.'

Kate looked at Barratt who was scribbling in his notebook. They would need to speak to the husband as a priority.

'They've not really got on since Mum stood for the local council. She's been especially vocal about immigration and Dad doesn't want to be associated with her views. He thinks it'll damage his reputation.'

'His reputation?'

'He's an artist. Lincoln Sullivan? Darling of the left. It's not good for him to be married to a right-wing councillor – especially one who seems… seemed to be lurching further to the right with each passing day.'

That's why the name was familiar. Julia Sullivan had appeared in the local press on a few occasions recently, mostly complaining about the number of refugee families being housed in the Doncaster area. Kate was also familiar with the work of Lincoln, Sadie's father, renowned for his detailed depictions of scenes from the industries which had built the region – steel and coal. The media were going to be all over this case.

'What made you come here this morning?' Kate asked. 'Why not see if your mother was here last night?'

'I'd started to get the feeling that she was having an affair,' Sadie admitted with a sigh. 'This wasn't the first time she'd not turned up to meet me. And she'd often go into a different room to answer the phone. I know it's not conclusive, but I know her – there was something odd going on.'

Sadie glanced at Barratt, the movement eerily familiar, as though she was making sure that he was noting everything down. It was something Kate often did during an interview.

'I thought I'd just leave her to it and come round in the morning, but I couldn't sleep so I got dressed and came round as soon as it got light. If it meant I woke her up well, serves her right, she shouldn't have stood me up.' The woman slumped to one side as she seemed to realise the significance of her words; that she would never have another chance to be disappointed by her mother.

'Can you tell me what you saw when you came into the house?'

Sadie shook her head. 'Nothing. I just walked in and went upstairs to see if she was in bed. That's when I saw the mirror. It's in the upstairs hallway, next to the bathroom door. It was broken, pieces of glass everywhere. I was going to go into her bedroom when I heard a noise from the bathroom, like a tap dripping into a full bath. It sounded odd, so I pushed the door open and I found her.' The last three words were distorted by a tremble in the woman's voice as she struggled to hold back tears.

Kate nodded. 'I was told there was a note. Where did you find it?'

'On top of the toilet cistern. It just said that she'd had a good life but it was time. I couldn't believe it. There's no way I would have expected her to kill herself.'

Kate glanced at Barratt to see if he'd noticed the discrepancy with what she'd said earlier. He frowned slightly. He'd heard it too.

'Sadie,' Kate said gently. 'Earlier you said something about writing a list of people who might have killed your mother. Now you're saying it was suicide.'

Those amber eyes fixed on Kate again. 'I *thought* it was suicide at first. That's what it was made to look like. Classic – wrists slashed in the bath. But when I saw her throat, I knew she couldn't have done it herself. It didn't make sense. Her wrists were deeply cut – how could she have raised a hand and then had the control to slit her own throat? And if she did the throat first how could she have had the strength to cut her wrists? She was murdered, I'm certain.'

It was exactly what Hollis had told her. She was about to ask more about Sadie's grisly discovery when she heard footsteps pounding down the stairs. Hollis stepped into the room wearing a white protective suit, his hair dishevelled as if he'd just tugged the hood down.

'Can you come upstairs for a minute? We've found something interesting.'

After mumbling an apology to Sadie, who seemed to have barely registered the interruption, Kate followed Hollis up to where Kailisa was waiting on the landing, a large digital camera in his hand.

'DI Fletcher,' he said, unsmiling. 'I'd heard you'd arrived.'

Kate nodded. 'You've found something?'

He handed her the camera, display screen facing her. 'It's a photograph of Julia Sullivan's ankle. This is the clearest image I have. If you want to see the real thing, you'll have to put on a suit.' He looked her up and down as if to say that white coveralls might be an improvement on her dark trousers and pale-grey blouse.

'What is it?' she asked, peering at the screen.

'A tattoo.'

Kate tilted the screen slightly to reduce the glare and made out a clear shape against the pale skin of Julia Sullivan's leg. It was crude, possibly done by a friend rather than a professional, but the shape was still clear. A cross below a circle. The scientific symbol for female. And a popular emblem for feminism.

'It's not recent, is it?' Kate asked.

Kailisa shook his head making the hood of his overalls flop around his face. 'Looks like it was done at least ten years ago judging by the blurring at the edges. The ink has dissipated through the surrounding flesh. And it's not very professionally drawn.'

Kate stared at the image again. It made no sense. Why would somebody who appeared to be the epitome of right-wing conservatism be tattooed with a symbol associated with views that were almost the exact opposite?

'Julia Sullivan.' Kate opened the briefing with a slide showing a picture of the councillor standing at a podium, her fist clenched at shoulder height as if to emphasise a point. Her short dark hair looked like it was sticking to her temples and her screwed-up face was flushed. 'Local councillor, independent rather than with a party, known for her anti-immigrant views and her fundamental Christian faith which she claimed confirmed her opinions on just about any subject. According to her daughter, Julia had some sort of religious conversion a few years ago. It caused a rift in the family, but she remained married to her husband. He's a painter.'

'Lincoln Sullivan?' DC Sam Cooper asked. 'And the daughter – is she Sadie?'

'You know them?' Kate sipped her latte, allowing Cooper time to explain. The DC spent a lot of her work time data mining to help with cases – was it possible she'd come across the family in that context?

'Sadie's a children's author. My sister's kids love her books. I don't know much about Lincoln.'

Blank looks all round. None of the team had young children.

'Well, she's fairly well known. Got a bit of stick about having help from her father but, as far as I've read, she does all the words and illustrations herself – it's nothing to do with him.'

Sadie hadn't mentioned her profession to Kate, only her father's, but the background didn't seem to help them.

'Moving on,' Kate said, tapping the keyboard of her laptop. In the next image Julia Sullivan looked much less aggressive – it showed her slumped forwards in a bath almost full of bloody water. The wounds on her wrists were clearly visible but the one on her neck was obscured by her hair, longer than in the first photograph, and the angle of the shot.

'Mrs Sullivan was found by her daughter who'd been concerned about her mother not turning up for a meeting with her and then not answering her phone. According to Sadie, she couldn't sleep so she went round to Julia's house and let herself in. This is what she found. And this.'

The next image showed the neck wound and the blood spatter up the tiles next to the bath.

'Whoa!' O'Connor said. 'That's a bit extreme.' He looked genuinely shocked, his red hair and beard standing out starkly against his pale skin. It *was* a startling image but she hadn't expected such a strong reaction. As her detective sergeant, Kate would have expected him to have seen much worse.

'And unlikely,' Barratt interjected. 'According to Kailisa she couldn't have made all three cuts herself.'

'Was there any sign of a struggle?' O'Connor asked. 'How could you get somebody to sit calmly in a bath while you cut them to shreds?'

'Nothing,' Barratt said. 'The only blood spatter seems to be arterial from the throat wound. Kailisa suspects she was drugged but we'll have to wait for the lab report.'

Kate raised her eyebrows at the four detectives who were now sitting to attention. 'Not a suicide then, despite this note.'

She projected the image of the A4 paper that had been placed on top of the toilet cistern and weighted down with a tub of hand cream.

Life has been a gift but I have to go now.

It had been printed in a clear font rather than written by hand.

'Strange wording,' O'Connor mused. 'I *have* to go. Almost like there's a compulsion or something forcing her to do this.'

'Or forcing the killer,' Hollis added. 'The use of "have" might suggest that the killer feels *compelled* to murder her. He *has* to get rid of her for some reason.'

'Good call,' Kate said. She'd had the same feeling. There was a reason for this murder, a purpose known only to the killer. If they could work out what it was, they might be able to find the perpetrator.

'Like a cleansing?' Cooper suggested. 'He's getting rid of her because he feels that she deserves it for some reason. Maybe a reference to some of the stuff she's said over the past few months.'

O'Connor snorted. 'Christ, just look on Twitter – lots of people make unpleasant comments about immigrants and transsexuals and gays. Our killer's going to be busy if he's going to wipe them *all* out.'

He's right, Kate thought – there had to be something more specific, some perceived slight or something that the killer found completely intolerable. This didn't feel random. The scene was intimate, the woman naked in the bath, and there had been no sign of forced entry. The more she thought about the note, the more convinced Kate was that the victim knew her murderer – possibly quite well. There were mugs and plates in the kitchen which had all been photographed and bagged to be swabbed for DNA and checked for fingerprints. She'd watched as one of the SOCOs had hoovered sections of the bedroom and bathroom floors and she knew that the doormat in the hall had also been taken away for analysis. Anything that might give a clue about the attacker's identity had been identified, bagged and sent to the labs. Unfortunately, the results could take days. There were other avenues to explore while they waited, and she needed to get her team focused and moving.

'Sam,' she said to Cooper. 'We need to find out about Julia Sullivan's social media presence. Find out what she'd been saying and how people were responding. Look at her Twitter feed if she has one, and Facebook. Did she have regular comments from one particular person? Were there any threats made?'

Cooper nodded and made a note on her tablet.

'Steve and Matt...'

'Post-mortem?' Barratt interrupted.

'It's this afternoon. This morning I want both of you working with the uniforms doing the house-to-house in Julia Sullivan's street. They'll be focused on who saw what, but I want you to get an impression of what they thought of the woman. Was she well liked, or did they find her views obnoxious? Had she argued with anybody? Ruffled any feathers for reasons other than political ones?

'Dan, with me to speak to Lincoln Sullivan. The daughter implied that they were separated – I want to know why and to find out what he can tell us about his wife's past.'

The job allocation felt insubstantial. They needed a strong lead, something to give the team focus and momentum but, in the absence of such a lead, all Kate could do was try to cover all bases in the hope that a pattern emerged from all the separate lines of enquiry.

3

L incoln Sullivan's studio was on the top floor of a converted factory just off York Road to the north of Doncaster. The building appeared to be Victorian in construction – red brick with arched, sandstone windows, all sandblasted clean of the black sootiness of the town's industrial past. Now, perched incongruously behind a KFC and a discount pet food superstore, the building had a prehistoric quality – an elderly relative presiding over a gathering of younger family members.

'I had no idea this was here,' Hollis said, craning his neck for a better view of the upper windows. 'And I use this road every day.'

'It's well hidden,' Kate agreed. 'Not the quietest spot for an art studio though. I would have thought he'd have wanted somewhere more peaceful to get the creative juices flowing.' She scanned the column of names next to the intercom system and pressed the button next to 'Sullivan'. After waiting for a minute, she pressed again. This time a voice responded.

'Yes?'

'Mr Sullivan?'

'Yes.' The middle vowel was drawn out, reluctantly acknowledging the name.

'I'm DI Kate Fletcher. I'm here with DC Hollis. We'd like to talk to you about your wife. I thought you'd be expecting us.'

A long pause. 'Of course. I'm sorry, I'm afraid I rather lost track of the time. Please, come in. Top floor. The door on the left.'

A buzz and a click and Kate pushed the door open.

'Nice,' Hollis breathed as he followed her into a large atrium. The huge arched window – which had probably once been the main door onto the factory floor – flooded the area with light. A dark-red steel staircase led up the right-hand wall to a door then continued, cutting across the window to a door in the opposite wall. Kate turned, following its progress along the wall above them to the third floor where it split to allow access to two more doors.

'Impressive,' she agreed. Their footsteps rang hollow tones as they ascended, and Kate wondered how annoying she'd find the sounds of her neighbours coming and going with each tuneless note. On the highest landing, the door to the left was ajar and Kate saw that her musings about the noise level had been anticipated by the building planners – the door was steel-fronted and at least three inches thick.

'Mr Sullivan?' Kate pushed the door further open and stepped into a bright hallway with white walls and blond wood flooring. 'Mr Sullivan?'

A head emerged from a door to the right. Kate had seen photographs of the painter, but they hadn't prepared her for his sheer physical presence. As he stepped out into the hall, she saw that he was heavily built and tall – taller than Hollis – his mane of grey hair was swept back from a broad face that, in the harsh light, was all lines and shadows. Wearing a baggy, dark-blue T-shirt and paint-spattered tracksuit bottoms that might once have been grey he looked like a giant toddler who'd been sent out of class for making too much mess with the colours.

'Sorry I didn't answer the door straight away, bit busy finishing my latest commission,' Sullivan said, splaying his huge hands in apology. 'Please, come through.'

As she followed Sullivan into his studio, she struggled to suppress a smile as Hollis whispered, 'Gordon's alive.' Sullivan's resemblance to Brian Blessed, another of South Yorkshire's famous sons, was hard to miss.

The studio was a huge room, lit from both sides by the arched windows that Hollis had spotted from below. The wood floor continued, scuffed and spotted with paint, to a kitchenette and an area hidden by a Japanese-style screen in a cream fabric. In the opposite corner a battered brown sofa and two plastic patio chairs crowded round a small coffee table. If Sullivan was living here it was an almost monastic existence.

'I'd apologise for the mess,' Sullivan said with a smile. 'But I'm not sorry. I don't have many visitors; this is my space, so I keep it how I like it.'

In the middle of the vast expanse of floor was a pair of easels holding a large canvas, at least four feet across and three tall. It was facing away from Kate, obviously to maximise the light from the arched windows, but her curiosity overcame her politeness. She'd seen prints of Sullivan's work but had never had a chance to view the real thing.

'May I?' she asked, already moving towards the painting. Sullivan shrugged, his indifference bordering on arrogance as he turned his back to fill a kettle and wash two mugs.

The piece was just as striking as the others Kate had seen in magazines, but seeing Sullivan's work in the flesh, newly painted and huge, was breathtaking. It depicted a modern mining scene with the coal face as a backdrop for a pair of miners, stripped to the waist, holding pneumatic tools. One had turned to the other, their faces caught in the light of an electric lamp suspended above the black seam of mineral, his expression grimly determined. The character of each man seemed to leap from the canvas amid the light and sweat and dust.

'That's amazing,' Kate said, lost for anything more profound to say.

Sullivan simply nodded and opened a jar of coffee.

'Drink?'

Hollis accepted but Kate shook her head, still transfixed by the painting. She moved position and the faces seemed more shadowed, the light emphasising the shine of the fresh coal. Another shift and her focus was drawn to the gloved hands of the man on the left. It was almost as though the work contained a series of optical illusions.

Reluctantly, Kate crossed to the sofa and sat down. Hollis followed her lead and plonked his lanky frame in one of the patio chairs, looking uncomfortable and out of place. Sullivan placed a mug in front of Dan and squeezed into the other seat, nursing his own drink between his huge hands.

'Firstly, can I say how sorry I am about your wife,' Kate began. 'It's...'

'Ex-wife,' Sullivan corrected her.

'Oh, I didn't realise you were...'

'It wasn't official, but I'd spoken to my solicitor. The machinery of divorce had been set in motion. Neither of us had told our daughter but we'd agreed that a permanent split was for the best.' He gave a rueful smile. 'And I suppose that makes me prime suspect in my wife's murder.'

'Can I ask why you split up?'

Sullivan took a deep breath and his eyes drifted towards one of the windows. 'Irreconcilable differences. Isn't that the phrase that's used? We'd stopped seeing eye to eye a while ago, but it was becoming increasingly acrimonious. I suggested that we live apart for a while, but Julia wasn't keen. I moved in here, leaving her the house – there wasn't much she could do to stop me.'

'These differences,' Kate asked. 'What sort of things did you fall out about?'

The man shifted in his seat, obviously struggling with the confinement of the rigid plastic chair. Kate's choice of the sofa hadn't been accidental – she wanted Sullivan to feel unsettled.

'She'd had a religious conversion. Two years ago, she was nearly killed in a car accident and her lucky escape changed her. She got it into her head that God had chosen to save her and give her a purpose. She stood for public office – as an independent – and got herself elected to the local council. I assume you've read some interviews with her? Seen her odious remarks?'

Hollis was scribbling in his notebook. He looked up suddenly. 'Right wing?'

'Her views were fairly intolerant of minorities, immigrants, anybody who wasn't just like her. It was quite a change. She never used to be like that at all. Whenever we spoke about it, she simply told me that I couldn't understand as I hadn't embraced Jesus.' Sullivan took a sip of his coffee and stared into the mug.

'You say she wasn't always like that. What was she like before her... conversion?'

'She was kind, tolerant. When she was younger she was quite outspoken, but her views were always in favour of the underdog. She hated Thatcher with a passion, loathed the privatisation of our services, supported the miners and their wives during the strike.'

It was quite an about-turn, Kate reflected. She'd heard the adage that, as we age, our waists get wider and our minds narrower, but this seemed much more dramatic and much more sudden. 'What did your daughter think of her mother's new world view?' Kate asked.

'She was as shocked as I was. But a lot more tolerant. It's easier to walk away from the person you've chosen to spend a life with than the person who you're tied to through blood.'

Out of the corner of her eye, Kate saw Hollis sit up slightly at the mention of blood.

'Have you spoken to your daughter since she found her mother?'

Sullivan nodded, his mane of grey hair tumbling around his shoulders. 'We went to the police station together yesterday evening to have our fingerprints and DNA sampled. We're not the best of friends at the moment. We chat on the phone from time to time but I often get the feeling that she calls out of a sense of duty rather than any genuine attachment. You'd think something like this might bring us closer together, but Sadie just rang to give me the facts, that her mother had been killed and that we had to give samples for elimination purposes. She didn't tell me how she was feeling. I suppose she might have been in shock. When I picked her up, she didn't say much, and we went our separate ways after leaving the police station. I take it you've spoken to her? Is she doing okay? She's not got a partner at the moment – I think she's a bit like me and gets lost in her work. I hate the thought of her having to deal with this alone.'

A rather strange image of the Sullivan family was developing in Kate's mind. Earlier she'd thought she'd detected a tone of disapproval when Sadie spoke about her mother's views but now it seemed as if it was the two women pitted against Lincoln. The background questions didn't seem to be taking them any further forwards – it was time to focus on the murder.

'Where were you last night?' Kate asked.

Sullivan smiled. 'I thought we might get round to that eventually. I've already given a statement – I was here, working.'

'Can anybody verify that?'

'No. I was alone. Unusually, I'm working to a deadline. This piece has been commissioned by the National Coal Mining Museum – they've got a big anniversary coming up and an Arts Council grant for a new display. It's being collected later.'

'Would your neighbours have been aware that you were here? Would they have heard if you'd gone out?'

'I doubt it. You've seen the thickness of these doors.'

'And when were you last at the house you'd shared with your wife?'

'The fourteenth of April – it was my birthday, so I chose to finally leave my wife as a present to myself.'

Hollis snorted in surprise and tried to cover it up with a cough.

'I know how that sounds,' Sullivan said, turning to Dan. 'But it really was the most sensible thing I could do for myself. We weren't getting on and there was no common ground left. My work was suffering and, honestly, there was no reason to maintain the pretence of a solid marriage. On my part at least. I didn't want to carry on sharing a house with somebody I didn't like. The woman I'd married was gone long before her death.'

'Your daughter thought Julia might be having an affair,' Kate said.

Sullivan threw his head back and let out a booming laugh. 'Sadie likes to see things that aren't there. I wasn't in the least bit surprised when she became a writer – she always had an overactive imagination. Julia's new religious beliefs wouldn't have permitted infidelity; I was about to test whether they would permit divorce.'

There was a germ of motive here, Kate thought. If Julia Sullivan had already refused her husband his divorce would it be reason enough for him to kill her? Or if he'd discovered an affair would he have murdered her out of rage, or to protect his reputation? Either scenario was vaguely plausible.

'Can you think of anybody who would want to harm your

wife... ex-wife? Had she had a recent falling out with a neighbour for instance?'

Sullivan snorted. 'I can think of lots of people who would have liked to give her a good slap – myself included – and I know, that's not very PC. But Julia had become infuriating in her conviction that she was right about everything and only people who shared her beliefs could possibly understand.'

There was something slightly pompous in his tone that was making Kate dislike the man. Her initial impression of him as welcoming and forthright was being replaced by distaste. She glanced at Hollis who was still scribbling in his notebook and could infer from his upright position that he was feeling something similar. Lincoln Sullivan might be innocent of his wife's death, but he wasn't a pleasant man to spend time with.

'I think that's all we need for now,' Kate said, struggling awkwardly to her feet from her position on the low sofa. Hollis snapped his notebook shut and pocketed it before following her to the door.

'Just one thing,' Kate said, turning back. 'We'll need someone to formally identify your wife's body. As next of kin would you be happy to do that?'

If he registered her deliberate choice of words, Sullivan showed no response, he simply agreed and ushered them out onto the landing.

'Well that was–' Before Hollis could finish his sentence Kate's phone rang. Cooper.

'What have you got, Sam?'

Cooper's voice on the other end of the line sounded shaky. 'I'd rather not say over the phone. I think you're going to want to see this.'

4

'Jesus, that's vile,' Hollis spluttered, reading over Cooper's shoulder. 'I thought it was usually extreme right-wingers who post this sort of shit.'

Cooper ran a hand through her blonde hair and seemed faintly puzzled when it got caught around her neck. She'd been growing it for a few months and it finally seemed to have settled into a style but, Kate could see, she still wasn't used to the length.

'It's anybody who feels safe hiding behind the anonymity of the internet,' Cooper said. 'There are a lot of people out there who feel it's fine to say anything they want as long as it's 'only' online. I doubt they have any particular opinion about Julia's views but she's a public figure and fair game in their minds.'

Kate leaned in and read the three tweets that Cooper had copied and pasted into a Word document. They were graphic and threatening. One said that they knew where Julia lived and would come round to her house and rape her. Another threatened to kill her by running her down in the street and the final one, the most chilling, was a threat to slit her throat.

'Bloody hell.' She sighed. 'There are some real nutters out there. How credible are these threats, Sam?'

Cooper tapped on her keyboard and pulled up the profile of the person who'd sent the final threat.

'This one's been the hardest to track down. The other two seem to systematically abuse women in positions of power whatever their political affiliation. I've flagged them up for further investigation, but they don't sound as personal as the other one – especially when you read them in the context of tweets to other women. The one who threatens to cut Julia's throat has three followers and doesn't follow anybody else. The account was set up in the last few months and the tweets are mainly innocuous, stuff about politics and how the people are being lied to by the government. I have no idea why they homed in on Julia Sullivan, but this feels a bit more personal than the others.'

'Killing somebody by cutting their throat is about as personal as it gets,' Kate observed. 'It's close contact and potentially messy.'

Hollis took a step back and settled into a chair. 'But it's also a common threat,' he said. 'There are plenty of reports about people being threatened with stabbing, rape and having their throat cut. There's something medieval about it that seems to appeal to a particular type of nutter.'

'I don't think it's medieval,' Sam said. 'It's more like something that would happen in hand-to-hand combat.'

'Like *Braveheart*?'

Kate smiled to herself. The two detective constables were getting side-tracked, but it was interesting to listen in on their conversation. They were both shrewd, and bouncing ideas off each other often led to some interesting insights. 'So, this is a war?' she suggested. 'A struggle for what? Dominance, justice?'

Cooper's eyes lost focus as she raised them to the ceiling, deep in thought.

'No,' Hollis said. 'That doesn't fit with the suicide note. Why would this person not want to claim their trophy, their handiwork?'

'But they must have known that we wouldn't be fooled. Unless they were completely forensically unaware and who's ignorant about evidence these days?'

'I still think it's personal,' Cooper said. 'How did the killer get the victim into the bath? Was he already in the house? There was no sign of forced entry, so it might have been somebody she knew.'

'Her clothes were in a pile on her bed. They weren't torn or cut, suggesting Julia took them off herself.'

'Or she was drugged and compliant as he undressed her,' Kate suggested.

'Or already dead.'

Hollis shook his head at Cooper's comment. 'No. There was arterial spatter on the tiles. She still had blood pressure when her throat was cut.'

Kate closed her eyes, trying to visualise the sequence of events. It was difficult to imagine Julia Sullivan allowing a stranger into her house, somehow being drugged, and then being led upstairs, undressed and killed. If the woman had been drugged, then how? Other than her family, they needed to find out who she was in contact with on a regular basis and to see if there was any truth to Sadie's suspicions about an affair.

'What church did Julia attend?' she asked Cooper.

The DC typed something into her computer. 'The Church of the Right Hand.'

'What the hell's that?' Hollis asked. 'What happened to Catholic or Protestant?'

Kate did a quick internet search to find the answer to his

question. 'Apparently, they're an evangelical group who believe in extending the right hand of friendship to anybody who shares their beliefs.'

'Which are?'

'"The sanctity of marriage; the holiness of conception; the oneness of man and woman as a unit" – whatever that means–'

'It means homophobia,' Cooper interrupted. 'Please don't ask me to go and interview any of the congregation.'

Kate smiled. Cooper had been guarded about her sexual orientation when Kate first took over the team, but she'd soon come to realise that her colleagues didn't care who she was in a relationship with as long as she could take some gentle teasing. It had amused Kate to see Cooper adapting well enough to give as good as she got on most occasions.

'They veer a bit towards the fundamental then?'

'Sounds like it,' Kate said. 'The Doncaster branch, group, sect, whatever, meets on Chequer Road near the museum. We could probably see it from upstairs.' The police station canteen was on the top floor and Kate did a lot of her clearest thinking sitting close to one of the windows clutching a mug of mediocre coffee. 'Hang on.' She clicked on a map of the town and then zoomed in on the address. 'Looks like a bog-standard terraced house. Nothing to suggest it's a religious building of any kind. Dan, grab your coat, you're taking me to church!'

5

The end-terrace house looked exactly the same as all the others in the row with a deep bay window and a thin strip of tarmac instead of a front garden. A low brick wall offered the pretence of separation from the street, but the short front path was only feet from the scuffed slabs of the pavement.

'Not very churchy,' Hollis observed, his hand on the tiny front gate.

'I'm not sure how official the Church of the Right Hand is,' Kate said. 'I got the impression from the internet they see themselves as "up and coming" in evangelical circles.'

Hollis jabbed the doorbell and they both stepped back in unison facing the front door.

A face appeared, indistinct behind the obscured glass, then the door opened.

'Can I help you?' The man who spoke was probably in his mid-sixties, shorter than Kate and completely bald. His blue eyes, deep within nests of wrinkles, looked suspicious and his lack of smile heightened this impression.

'Is this the Church of the Right Hand?' Hollis asked, his tone suggesting doubt.

The man nodded tersely.

Kate introduced herself and Hollis and explained that they wanted to talk about Julia Sullivan.

The name seemed to change the weather in the man's face as he gave them a jowly grin and pushed the door open wider to invite them inside. 'She's such a valued member of our group. Has she been threatened again?' he said, leading them down a dingy hallway to a kitchen at the back of the property.

Kate ignored his question. From the rear she could see that his clothes hung loose on his shoulders and bottom and the turn-ups of grey trousers scuffed the floor tiles as he walked. His untucked checked shirt was frayed around the hem and the sleeves were unevenly rolled.

'Can I get you a drink?'

The kitchen was in a much cleaner state than its owner, but Kate still refused and Hollis followed her lead. 'If we could just ask a few questions Mr...?'

'Greaves,' the man said, filling the pause as expected. 'Alistair Greaves.'

He told them to sit and then left the room.

'Should we be scared?' Hollis whispered.

Kate was about to respond when a woman bustled through the kitchen door, her appearance the opposite of Greaves's shabbiness. She wore a tan blouse and navy-blue A-line skirt which gave the impression of a 1950s housewife. Her make-up was subtle but flawless and her greying blonde hair was tied back in a neat bun. 'I'm Cora Greaves,' she announced, striding over to the kitchen counter and putting the kettle on. 'Alistair's wife.'

Greaves hovered in the doorway. 'They don't want drinks, Cora.'

The woman looked around as if suddenly at a loss.

'We'd like to talk about Julia Sullivan,' Hollis said gently. 'We understand she attended church services with you.'

Cora glanced at Greaves as though seeking permission to speak. Whatever she saw in the man's face it was obviously enough. 'We don't hold church services,' she said, smoothing a strand of hair that was threatening to break free from the bun. 'We hold counsel. Our members sit until the spirit moves them to talk about their relationship with God.'

'Like the Quakers?' Kate asked.

Cora's eyes narrowed. 'We're *nothing* like the Quakers. We seek direction and instruction. God speaks to our group and we follow his teaching.'

'So you don't read the Bible?'

'Brothers and sisters are free to read whatever they like. We provide our own tracts based on God's own word, not translations by those looking to dilute the message. We believe that our way is the true way to God's right hand.'

'And what is your way?' Hollis asked. Something about his tone seemed to irritate Greaves who crossed his arms and leaned on the door jamb, scowling.

'Purity,' Cora said simply. 'Purity in all things. Purity in the way we live our lives.'

'I read online that your group doesn't agree with sex outside marriage,' Kate prompted.

'No. Man and woman are designed to fit together within the sanctity of marriage. Modern society is too lenient, too tolerant and it's dangerous. How can people find their way back to God if they go against his word?'

'What about purity of race? Are mixed-race relationships permitted?'

Cora's mouth tightened. 'Of course. God created all races equal.'

She was lying. Kate suspected that they were being given the sanitised, user-friendly version of the Church of the Right Hand which kept within the letter of equality laws in public but, in private, encouraged views like Julia Sullivan's.

'How did Julia come to join you?' Kate asked, trying to steer the conversation away from the specifics of their beliefs for the sake of her own blood pressure.

'I met her in hospital. One of our ministries is to help heal the sick so a number of us volunteer at the Doncaster Royal Infirmary. She'd been in an accident and was feeling low, so I gave her support and space to talk. She was unhappy about the state of the world and confused about what she wanted for the future. It was very clear that she was floundering even before the car crash, so I offered her direction. When she was well enough, she joined us here for regular meetings.'

'Did you approve of her political career?'

A quick glance passed between Cora and her husband.

'Generally, we feel the woman's role is in the home, but it was important for her to get her message across. And, besides, her husband is–'

'Cora!' Greaves snapped.

'My apologies,' the woman continued. 'It's not my place to speak about another woman's husband. Our group supported Julia.'

'What about suicide?' Kate asked. 'How does your church feel about that?'

Cora visibly turned pale. 'Has something happened to Julia?'

Hollis leaned towards the woman. 'I'm sorry to have to tell you, Julia Sullivan is dead. Her body was found in her home in the early hours of yesterday.'

'No. We'd have heard. Somebody would have told us. How did she die? She was always so full of life. I can't believe this.'

She stood up and then sat down again as if unsure what to do or how to react. Greaves moved from his position by the door and crossed the room to place a soothing hand on his wife's shoulder.

'We can't give you any details about the case,' Kate said. 'When we arrived, you mentioned that Julia had been threatened. Were there many threats?'

Greaves nodded. 'There were a couple of things on the internet saying that she was evil and should die. She showed me on her phone.'

'But nobody in your organisation bore her any ill will?'

'Of course not,' Cora spat. 'We preach love! The only people who wished her ill are those ones who left threats. Those cowards who hid behind their fake names and pictures.'

'You mentioned suicide,' Greaves said, looking up and placing his free hand on his wife's other shoulder. 'Is that a possibility?'

'It's too early to say,' Kate lied. 'We're just trying to get a complete picture of Julia's life at the moment.'

Cora nodded as though Kate's statement made perfect sense. 'I'm sure you're doing everything you can. She was a good woman. Make sure you look closely at her husband – he wasn't exactly supportive of her joining our group or of her political career.'

'We're speaking to everybody in Julia's life,' Kate said. 'It has been suggested she was having an affair. Does that seem likely?'

'No!' Greaves snapped. 'That would go against everything we believe in.'

His wife closed her eyes as if in pain and began to mutter to herself. It took Kate a few seconds to realise that she was praying. Greaves nodded to himself and joined in as Kate stood up and slid her business card onto the table.

'Please, get in touch if you think of anything that might help,' she said but the couple ignored her. She raised her eyebrows quizzically to Hollis who gave a tiny shrug and pointed to the door. Kate nodded and walked down the hallway to the door with the voices of Cora and Alistair Greaves following them like a swarm of angry bees.

6

S tretching her arms above her head, Kate groaned and looked at her watch. She'd spent nearly two hours researching the Church of the Right Hand and Julia Sullivan. She looked around at her flat, at what she'd been avoiding since she'd walked in, grabbed a beer and flopped on the sofa. There were boxes everywhere. Some were full and labelled, more were empty, gaping mouths waiting to swallow her possessions and spit them out somewhere else, in another life.

She loved this flat, with its view across Town Field and its quirky corners and angles. It was a five-minute drive to Doncaster Central and there was an off-licence on the corner just 100 yards away. What more could she want? Maybe guaranteed parking – trying to find a space after 5pm was a nightmare. What she was feeling had little to do with the flat, if she was honest. It was more to do with Nick. They'd been seeing each other for over two years and moving in together was the next logical step – she'd taken marriage off the table early in their relationship, still bruised from her divorce from Garry – but there was still a sense of losing freedom. Kate loved Nick, there was no doubt about that, and they were well suited. Both career-minded – he'd been appointed senior consultant the previous year – and both at an age and a time in their lives when they wanted things to be easier, more straightforward.

It had taken a while to admit to herself that the real issue was her age. Turning fifty had been a celebration but had also forced Kate to take stock and lurking among her plans and hopes was the dark spectre of retirement. She knew that there was no rush. She'd taken some time out when her son, Ben, was small so she had few years of her pension to make up – if that's what she chose to do. But the job was getting more difficult, more complex and she didn't want to be a burden to her younger team. She had considered going for promotion but that seemed to offer the promise of more paperwork, more media liaison and less time in the field so she'd come round to accepting that DI was to be the pinnacle of her career.

And then there was the menopause. It had been creeping up for a couple of years, but she was now in full-blown hot sweat and insomnia territory. She knew her colleagues had noticed but not even Dan had been brave enough to comment when she opened windows or cranked up the air con in the car. She'd started to keep a spare blouse in her locker at work and a travel-size deodorant in her desk drawer, but she still felt caught out and thrown off guard by the hormonal changes.

The house she'd bought with Nick was a compromise. He'd wanted an old property with a rich history and a rambling mess of a garden; Kate wanted modern and absolutely no work to be done. They'd looked at a former pub, a converted chapel – no outside space – and an old rectory, but if Nick had been hoping to infect her with his enthusiasm, she'd remained stubbornly immune. She was about to give up and agree to move in with him, even though she was increasingly convinced that wasn't what he wanted either, when he texted her an address and a time. Kate hadn't known whether to feel annoyed or intrigued but she'd gone along with Nick's ploy and driven to a quiet lane in Austerfield near Bawtry – timing the journey so she could assess it as a commute.

Twenty minutes after leaving work she was standing in front of a beautiful barn conversion on a big plot, surrounded on three sides by beech hedges. It was gorgeous. Kate didn't regard herself as the sort of woman who was interested in interior decoration, but she couldn't quite believe her reaction to the place. The interior was modern, but it retained some original features while avoiding the clichés of dusty beams and odd patches of bare stone. The main bedroom had views over open country beyond the hedges and a huge en-suite bathroom. The lounge was enormous with under-floor heating and a wood burner – two things Kate hadn't known she'd needed until now. The kitchen wasn't of much interest to Kate. She wasn't a great cook, but Nick was excellent and tended to make most of their evening meals.

Nick hadn't met her at the house. He knew her well enough to allow her the space and time to get a feel for the place. Half an hour after arriving she'd texted a simple 'Yes!' and three weeks later they'd put down a deposit.

Kate knew it was a positive move for them. It would be good for their relationship and living further from work would allow them some decompression time before arriving home. She just didn't want to pack, and she didn't like change.

Pulling her laptop towards her, Kate went back to her research. The website for the Church of the Right Hand was very vague about the group's aims and beliefs and there was little mention of them elsewhere on the net. She'd found a few references to them being founded in 2009 in the USA but searching on the names of the founders had yielded nothing of interest. It looked like the church was legitimate and had managed to keep out of the news.

She typed the name of the church and 'forums' into the search bar to see if there were any discussions involving the members or the methods of the group and was excited to see Church of the Right Hand mentioned with a reference to a forum called 'LiFlight'. Clicking on the link took her to a post on the third page of a discussion which appeared to be about unethical religious practices. A member called 2Tru had written about their experience of the Church of the Right Hand and their experience had obviously resonated with other former members.

2Tru– They seemed so nice at first. I'd been on the street for a few months when they found me and took me in and they really helped me to get back on my feet. I found a job in a café and I got a bedsit and was ready to get back in touch with my family. That's when I saw what they were really about. The pastor told me that if I wanted to stay in the group I needed to renounce my past and that included my mum and sister. It didn't feel right but I went along with it because they'd been so kind.

Bev87– That's how they work. Same happened to me. I'd split up from my boyfriend and was in a bad place and they gave me a focus. But they tried to isolate me from my family and friends. I fell for it. I believed their bulls**t about what God wants and how only the pure go to heaven. Did they try to persuade you that white people are superior to everybody else?

2Tru– I got a hint of that. My group were always going on about homosexuals and fornicators. They had me believing all sorts because I had nobody else to talk to.

Bev87– Glad you're safe now. Stay strong.

2Tru– ThnX

It wasn't much, but it was disturbing. Cora had said that she met Julia in hospital. Had she preyed on the vulnerabilities of Julia after her accident? If she had a head injury, she may have been easy to manipulate and open to suggestion. While it didn't give anybody from the Church of the Right Hand an obvious motive for murder it did imply that Julia's views weren't necessarily formed honestly, and the church had opened her up to online abuse and threats. Had she unwittingly become the spokesperson for some very suspect people?

7

Cain Powell's phone died just as he rounded the corner of the lane heading up to the Beacon. One minute his feet had been pounding along to Florence and the Machine, the next, silence. It wasn't just the lack of music that pissed him off: a dead battery meant no Strava app. No Strava meant no bragging rights that he'd done the Turton circuit in less than an hour. He slowed to a trot and then stopped completely, Velcro rasping as he tore the phone holder from his upper arm.

'Shit!' he swore, jabbing at the screen of his mobile as though he could poke it to life. 'Bloody thing!'

He peered through the mist, trying to work out how much further he had to go to reach the downhill section that signalled the easier return leg of the route. Probably less than a quarter of a mile – not worth turning back. The anticipation of impressing his friends over a pint in the Plough later made him think he might as well carry on even though running was a bit of a lonely occupation without music.

'Sod it,' he muttered, strapping the armband back on and setting off at a fast jog. The mist gave way to low cloud as he slogged his way up the hill towards the television mast on the site of a medieval beacon. As he got nearer to the mast, he could only see the bottom half – the rest hidden by grey dampness. He hated running in the wet. It settled in his hair and made him sweat much more than on a dry, warm day, making him look like he was struggling and out of condition.

There was a vehicle in the small parking area at the end of the lane with its engine running. Cain could feel the vibration before he actually heard anything, and the rear lights got brighter as he got closer. It was a popular spot due to its elevation and the expansive views across the River Don towards the Peak District but on a morning like this, Cain couldn't see the point of parking up. Unless they were dogging. There had been a few complaints from locals that the area around the Beacon was being used for illicit sexual activity but usually at night, not at half past seven on a gloomy summer morning.

Curious, Cain slowed a little as he drew level with the car. It was a Range Rover, dark blue, two years old. The inside seemed to be as foggy as the surrounding air, obscuring his view of the occupants. He stepped closer, puzzled. Had they opened the door and allowed the fog inside?

Then he saw the plastic hose that had been taped to the exhaust and the duct tape across the back window where the end of the hose disappeared. This wasn't sightseeing or dogging; this was suicide.

'Bloody hell,' Cain whispered to himself as he wondered what to do.

He walked slowly round the car, trying each of the doors in turn. All locked. He could break a window but there was nothing on the ground that would have the weight and heft to smash through the glass, just gravel and small stones. As he looked around, hoping for inspiration he noticed that there was something propped up against the windscreen – something white. A note.

Please leave us alone. We've had a good life but it's time to go.

An instruction – or a plea?

There wasn't much he could do here, Cain decided. He'd have to go and get help. His phone was dead, but the nearest public phone box was close – just outside Turton – no more than five minutes at a fast jog.

Swearing under his breath, Cain set off back the way he'd come, picking up pace until he was running flat out. Less than three minutes later a splash of red in the white mist was pulling him towards the phone box.

8

'Who's he?' Kate asked, nodding towards a largeish man in shorts and T-shirt, shivering despite the silver blanket he was wrapped in and the increasingly warm morning sun.

Barratt flicked back a page in his notebook, squinting as he peered down at his own scrawled handwriting, the hood from the protective suit he was wearing flopping down over his balding head. 'Cain Powell. He found the car, saw the note and ran to the phone box to call for help.'

'Note?' Nobody had mentioned a note to Kate when she'd got the call about two bodies in a car on Beacon Edge.

'There's a note propped up against the windscreen asking to be left alone.'

Kate turned, taking in the car, the television mast and then the view which had been revealed as the early low cloud burned off. 'Not a bad spot to end it all,' she mused. 'Bit rough on the jogger though.'

'Except they didn't want to end it all,' Barratt said.

Kate had guessed as much as soon as she'd been summoned to what appeared to be a straightforward suicide and she was keen to see what had got the pathologist so interested in the case. She suspected a link with Julia Sullivan.

A taped cordon had been set up around the car using the fence and two small trees, the blue-and-white police tape fluttering in the light breeze that had helped to disperse the mist. Inside the cordon, white-clad figures were busy with brushes and other tools, collecting samples and recording everything using digital cameras. Kate could see the rear half of a small figure protruding from the passenger side, the upper half obviously busy with one of the bodies.

She walked over to the tape and flashed her ID at a uniformed officer who was standing guard. He seemed to be desperately trying to avoid looking at the bodies in the car, his eyes drawn to the expansive view and occasionally flicking to the pool car that Kate had driven to the scene. There didn't seem much point in his presence as the end of the lane had been blocked by a row of cones and another uniformed officer was stationed there to keep out nosey members of the public.

'Can I speak to Doctor Kailisa?' Kate asked. The man looked at her uncertainly before turning to the car.

'I think he's still working on the bodies,' he mumbled, turning back to Kate. 'I can't disturb him if he's busy.'

Scared of the pathologist's famed bad temper, Kate thought and smiled to herself. She'd been on the receiving end of Kailisa's sharp tongue on many occasions and it wasn't pleasant.

'Okay,' Kate said. 'I'll just have to ask him myself.'

She grabbed a sealed packet of overalls and wriggled the thin protective suit over her clothes before snapping on a pair of shoe covers. The reluctant sentry raised the tape just far enough for her to duck underneath and she followed the line of step plates to the vehicle.

'What've we got?' she asked as Kailisa eased himself out of the car. 'Any obvious signs that this isn't a suicide?'

'DI Fletcher,' Kailisa said, turning to her, eyebrows raised above the surgical mask that covered the lower half of his face. 'Good morning to you too.'

Kate smiled. Kailisa wasn't known for his politeness so she rarely bothered with pleasantries when they met at a crime scene.

'Can you talk me through the scene?'

Kailisa straightened up and pointed at the vehicle.

'Dark-blue Range Rover. Two years old. Registered to a Peter Houghton. Two bodies in the two front seats. The male had a wallet in his pocket with a driving licence in the name Peter Houghton with an address in Turton. Female unknown but her age suggests that she's likely to be his wife Eleanor.'

'So why am I here?'

Kailisa continued as though he hadn't heard the question. 'The engine of the car was running – fuel tank registers a quarter full. A length of hose had been attached to the exhaust pipe with duct tape and fed through one of the rear windows – the gap was sealed with more tape.'

'So...?'

Kailisa held up a gloved hand, palm towards Kate, preventing her from repeating her question. 'We don't know how long the car was running for, but the cabin was full of exhaust fumes – preliminary readings suggest high levels of carbon monoxide.'

Kate waited. She knew the pathologist was methodical and wouldn't be prevented from presenting the evidence in his own way and in his own time. Her interruption had been more instinctive than a serious attempt to divert him from his narrative.

'However, close examination of both bodies suggests that they were dead, or close to death, when the tubing was inserted into the window. Carbon monoxide poisoning produces a particular red lividity and neither body has evidence of this. I've checked shoulders and legs where there was pressure contact with the seats but there is nothing to suggest carbon monoxide was the primary cause of death. Of course, post-mortem examination will be necessary to confirm this. Both bodies appear to be in the early stages of rigor mortis which suggests they have been dead for a few hours.'

'Could they have taken something – pills, drugs – and used the exhaust as backup? Sort of a belt and braces job?' Kate asked. 'The presence of a note suggests that they didn't want to be rescued so perhaps they made doubly sure.'

Kailisa tilted his head on one side, studying Kate's face intently until she looked away, uncomfortable with his scrutiny. She knew from experience that he was giving her time to dig a hole before he could give her a hefty shove into it.

'That might make sense except for one other piece of evidence.'

Now it was Kate's turn to stare and wait. Kailisa turned and pointed to a yellow evidence marker about a hundred feet away next to one of the four metal posts driven into the concrete that formed the bottom of the television mast.

'The car keys were found over there, hanging from a rivet in the metalwork.'

'Could one of the car's inhabitants have thrown them and they landed like that?'

Kailisa shook his head. 'Even if they'd stood at the fence it would have taken a huge effort and neither person looks like they had the upper-body strength. The odds of the keys landing on the rivet are vanishingly small.'

Kate thought for a second, trying to picture the scene. 'Could one of them have walked over to the tower and put the keys there for some reason? So there was no temptation to drive away.' Even to Kate's own ears, the explanation was thin.

'The gate to the area around the mast is locked. I doubt either victim would have been able to climb over and the fence is too high, and secure – it's been checked. There are no gaps in the perimeter.'

'How did you find the keys?'

'One of the SOCOs saw the sunlight catching something metal. He took a photograph and enlarged it on the screen of his camera. The area was thoroughly processed, the gate tested for fingerprints and shoe impressions and the ground carefully photographed. There were some impressions in the damp grass but no detail. Whoever left the keys didn't walk on the track.'

Kailisa pointed to the rough gravel track that led to the concrete base of the mast. 'Even if they had, it's unlikely that we would have recovered impressions. The ground is relatively dry apart from a light coating of damp from the drizzle earlier.'

'So, somebody locked the car, climbed over the gate and went to hang the keys on the TV mast?' Kate was thinking aloud, trying to make sense of the findings. 'But the two people in the car wouldn't have been locked in; all one of them would have had to do was open a door; the central locking wouldn't prevent a door being opened from the inside.'

Kailisa nodded.

'And why hang up the keys? Why not just throw them away?' Kate looked around again. 'And where did they go after they'd left the keys? Unless they brought their own vehicle, but then how did they get the people in the car up here in the first place?'

'It's a conundrum, wrapped in a mystery,' said a voice from behind her.

Kate turned to see the tall, lean shape of Hollis silhouetted against the mid-morning sun.

'Where've you been?' she asked as Hollis stepped closer to the cordon tape and came more clearly into view. He was dressed in a dark T-shirt and jogging bottoms rather than his customary suit. His blond hair was damp, whether from sweat or a recent shower, Kate couldn't tell, and his face was ruddier than normal.

'I was at the gym. Day off for the overtime I did last weekend.'

Kate grinned. She'd forgotten that he had booked time off. It was just like Hollis to drop everything at the slightest hint of an interesting case, even on his day off.

'FOMO getting to you again?' she teased.

Hollis smiled back. 'Fear of missing out? Something like that. Matt's already given me the broad strokes. The thing with the keys is interesting. And the note. The wording is very similar to the Julia Sullivan case.'

'I haven't seen it,' Kate said.

'The wording's almost identical. Hard not to think there's a connection.'

Typical Hollis. Of all her team, Dan loved the mystery, the slow unravelling of events that would lead them to a killer. She was about to respond when a shout from the direction of the car caught her attention – Kailisa had obviously authorised the removal of the bodies and she was needed. She trotted over, taking in the stretchers and body bags placed next to the car's doors and the silence as the team awaited instruction.

'The male first,' the pathologist said. 'Gently.'

Kate watched as two of Kailisa's team eased the body from the driver's seat of the car, struggling with the tight space and the reluctance of the limbs to give up their hunched position as the rigor advanced. Finally, the body was zipped into a body bag and the men turned their attention to the female. Kate followed them round to the other side of the car and watched as they repeated the complex movements – the zipping of the second body bag adding a sense of finality to the operation.

'Right, we'll probably get to work on the first victim in the morning if you'd like to be present. You may be able to confirm identification before then but if not I will probably be able to help,' Kailisa said. It was a courtesy rather than a genuine invitation – he knew that Kate would probably send Barratt or Hollis. 'A vehicle recovery team should be here within the hour to take the car once the team have finished processing it *in situ*.'

The removal of the bodies had caused a surge in activity around the vehicle as the forensics team checked the empty seats and footwells now they were unencumbered by the probable remains of Peter Houghton and his wife. Kate leaned closer to the passenger side, her attention caught by something odd.

'Was the rear-view mirror like that when you opened the car?' Kate asked, pointing to the unusual position. The mirror had been turned round so it would have reflected the passenger rather than the driver. There was also a crack running diagonally across the surface. Kate remembered the irritation she caused her ex-husband when she used the rear-view mirror to check her make-up while he was driving. It was as though the female had wanted to take one last look at herself even if the image had been distorted by the crack.

Kailisa followed her gaze then summoned one of the men who'd removed the body.

'Did you knock this mirror?' His tone was faintly accusatory.

The man's face, framed by the tight elastic of his hood, coloured. 'Don't think so.' He sounded uncertain. 'We can check from the photographs.' He trotted away and returned with a large digital camera clasped tightly in both hands. 'It was like that when we opened the door,' the man confirmed, showing the digital image to Kate on the camera's display panel. The position of the mirror and the crack were clearly visible.

Kate thanked him and walked back to the line of tape. If Kailisa was correct and the bodies were murder victims, then why would the female have checked her reflection? She couldn't have if she'd already been dying. The killer must have turned the mirror. Had he or she knocked it reaching over for the keys and managed to crack it at the same time? It seemed unlikely but they didn't know yet if somebody else had been in the car. Was it a message? Julia Sullivan had been murdered with a shard of mirror.

'Who's got the note?' she shouted in the general direction of the SOCO team. One of the men jogged over, holding an evidence bag which he passed to Kate. She could make out the words through the clear plastic.

Please leave us alone. We've had a good life but it's time to go.

This couldn't be a coincidence – the wording was too similar. Whoever killed the Houghtons had also killed Julia Sullivan. Kate was sure of it.

9

'DVLA gives us a preliminary ID of the driver as Peter Houghton of Turton. It seems likely that the female is his wife Eleanor,' Kate began, opening the briefing. She tapped the keypad of her laptop and an image appeared on the whiteboard.

'This is Houghton and his wife at a recent function for leading local businessmen. A fundraiser for an MS charity. Apparently, Mrs Houghton's sister died of the disease eight years ago. The photograph matches the physical characteristics of the two bodies but we're still waiting for a positive ID. The couple lived alone and there is no known family at this stage.'

Kate looked around the assembled group as they absorbed the information. Hollis had changed into a dark-grey suit although it was too warm for the jacket which was draped carefully across the back of his chair, and his shirtsleeves were rolled up to the elbow with almost military precision. She noticed that Barratt had also managed to tidy himself up after being encased in a protective suit for most of the morning. Cooper was frowning at the screen as though trying to absorb every detail and O'Connor was stroking his scrubby, dark-red beard meditatively.

'Is this Peter Houghton the haulage chap?' O'Connor asked.

Kate nodded. 'South Yorkshire's answer to Eddie Stobart.'

'And a bit of a git, by all accounts,' O'Connor continued with a grin. 'When there was a move to widen the M18 he allowed the police access to his land near the site so they could forcibly remove protesters from the trees. He's one of those climate-change deniers – doesn't believe in renewables and has never even tried to update his fleet to make them more environmentally friendly.'

Kate had already done a bit of research herself. Houghton was unpopular with his neighbours due to his drive to acquire as much land as possible in the small village. He'd even bid on land next to the nature reserve – against the RSPB – and won, preventing the expansion of the conservation area. He'd acquired planning permission for the land but, so far, he'd not started to build. Was there a possible motive there for his murder? There was certainly a similarity to Julia Sullivan. Both she and Houghton held unpopular opinions and weren't afraid to voice them. Or, somebody might have objected to Houghton's plans and wanted him out of the picture in the hope that the land could be saved from development. It was a bit of a stretch, though, given the similarities between the two notes.

'What I don't get,' Sam said, 'is why make it look like suicide when it obviously isn't? Why not just kill them both? Staging something so elaborate takes time and effort and increases the risk of being caught in the act. Same with the Sullivan case, if we're connecting them.'

Kate moved the slideshow on to a photograph of the scene showing the position of the car relative to the television mast and the gated enclosure.

'I think we have to assume that the area or the method meant something to the killer. Why would somebody go to the trouble of getting the couple up there – it's three miles from their home – and setting up this elaborate scene?' Kate already had a couple of ideas, but she wanted to see if anybody on the team came to a similar conclusion.

'It's a message,' O'Connor said. 'The keys, the car, everything is meant to send a message.'

Kate nodded, pleased. 'And if we can understand the message, we might be able to work out who the killer is. Let's look at the elements. There's the car and the suicide paraphernalia.'

'Could be a reference to Houghton's lack of concern for the environment,' Sam suggested. She was good at this kind of puzzle, despite her relative lack of experience, and often spotted patterns that were invisible to the rest of the team.

'Go on,' Kate prompted.

'Well,' Sam ran a hand through her shaggy blonde hair. 'If he's seen as an environmental vandal, there's poetic justice in him being poisoned by exhaust fumes. Taking away the car keys might be a way of saying he can't escape?'

This last suggestion was more tentative and earned a wry twist of Barratt's lips.

'I don't see it,' he said. 'The car thing, yes, but not the keys. Why not just take them away? Why display them? Whoever did this wanted the keys to be found to remove any doubt that this was suicide. They're telling us that they've got away with murder.'

Kate thought about both suggestions but neither felt quite right. She had no doubt that the keys were a message, but it was one that they didn't understand fully. Yet.

'What about the practicalities?' Hollis asked, never overly comfortable with speculation and vagueness. 'How did he or she get the Houghtons into the car? And who drove it up there? It's the middle of June, it's only dark for a few hours so the risk of being seen is fairly high. And then how did they get away? Unless the killer met them there in another vehicle.'

Kate had anticipated this question. She flicked to a satellite image of the scene and zoomed out to show Turton in relation to the television mast.

'The scene is just over three miles from the Houghtons' home by road – ten minutes max. It's less than two miles if you follow this footpath.' She swapped to a section of OS map that corresponded to the satellite imagery and pointed to a green dotted line. 'And then you can access this track which leads directly to the village and comes out opposite the Houghtons' house.'

Her colleagues stared at the screen, studying the map, obviously trying to work out the logistics of dumping Houghton's car and getting back to the village without being seen.

'If they left their own vehicle somewhere near the Houghtons' house and then went back for it after setting up the supposed suicide, somebody would have noticed an unusual vehicle parked in the village – there's only about a dozen houses. And there's no public transport. They must have left their car up near the television mast and walked down to the village.'

'I wouldn't have left a car in the village. Looks like prime Neighbourhood Watch territory,' O'Connor mumbled. 'Probably curtain-twitchers on every corner.'

'What if it was one of the neighbours?' Barratt suggested. 'Get yourself invited in for drinks, spike the old couple's sherry, bundle them in the car after dark and then jog back to the village at first light. It looks like Julia Sullivan let her killer into the house; maybe it was somebody known to all three.'

It was a possibility that Kate had considered but it was high risk. Anybody living near the Houghtons would be under the spotlight of suspicion as soon as the bodies had been found. If it was somebody local, surely they'd have left the car much further away to divert attention from themselves.

'You don't shit where you eat,' O'Connor said. Cooper frowned her disapproval, but he continued regardless. 'If you're going to kill your next-door neighbour you don't dump the body in your back garden and wait for it to be found. I can't see it being anybody from the village.'

Kate wouldn't have expressed it in the same terms, but she shared O'Connor's misgivings. Unless they were very lucky, Kate doubted that this was going to be the work of an irate neighbour as a result of a disagreement. How did that connect with Julia Sullivan? There was something deeper about the symbolism of the scene. She clicked through the photographs until she found one of the rear-view mirror.

'This was a bit weird as well,' she said. 'The mirror was cracked and turned to face the passenger rather than the driver. I wondered if one of the tech crew had knocked it, but this image was taken before they moved anything. Given that Julia Sullivan was murdered with a sliver of mirror we have to consider the link.'

'Could have happened when Houghton was placed in the driver's seat,' Barratt suggested. 'An accident? I've turned mine round a few times when I've been cleaning the inside of the car. Maybe the killer was giving everything a wipe down before he left and knocked it out of place. Just a coincidence that there was a mirror in the Sullivan case?'

'Was there anything else in the vehicle that was unusual?' Cooper asked. 'Anything to suggest how they really died?'

'Kailisa couldn't say what the real cause of death might have been. My guess would be drugs. Maybe an overdose of an opiate but we'll have to wait and see. If they were poisoned or drugged, it's unlikely it happened at the scene. How would somebody convince them to eat or drink something?'

'Back to the poisoned sherry,' O'Connor quipped.

'If they were drugged at their home that suggests somebody with a degree of upper-body strength. The killer had to get them in the car and one body had to go in the back seat or the boot while he drove up to the dump site.'

'Kailisa isn't sure that they were dead when they were left in the car. His exact words were "dead or close to death",' Kate said. 'It's possible that the killer was able to get them both to walk at least part of the way to the vehicle before the drugs took full effect. If he put Houghton in the back, he'd have only had to move him out of the back door and in through the driver's door. Hopefully there'll be something on the body, bruising or scuffing, to give us a clue.'

'If somebody drugged them in their home it suggests that the killer might be known to one or both of them,' Barratt mused. 'The house has a high wall round it and I'm fairly sure there's a decent security system in place – maybe even automatic locking on the gate with an intercom for access.'

It's a good call, Kate thought. Few people, especially if they were vulnerable or elderly, would allow a stranger into a well-protected house. It was yet another similarity. There was no sign of forced entry at the Sullivan house – it appeared that the killer may have been known to all three victims.

'Could have been an old friend or one of Houghton's employees,' Hollis said. 'Even a family member that we don't know about yet.'

'So, we need to get digging,' Kate said. 'Jobs. Steve, you and Matt get yourselves over to Houghton Haulage – the depot's just outside Thorpe on the Rotherham road. Find out who runs the business, who's unhappy, who might be bearing a grudge. Sam – finances, personal and for the company. See who owed Houghton money and who he owed money to. And see if you can dig up any family members. And see if there's anything connecting the Houghtons and Julia Sullivan. Dan, we're going back to Turton to have a poke round the Houghtons' house – the SOCOs should be there by now and I want to be there when they gain access. I haven't been able to track down a key holder so I've authorised use of the battering ram. We might have a chat with the neighbours as well. If O'Connor's right about the curtain-twitchers, then I'm sure there'll be plenty of people who can tell us something about Mr and Mrs Houghton.'

Kate watched as O'Connor and Barratt grabbed their jackets from the backs of chairs and headed for the door. Cooper remained seated, typing something onto the screen of her tablet – probably notes from the meeting.

Hollis stood up and rolled down the sleeves of his shirt, buttoning them carefully before slipping on his suit jacket. 'Hell of a day off,' he said with a grin as he led the way to the stairs.

10

'Wow!' Hollis said as they pulled in through the double gates and got their first look at the Houghtons' bungalow. The brick-paved drive led to a gravelled parking area on one side of a deep-red front door which was flanked by mock-Corinthian pillars. The other half of the front garden was a rectangle of grass, recently mown with perfectly trimmed edges, but strangely dull as though the owners didn't want the garden to detract from the splendour of the house.

An unmarked van was parked next to a liveried police car, matching the one stationed on the road outside, indicating the presence of a forensics team and at least one uniformed police officer. Kate hoped to have a look around before the SOCOs caused too much disruption. She parked next to the police car and the driver got out as she was reaching into her pocket for her ID.

'DI Fletcher, DS Hollis,' Kate said. 'Are you going to get us into the house?'

The man nodded and opened the hatchback of the car to reveal an immaculately tidy boot space containing a black plastic case. He reached in, opened the case and removed the 'enforcer' otherwise known as the 'big red key' – a small but effective battering ram weighing sixteen kilos. The officer put on a helmet and thick gloves before hefting the object out of the boot and marching towards the front door.

Kate reached into the boot of their pool car and removed packages of coveralls and shoe covers. 'Here,' she said, passing a pack to Hollis. 'This is a crime scene until we know otherwise.'

The uniformed officer waited until they'd donned the protective clothing and then swung at the door, fracturing the frame and causing the door to lean inwards.

Kate heard a van door open and she turned to see one of the forensics officers approaching. She recognised the bald head and broad shoulders of Martin Davies, one of the newer additions to the SOCO team.

'Give us a few minutes,' she instructed, slipping on shoe covers and stepping into the hallway of the bungalow, avoiding the jagged edge of the door frame where the lock had given way under the force of the battering ram.

Davies nodded. 'Your call. Yell when you're ready for us.'

Kate shuffled along the wide hallway peering through doors, looking for the kitchen. If the Houghtons had been poisoned, that was the most likely place to look for evidence – she was hoping for half-empty glasses or residue left on mugs, possibly even the DNA of the killer if he or she had eaten or drunk anything.

'I wonder if they had a cleaner,' Hollis mused behind her. 'The place is spotless.'

Kate looked down at the deep green carpet shot through with a mustard-coloured Prince of Wales feather motif. She held out her arm, stopping Hollis in his tracks. 'This carpet's been hoovered recently,' she said, pointing at the parallel marks of wheels just discernible in the nap of the wool. 'Looks like nobody's walked this way since.'

'Maybe he came in and out of the back,' Hollis suggested.

'Or maybe he tidied up after himself. There might have been debris or residue left behind from his shoes. If there was it'll turn up in the car as well, hopefully. Might give us a clue as to where he came from.'

The door at the end of the hall was closed. Kate slipped on a pair of nitrile gloves and turned the handle. The door swung open to reveal a huge kitchen with white units and black marble worktops.

'Looks like there's plenty of money in the haulage business,' Hollis whispered as they stepped into the room. 'There must be over fifty grand's worth of kitchen here. Jesus.'

Kate turned slowly taking in the espresso machine that wouldn't have looked out of place in a flashy hotel bar, the huge, American-style fridge and the twin Belfast sinks. A red light was flashing underneath one of the worktops.

'Oh, shit,' she said.

'What?'

Kate crossed the kitchen floor and opened the dishwasher to reveal two mugs and three glasses. No plates, no pans and only a teaspoon in the cutlery basket. Why would anybody put the machine on for such a tiny load? Unless they wanted to be certain that the items were thoroughly cleaned.

'I think whoever vacuumed the carpet also put the dishwasher on. If the Houghtons were poisoned there'll be no trace on the crockery or the glasses.'

'Three glasses,' Hollis said. 'Looks like the killer had a drink with them. Maybe O'Connor's right about the poisoned sherry – it could have been somebody they knew.'

'Whoever it was spent time here, cleaning and tidying. He must have been confident that the Houghtons were incapacitated. There's a level of forensic awareness and thorough planning. We'll be lucky to find anything significant. Very different from Julia Sullivan's house.'

Hollis looked round the kitchen. 'Rubber gloves on the sink,' he said, obviously thinking aloud. 'Maybe the killer used them – they'll have left DNA inside. And a domestic vacuum cleaner isn't going to pick up everything – he might not have emptied it afterwards. Worth a look.'

Kate smiled, appreciating the DC's optimism. He might be right. Even the most careful criminals could slip up, especially if they thought they knew better than the police and scientists. Was that what they were dealing with – an arrogant personality who didn't expect to be caught? The positioning of the car keys and the cleaning of the house strongly suggested they were being taunted.

Hollis was opening and closing cupboards. 'Nothing unusual. The cupboard above the fridge has a selection of spirits – looks like the gin's open but the others still have intact seals. Probably worth checking for prints.'

Kate decided to leave him to it and stepped back out into the hallway. Four doors had been left ajar. The first one she approached led into an expansive sitting room flanked by a large conservatory with a view nearly as stunning as the one from the Beacon. *Amazing how money can make this part of South Yorkshire seem attractive,* she thought, watching heavy lorries struggling up a steep section of the M18.

The carpet in the hall continued in the sitting room, the same colour and pattern but here the décor had obviously been chosen to match. The two large sofas were pale green with ochre cushions and the walls were a cream colour with a racing-green dado rail part way up. Kate scanned the display cabinet that dominated one wall – it seemed that one of the Houghtons liked to collect glass animals; the shelves were dotted with fragile-looking deer and butterflies in various levels of transparency.

The bottom shelf housed two replica lorries, both decorated in the maroon and gold of Houghton's Haulage company.

There was no trace of dust in the cabinet and the glass front was so clean that it was practically invisible. Kate sighed as she took in the sofa cushions that lacked the telltale dents of recent occupants and the familiar stripes of the vacuum cleaner across the carpet. She wandered over to the mantlepiece, attention caught by an array of photo frames, hoping to find a clue about the wider family or the identity of close friends but each image showed the couple in an exotic location; Venice, a Mediterranean island, Bangkok. It was as if they lived in their own bubble and needed nothing but each other. Part of Kate thought it was sweet but the other part, the detective part, was frustrated by the lack of information in the room.

There was another photograph on the windowsill to the right of the conservatory, bigger, nearly A4 size. As Kate moved closer, she saw that it was a wedding photograph showing Peter and Eleanor Houghton dressed in formal wear, toasting each other with full glasses of champagne. Kate was surprised by the backdrop of the London Eye and the ages of Peter and Eleanor. She'd assumed that they'd been married for decades. Perhaps it wasn't a wedding – could have been a renewal of vows or a different form of celebration.

The dust-free television dominated the back wall of the room. It was hooked up to a surround-sound system and it was almost big enough to turn the living room into a home cinema. Shelves of DVDs stood at either side and Kate smiled as she scanned the titles. There were clearly two very different film fans in the house. One side was almost exclusively Westerns while the other was romantic comedies and the odd thriller.

There wasn't much else to see in the sitting room. A copy of the *Radio Times* was folded to the previous day's listings and a

Mills and Boon novel was half hidden under one of the sofas as though it had been kicked there by accident.

Disheartened, Kate went to explore the three bedrooms and was only mildly surprised to find that the Houghtons didn't appear to share a bed – two of the rooms contained fully made-up doubles and both had a range of books and a pair of spectacles on the bedside tables. She opened drawers and wardrobe doors but there was nothing that immediately struck her as out of the ordinary.

The third bedroom was obviously used as a study with a PC set up on a dark wood desk. The shelves contained a range of British road atlases which appeared to be collectables – the most recent was dated 1948 – and more plastic replicas of Houghton's fleet of lorries. There might be something interesting on the computer but accessing it was well beyond Kate's skill set and she didn't even bother switching it on. The techies would soon find out if there was anything important on the hard drive.

'Anything interesting?' Hollis asked from the doorway. 'I've had a nose around the garage, but nothing jumped out at me. The door was closed, it's one of those where you use a remote control which was on the kitchen counter. Looking at some of the clutter, I'm not sure the car was kept in there anyway. There's not much room.'

'The place is spotless,' Kate said. 'Separate bedrooms but I don't suppose that's unusual at their age.'

'Ugh, too right. Sex should be banned for the over-fifties.'

'Oi!' Kate said but she could see from his grin that he was teasing her. Her fiftieth birthday had caused her team much hilarity and was still a topic to be mined for comedy gold at every opportunity.

'Oh, I don't mean you and Nick,' Hollis said with mock innocence. 'Just the old fogies.'

'Thin ice, Dan,' Kate warned with a smile. This time Hollis

took the hint. Kate didn't mind being teased about her age, but she tried not to share details of her private life with her colleagues.

'So, what now?' he asked. 'Let the techies do their job?'

Kate nodded. 'There's nothing obvious here and we'll only be in their way so I think we should try a spot of door-knocking and see what the neighbours make of Mr and Mrs Houghton. You never know – one of the curtain-twitchers might have seen something.'

She sincerely hoped so because, if the state of the house was any indication, their killer was organised and very thorough.

11

'You want to lead, or should I do the talking?' Barratt asked O'Connor as they pulled up outside the main depot of Houghton Haulage in Thorpe. A former food-packing factory, it had been the centre of Peter Houghton's operations since the early eighties and little of the former structure remained. Barratt leaned forward, peering through the windscreen at the modern, single-storey office block that had been erected next to what was left of the Victorian red-brick building that once housed one of the largest conveyor belts in the country – if Wikipedia was to be believed. The narrow windows and gently sloping roof reminded him more of a chapel than a workplace. Most of the fleet of 600 trucks must have been out on the roads and motorways of Britain as only half a dozen were parked on the huge expanse of concrete which had replaced most of the Victorian construction.

'They're a bit fifties looking,' he said, referring to the maroon-and-gold livery of the lorry cabs.

'What?' O'Connor was looking at his phone, not really listening.

'The lorries. Like something out of a *Carry On* film. The colours are a bit old-fashioned. I'd have thought he'd have modernised the look at some point.'

O'Connor looked out of the window then back at the screen of his mobile. 'It's a brand. If you change it, it's not as recognisable.'

'I get that,' Barratt said. 'But...'

'You lead,' O'Connor said, opening the passenger door and slipping his phone into the inside pocket of his jacket. 'I might have a look around when we're done. The manager's called Tony Sims – Cooper just texted me the most up-to-date staff list – she's not found any family connection to Peter Houghton.'

Barratt led the way to a door marked 'Reception' and they stepped into an area which looked more like the lobby of a chain hotel than the front office of a hauliers. The carpet was a deep maroon, broken up by thin gold stripes and the light-wood reception desk was stencilled with the name of the company in letters at least six inches high. The woman speaking on the phone behind the desk gave them a brief wave and then turned her back to continue the conversation for a few seconds.

'Sorry about that,' she said, turning back around and carefully placing the telephone receiver back in its cradle. 'Can I help you?'

Barratt showed her his ID and introduced O'Connor who gave her a half-second smile. The woman ran a hand over her hair and Barratt could sense her wishing she had a mirror so she could check her appearance. In her mid-fifties with a blonde bob and less-than-subtle make-up she was exactly the type of woman who seemed incapable of resisting O'Connor's charms. Women his own age seemed put off by the dark-red biker-style facial hair and generally unkempt appearance, but middle-aged women seemed to want to mother him. O'Connor must have picked up on the woman's interest and ignored his previous instruction to Barratt.

'We'd like to talk to whoever's in charge,' he said with a lopsided grin.

The woman fiddled with the open top button of her maroon blouse as she looked from O'Connor to Barratt. 'Can I ask what it's about?'

'I'm afraid not. We just need some information regarding a recent incident. Background, that's all.' O'Connor didn't bother to smile this time, but it didn't seem to matter to the receptionist.

'Well, Mr Sims is in charge of the day-to-day running of the company. I'm his PA.'

'And can we speak to Mr Sims...?' O'Connor left a pause, waiting for the woman to fill it with her name.

'Maggie. Maggie Richardson. I'll see if Mr Sims is available.'

She picked up the phone again and tapped twice. 'Mr Sims? I have two police officers here who'd like to speak to you... I don't know, they said something about a recent incident.' She listened for a few seconds then fixed her grey eyes on Barratt. 'Is it something to do with one of our drivers?' she asked.

Barratt shook his head.

'Apparently not. They won't give me any more information.' She listened again then put the phone down. 'If you take a seat Mr Sims will be with you soon.'

Barratt led O'Connor to a row of wooden chairs arranged along one wall of the reception area but, before he could sit down, his attention was caught by a series of black-and-white images mounted on the wall behind the chairs. They showed Houghton Haulage lorries through the ages and all were scenes around Thorpe. Although he didn't know the village as well as his boss did, Barratt recognised a pub and the quarry that had long since been filled in with debris from the steelworks in

Sheffield. The site had been the scene of the first murder he'd worked with Kate and his first real success. Two of the images showed pubs that he didn't know, and one was taken from a high point with a background of rolling fields, a view Barratt recognised despite the lack of motorway.

'Look at this,' he said to O'Connor. 'It's near where the car was found, before the television mast was put up there. Somewhere near Turton.'

O'Connor stepped closer and peered at the image.

'Houghton's favourite spot? Maybe that's why he built a house up there.'

Barratt took out his phone and took a quick picture of the photograph.

'You never know – could be significant,' he said.

'What could be significant?'

Both detectives turned to see a tall, dark-haired man standing next to the reception desk. His arms were folded across his chest and he was frowning at the two police officers. Obviously, he didn't appreciate being disturbed.

'Mr Sims?' Barratt held out his hand, but Sims's arms remained resolutely folded. Unfazed by the man's reticence, Barratt introduced himself and O'Connor and asked if there was somewhere they could go to talk.

'Come through to my office,' Sims said, heading for the door next to the reception desk. As they passed Maggie Richardson, Barratt saw her give O'Connor an apologetic smile as though to make up for her boss's rude behaviour. Not that O'Connor would have noticed; the DS was usually oblivious to people's manners, especially his own.

'What's all this about?' Sims asked, gesturing to two chairs opposite a huge, pale-wood desk which matched the one out in the reception area. 'I really don't have much time.'

Barratt sat down but O'Connor chose to stand by the door in a pose that echoed Sims's earlier posture, arms folded as he leant against the wall. Sims undid the buttons of his suit jacket and sat opposite Barratt, his eyes expectant. Barratt studied the man, noting the deeply tanned, clean-shaven skin, dark-blue eyes and a nose that somebody more charitable might have described as Roman but Barratt thought just a bit too big for the man's face. In his early to mid-forties, Sims was a picture of good health, with a physique which suggested he exercised regularly to compensate for his sedentary job.

'How well do you know Peter Houghton?'

Sims smiled. 'I've known Peter since I was a boy. I used to come here and watch the lorries being cleaned and maintained. Started work here when I was sixteen, cleaning the cabs. Peter put me through an apprenticeship to become a mechanic and I worked my way up through the company.'

'So, he's been a mentor to you?'

'I suppose so. We're more like family now though. He trusts me to run the company and I trust him to make sure I get paid.' Sims sat back in his chair as though he'd said everything he could on the subject.

'What about the company finances?' O'Connor asked from his position next to the door. Barratt bristled – the DS had pulled rank and decided to ask questions of his own rather than leaving it to Barratt as agreed. The question seemed to unsettle Sims, or perhaps it was the fact that it came from O'Connor and his tone wasn't exactly polite.

'Finances?'

'Money. Incoming and outgoing. What sort of state is the company in?'

Sims sat back again and clasped his hands together on top of his desk. 'The company is in a good position. There isn't much competition in the local area, so we get a lot of new business. We also have our long-standing clients some of whom have been loyal through thick and thin for nearly seventy years.' His response sounded rehearsed and more than a little pompous as though he were giving a presentation to the board of directors.

'Why you?' O'Connor asked, changing tack.

'Why me what?'

'Well, I assume the company has been in the family for a couple of generations – hence the name and the livery – so why did Houghton choose you to manage it when he retired, if he has retired? Are you a relative?'

'No. I've already explained, I've been with the company all my working life and Peter appreciates loyalty. Can you tell me what this is about?' The man was clearly growing agitated. Looking from O'Connor to Barratt, seeking answers.

Barratt looked at O'Connor who gave him the briefest of nods. 'I'm sorry to tell you that Peter Houghton is dead,' he said.

'Dead? I only saw him yesterday and he was in the best of health...' Sims stopped speaking as he obviously realised the implication of two detectives telling him that his boss was deceased. 'How did he die? You wouldn't be here if it was a heart attack or something like that.'

'We really can't give you any details at the moment. Mr Houghton and his wife were found dead in their vehicle early this morning.'

'In their vehicle? It was a car accident?'

Barratt didn't respond and O'Connor just sniffed loudly and stared at the manager.

'I can't believe it,' Sims continued. 'Eleanor as well?'

'Did they have any family?' Barratt asked. 'Children, nieces, nephews?'

Sims shook his head. 'No. That's one of the reasons that I ended up managing the company. They married late in life – I think they were both in their fifties – and neither had been married before as far as I know. I don't know about extended family, though, but I've always assumed that there wasn't anybody.'

'Okay,' Barratt said, taking out his notebook. 'I'm going to need your details. It's possible that you may have to formally identify the bodies if you can do that?'

Sims nodded shakily.

'I also need to know if Mr Houghton had any enemies. Business rivals, disgruntled ex-employees, that kind of thing. Any arguments about how the company was being run?'

'Enemies? You think somebody killed them?' His eyes widened with incredulity.

'It's one line of enquiry,' Barratt said. 'Can you think of anybody with a grudge?'

Sims's eyes drifted as he seemed to be considering the question. 'I can't think of anybody,' he said. 'As far as I know, Peter was well respected.'

'What about you?' O'Connor asked. 'Do you have any enemies? Anybody who might want to send you a message?'

'Of course not! I run a haulage business – it's not the Mafia. It's not like me and the boss of Eddie Stobart go around letting each other's tyres down and decoupling rigs.'

Barratt slipped his notebook into the inside pocket of his suit jacket and stood up. 'Thanks for your time, Mr Sims. If we need anything else, we'll be in touch. And I'd appreciate it if you'd think about helping with the ID of the bodies.'

Sims nodded. 'Of course, anything I can do to help.'

Barratt followed O'Connor back to the car but wasn't surprised when the other man continued towards the yard where the lorries were parked.

'Still want to have a look around?' he asked.

O'Connor's moustache twitched. 'Obviously.'

'You saw it as well?'

'Couldn't miss it.'

Barratt was glad of the confirmation that what he'd seen wasn't his imagination. When O'Connor had asked Sims about arguments within the company, the man had flushed slightly and couldn't look at either of them. He was lying.

12

'It's a bit posh round here,' Hollis said as Kate pressed the doorbell of the Houghtons' nearest neighbour. The house, like Peter and Eleanor's bungalow, stood on its own plot but this one was smaller, and the gates were waist-high rather than over six feet. Built from the same red brick as the council estate five miles away where Kate had grown up, the two-storey building was double fronted and well set back from the road that passed through the village. As a child, Kate had occasionally walked to Turton with her parents on long summer days. One of the local farmers grew strawberries in the fields surrounding the television mast and they were cheap and plentiful enough to be worth the two-hour walk in the heat and humidity.

Later, in her teens, Kate had cycled the roads around the village, stopping often on the motorway bridge and musing about the destinations of the increasing number of cars using the newly built M18. Home to ex-footballers and at least one star of a daytime soap opera, Turton had always seemed like somewhere that would always be just beyond her reach, just a bit too exclusive for a girl from the Crosslands Estate.

'Always was,' Kate said. 'One of my school friends lived here. Snobby cow.'

Hollis barked a laugh, whether at Kate's comment or from surprise that she was sharing details of her childhood, Kate didn't know.

They both stepped back as the door was opened by a tall woman in her late twenties or early thirties who could have just stepped off the set of a television programme about perfect people and their perfect homes.

'Can I help you?' the woman asked, looking from Kate to Hollis as though unsure which of them to address. 'If you're Jehovah's Witnesses I'll tell you straight away that I'm a Satanist and I drink the blood of puppies.'

The comment was so unexpected that Kate couldn't suppress a grin. 'We're not. But we might have to arrest you for animal abuse,' she said, flashing her warrant card.

The woman's face relaxed. Not the most common reaction to finding police officers on your doorstep but Kate was glad of the suggestion of openness.

'Ah, I should have guessed given the amount of activity around my neighbours' house today. What's happened?' She held up a hand, palm outwards. 'No. I know, you can't tell me.'

'Can we come in?' Kate asked. 'It's probably easier than talking on the doorstep. And a lot more private.'

'Of course.' The woman turned and led them down a short hallway, painted a calming shade of pale blue. Kate appraised her as they walked. Lilac cashmere cardigan and black trousers seemed an unlikely combination for lounging around at home and a slightly odd choice for a young woman. Kate wondered if she'd been out somewhere special.

'Through here.'

The living room was painted in an off-white that Kate knew would have been called Calico or Barley and the leather suite was cream-coloured and immaculate. The carpet was a deep burgundy and held the shape of their footprints as they went to sit down.

'Lovely home,' Kate said, meaning it for once. 'Have you been here long Ms...?'

'Knowles, call me Adele,' the woman responded. 'And yes, you could say I've been here a while. I was born in the front bedroom of the house – thirty-four years ago.'

'You've lived here ever since?'

Adele nodded. 'Apart from three years at university in Leeds. I came back to care for my mother, but she ended up caring for me – until she died a few years ago.'

Kate waited for an explanation for the cryptic comment, but none was forthcoming. 'Do you work or are you at home most of the day?'

'Yes. And yes. I work at home. I'm a translator. Mainly technical journals. English to German.'

'Sounds interesting.'

Adele smiled. 'It's not but it pays well and there's no commuting involved. I'm sorry, I haven't offered you a drink. Tea? Coffee? A cold drink? I've got a lovely elderflower cordial that one of my neighbours makes.'

Hollis asked for cordial, but Kate declined the offer, and both waited while Adele disappeared into the kitchen for a couple of minutes.

'Sounds like she's got a good life,' Hollis said. 'Nice house, decent job and hours to suit.'

'You'd hate it,' Kate responded. 'Nobody to talk to. No reason to put a suit on and gel your hair. You'd be climbing the walls after a fortnight.'

Hollis laughed. 'You know me so well.'

'Here we go,' Adele announced, breezing back into the room holding a tray containing two glasses which rattled with ice cubes and dripped with condensation. Kate found herself regretting not asking for a drink as she watched Hollis take a large gulp. Despite the open windows the living room was getting warm as the midsummer sun moved round to the west.

'Can I ask you about your neighbours?' Kate began. Hollis carefully placed his drink on a coaster and took out his notebook.

'I assume you mean the Houghtons,' Adele said, taking a sip of her cordial. 'As that's where all the police activity has been focused.'

'Did you know them well?'

'Well enough.' Something about the woman's tone suggested that she didn't like her neighbours very much. 'They've lived next door since I was a teenager. They bought the plot and built their own home.'

'What were they like?' Hollis asked. 'Friendly, helpful? Were they an active part of the community?'

'Were? You're using past tense. Has something happened to them?'

Hollis glanced at Kate.

'A couple were found dead in their car this morning,' she said. 'It seems likely to be the Houghtons.'

'In their car? That's a bit odd.' The woman didn't seem upset or concerned about the deaths of her neighbours, more curious than dismayed. 'Was it an accident? A car crash?'

'We really can't give you any details,' Hollis said. 'When did you last see your neighbours?'

Adele shrugged. 'Maybe last week when I was putting out the bins. I usually saw *him* on bin day. Can't remember when I last saw *her*.'

'Did you speak?'

'No. I haven't spoken to Peter Houghton for years.'

Kate sat back in her seat, shocked. How could you avoid your neighbour in such a small community? 'Had you fallen out?'

Adele snorted. 'Fallen out? Not really. That would imply that we were friendly at some point. I couldn't stand Peter Houghton, and his wife wasn't much better.'

'Was he not generally liked in the village?'

'No idea. You might find it hard to believe but there's not a lot of gossip in Turton. At least, not that I know of. If there is, I'm more likely to be the subject of it rather than sharing it. I'm sure Peter Houghton wasn't one to keep his foul comments to himself.'

This was unexpected. The woman's vitriol was apparent in the way she spat Houghton's name every time she said it.

'Foul comments?'

'Transphobic crap. At first he'd just dead-name me.'

Realisation dawned on Kate, but Hollis was a bit slower on the uptake.

'Dead-name?' he asked, frowning. 'I'm not sure...'

'It's when somebody calls a trans person by their birth name. Houghton's known me since I was about fifteen years old. He insisted on using my birth name. Then it was loud comments whenever I went past. *Freak*, *weirdo*, that kind of thing. Always addressed to his wife, never directed at me, but loud enough for me to hear. He was a nasty old bigot and, while I'd never say I was glad somebody was dead, I can't say I care.'

'What about his wife? Did she make offensive comments?'

Adele shook her head. 'She hardly spoke. I got the feeling that she might be afraid of her husband – that she would never voice an opinion of her own and certainly not one that went against what he thought. I've got no evidence for that – it's just a gut thing. She always struck me as meek, servile. He was just an arrogant sod. His attitude about the environment was pretty appalling as well – I suppose you've heard. Buying land that could have been used for conservation and laughing when the local paper asked if he'd be making his lorry fleet more environmentally friendly.'

'Did other people in the village feel the same way about the Houghtons?' Hollis asked.

Adele took another sip of her drink, the musical tinkle of the ice cubes a torment to Kate. 'No idea. Like I said there isn't much gossip, as far as I know, and nobody said anything to me. You'll have to ask the rest of my neighbours. I'm probably the person who liked the Houghtons the least though. It was more personal with me. I hope it isn't a murder investigation because I'll probably be your prime suspect.'

Adele smiled, until she caught the look between Kate and Hollis.

'Oh. Oh, shit.'

1983

Mum was crying in the back of the van after the women picked us up to take us back to the camp. She kept saying, 'I can't believe it.' And 'I thought they'd listen.' The other women nodded in agreement, but I didn't know what they were talking about. The driver seemed to be going faster than last time but her urgency didn't seem to have infected the women in the back. There was a lot of sighing and shaking of their heads as they spoke in hushed voices. I couldn't work out any of the details but there was something going on at the camp and it was something very important.

It was dark when we arrived but there were lights everywhere inside the fence – really bright ones that hurt my eyes when I looked at them for too long. There were women everywhere, blocking the roads, clinging onto the fence, gathered around the tents and shelters. Mum ran straight up to the fence and started shouting swear words, really bad ones, and two of the other women from our van joined her. I wasn't sure what to do. Part of me wanted to join in with the swearing – Mum was so worked up that she probably wouldn't have minded – but I felt too small, too unimportant so I sat down next to one of the strange shelters that seemed to have sprung up since we were last here. The women make them out of branches and plastic sheets and old blankets.

A young woman tumbled down from the fence and landed almost at my feet, laughing and crying at the same time. 'Hey, kid. What's up?'

I just shrugged. I didn't know who she was, but she seemed a little too friendly and that made me wary of her, at first.

'I'm Taz,' she said. 'I've been here for a few months. I saw you get out of that van a couple of minutes ago. Are you new?'

'No!' I don't know why I shouted but I didn't want her to think I didn't belong. 'I've been here before. I came down with my mum a few months ago and we all held hands around the fence.'

Taz smiled as though I'd said something funny. 'That's great. I was here for that too. We called it 'Embrace the Base'. It was in all the papers. Did you have a good time?'

I didn't know how to answer that. I'd enjoyed being part of a big gang, but I didn't like all the cold and the mud. And I didn't like the feeling of not really knowing what was going on.

'It was all right,' I said.

Taz gave me a funny look. 'You don't want to be here, do you?'

I shrugged again. I was scared to say no in case she got mad.

'I get it,' she continued. 'I didn't like it at first. It's cold, and wet and muddy and there's not much to do. But it's *so* important that we stay. That we all stay. We're trying to change the world for the better and we're doing it for you, the kids.'

I didn't know what to say so I kept quiet. Taz sounded like Mum, like all the other women. They knew why they were here, and they seemed to have a plan. I just wished I knew what it was all about. Maybe, if I got to be friends with Taz she'd tell me.

13

'Other than Adele Knowles, the neighbours' comments about the Houghtons were fairly banal,' Kate said, opening the team briefing the next day. 'Kept themselves to themselves. Nice enough. That kind of thing. There were a couple of mentions of the land that Peter Houghton bought but nothing especially resentful.'

'Usual bland crap,' O'Connor muttered. He was right. Kate had lost count of how many cases she'd worked where the neighbours were shocked to learn that the man opposite was a drug dealer, or the woman next door beat her children. For such a nosey society, it seemed most were still very quick to judge on appearances and keep themselves to themselves.

'None of them saw anybody arrive at or leave the Houghtons' bungalow the night before last and there were no reports of an unfamiliar vehicle parked in the village.'

'So, our killer either arrived on foot, which seems unlikely, or was parked on the Houghtons' property? That suggests it was somebody they knew or trusted,' Hollis pointed out. 'So far we've found no family–'

'There's a nephew,' Sam interrupted as she entered the room

with her laptop under one arm and a mug of coffee in the opposite hand. 'Sorry I'm late. Got a bit distracted.'

'A nephew?' Kate prompted.

'Son of Eleanor Houghton's sister who died from MS. He lives just outside Adelaide.'

'Australia?'

'Unfortunately. That's why I was late – I was chatting with him on Skype. He's not been back to the UK for eight years – since his mother died – but he was in regular contact with his aunt and her husband. He claims they were settled, comfortable. Neither was in especially poor health and, the last time he spoke to them, they were looking forward to a holiday in Greece later in the year.'

'That just supports the theory that it wasn't suicide,' Barratt said. 'But we already know that. Did the nephew know of any enemies, competitors, threats to the couple?'

Sam shook her head. 'Nothing. Eleanor always said that business was good – she wasn't even worried too much about post-Brexit changes as most of Houghton's business is domestic.'

Kate held up her hands to silence the inevitable speculation between the members of her team. She could see that they were all eager to get started, to get digging into the details of Peter and Eleanor Houghton's lives but she needed them to focus, to start at the beginning – the crime scene.

'Right. I've got a preliminary tox report on Julia Sullivan which shows high levels of a benzodiazepine, I'm guessing Rohypnol but we need confirmation. I've also got *all* the Houghton images through from the SOCOs and the forensic team,' she began. 'I want to go through, photo by photo, and see what we've got before we go down the route of wild speculation and hearsay. Keep the Sullivan scene in mind as well. Look for similarities.'

Four faces turned to the screen as she tapped a couple of

keys on her laptop to project the first image. It showed the car with the doors open to allow the fumes to escape but with both bodies still *in situ*. Apparently, medics had established that both occupants of the car were beyond hope of resuscitation and so had left everything in place for the police and forensics teams.

'They look relaxed,' Sam said. 'Both heads tilted back like they've just stopped to admire the view.'

'All they need is a flask and a couple of sandwiches,' O'Connor said.

The next few images were close-ups of the couple from various angles none of which showed any marks or injuries on the bodies. Nothing to suggest that this wasn't suicide. There were close-ups of the tubing taped to the exhaust pipe and the rear window where it entered the car.

'Prints from the duct tape?' Barratt asked hopefully.

'Nothing yet.'

'If one of the Houghtons had attached the tubing, their prints would have been all over it. Do we know where the piping is from?'

'Not yet,' Kate said again. She made a note. It was a good question. If the plastic tubing wasn't from the Houghtons' house or garage, then they might be able to trace it to a source which could lead them to the killer.

Three pictures showed the 'suicide note'. Kate had already had confirmation that the paper matched that in the printer in Peter Houghton's home office, but it had no distinguishing marks and was probably from a supermarket or office supplies shop. More analysis was needed to match the ink to the printer but, again, the printer was a common brand and model. The note could have been printed by the killer and taken to the house.

'The phrasing's weird,' Sam commented. 'Why the explanation? Why not just a request to be left alone?'

Kate studied the words. It was polite – *please leave us alone* – and the second sentence did seem a little unnecessary. Why bother to tell whoever found them that the couple had had a good life? Exactly the same as the note in Julia Sullivan's bathroom.

'*We* and *us*,' Hollis commented. 'They're in this together, like it's a joint decision. We're being drawn to Peter Houghton because of his business and his profile in the media but the note suggests that they're both the target.'

'They're both as much to blame,' Sam mused. 'Both as guilty.'

'What about *time to go*?' Kate asked. 'To me it suggests that they've been set a deadline and they've not met it. Maybe a ransom request or they were being blackmailed and didn't pay? Could they have some link with Julia Sullivan's politics? We know Peter was unpleasant to Adele based on her being trans. Not that different from Julia's comments on homosexuality.'

Blank looks from her colleagues. Kate enjoyed these morning brainstorming sessions – they often set out a plan for the day, each team member following up on promising ideas – but this time it didn't seem to be working.

'What about their time being up in the sense of it being time the world was rid of them? Or am I reaching a bit too far?' Barratt asked.

Kate shrugged. It seemed as likely as anything else that had been suggested. Sam was tapping on her keyboard, engrossed in something. The young DC often seemed oblivious to the world around her when she was chasing something in cyberspace and Kate knew better than to disturb her.

She moved on to the next image, the keys hanging from a rivet of the television mast. 'Car keys,' she said. 'About fifty yards from the vehicle. Whoever left them there climbed the gate of the compound. It's six feet high and well beyond the capabilities of either of the Houghtons.'

'Are we sure about that?'

Kate nodded. 'They were elderly, Eleanor usually walked with a stick.'

'So even if the couple had survived, they couldn't have driven home,' Barratt said. 'But it's not far to walk. This isn't about making sure they couldn't reach the keys – it's symbolic. It means something to the killer.'

O'Connor sighed heavily. 'Just what we need. Another psycho. If it only means something to him, how the hell are we supposed to understand it?'

Kate smiled. O'Connor wasn't a fan of the use of psychology in police work. He liked his villains to be bad – end of story. He understood means and motive but anything more 'airy-fairy' and he tended towards open scepticism.

'If we can work out what it means it might speak to motive. Like the mirror.' Kate switched to a photograph of the rear-view mirror in its unusual position, a different image from the one they'd seen previously. In this one the crack was clearly visible and it caught a portion of Eleanor Houghton's face.

'I still think it was an accident,' O'Connor said dismissively.

'Maybe. Or maybe our murderer wanted Eleanor Houghton to take one last long look at herself,' Hollis said. 'Perhaps that's why he used part of a mirror to kill Julia.'

Kate displayed a photograph of the broken mirror on the landing of Julia Sullivan's home. If it had fallen it would have landed on carpet and probably have remained intact. It looked as though somebody had taken it down from the wall and deliberately broken it.

The positioning of the mirror in the car was interesting – shifting the focus from Peter to Eleanor – an idea they couldn't ignore. Kate was about to show the last two images from the Turton scene when Cooper sat up suddenly.

'Look at this,' she said, turning her laptop round so they could see what was on the screen. It was an image of another suicide note held down by a chunk of rock. Two sentences.

I'M SORRY. I'VE HAD A GOOD LIFE BUT IT'S TIME TO GO.

'Where was this?' Kate asked, intrigued by the similarity.

'Suicide on Burbage Edge earlier this year. Olivia Thornbury. Found hanged by a couple who were out on a hike. Nothing to suggest suspicious death.'

'Doesn't sound much like our case,' Barratt said. 'Apart from the wording of the note.'

'Or our killer could have a link to this woman and used words from her note,' Sam suggested.

Kate was already accessing the case file, intrigued by the similarity. 'She was one of us. A retired DCI. Hang on.' She skimmed the notes, trying to absorb the most important details.

'Partner hadn't reported her missing. Thought she was out for an early walk, but she was found hanged from a climbing rope on one of the steep pitches on Burbage Edge. She'd been a bit down because she'd been forced to give up climbing due to ill health. PM reports diazepam in her system which partner confirms was prescribed by her GP. Nothing to suggest it wasn't suicide.'

'Nice try, Cooper,' O'Connor said with a grin. 'I still think it's to do with the haulage company. There's something going on there and I reckon that's why Houghton was murdered. The wife's just collateral damage. I reckon we'll find some sort of link with the Sullivans before long.'

'Hang on,' Kate said, still reading. 'There's a statement from her sister that says Olivia wouldn't have taken her own life. They were raised Catholic and it went against everything she believed in. There's also a question mark about the veracity of the note. It's in block capitals so nobody could confirm it's Olivia's handwriting.'

'Religion again,' Hollis mused. Kate had given the others a brief account of their visit to the Church of the Right Hand but they hadn't been able to use it to move the Sullivan case forward beyond Kate's suspicion that Julia had been manipulated in some way.

'We hear that all the time though,' Barratt said. 'Family members often claim that their husband or father or whatever would never have killed themselves for whatever reason. It's just denial.'

'She's an ex-copper though,' Hollis said. 'Probably lots of people out there bearing a grudge against her. But how would that link to the Houghtons? Or Julia Sullivan?'

The group sat in silence for a few seconds as they pondered a possible link. Kate could see that O'Connor had already dismissed it and Barratt seemed to be inclined to side with him. They'd spent some time poking around the haulage yard and the DS was convinced that something was amiss in Houghton's company, despite the lack of concrete evidence. Cooper would want to find more – data mining until she struck gold, or bedrock. Kate looked at the note again trying to feel what her instinct was telling her because, really, that was what connections like this came down to – her gut. Two sentences and there it was, that niggle, that faint electric current in her brain that told her not to ignore this even if it amounted to nothing.

'Right, jobs,' she said, decision made. 'Sam, keep on with background for the Houghtons – especially the money. Find out more about this nephew as well – did he stand to gain anything by their deaths? And see if you can find a connection between either of the Houghtons, Julia Sullivan and/or Olivia Thornbury.'

O'Connor shook his head, but Kate knew he wouldn't dare to comment. 'Steve, Matt, I haven't forgotten it's your lucky day. Get over to Doncaster Royal Infirmary for the PMs on Peter and Eleanor Houghton. Give Kailisa my regards.'

Barratt stood up, grinning, and grabbed his suit jacket from the back of his chair. 'I'm sure he'll appreciate that.'

Kate waited until she was alone with Hollis before revealing his assignment for the morning. She wasn't entirely certain of his support, but she knew he wouldn't voice his doubts until the job had been done. He was looking at her, half expectant, half apprehensive. He knew what she was going to say.

'Okay, Dan. We're off to Sheffield to talk to DCI Thornbury's partner. If I'm right and there is a link to the Houghtons and Julia Sullivan, it might help us find our murderer. And, if I'm wrong, lunch is on me.'

14

Barratt smiled as O'Connor wrinkled his nose in disgust. 'I hate the smell of this place. It's so clean. All you can smell is chemicals.'

'You'd prefer rotting flesh and body fluids?'

O'Connor nodded. 'It'd be a bit more real.'

Barratt snorted. He knew it was all bluster. Nobody liked attending a post-mortem – and three in a couple of days was a bit much – but after your first, which was a rite of passage and you were lucky if you didn't pass out, they got better. He didn't actually mind the cutting and weighing and measuring – it was fascinating how much the body could tell them about manner of death – but he still hated the first few minutes where he had to adjust to being around the remains of a human being. Once the cutting started it was easier to see the flesh as meat and the organs as clues.

The pathology suite at Doncaster Royal Infirmary was state-of-the-art, a stark contrast with the 1960s pebble-dashed exterior of the bulk of the building. It housed laboratories and a sealed area where observers could watch and listen without being exposed directly to the bodies. The two men made their way to the viewing gallery and waited for Dr Kailisa to appear in the pathology lab below – an audience of two awaiting an especially grisly play.

'Gentlemen.' Kailisa greeted them with only a slight glance up to where they were sitting and a tiny nod. Barratt had a lot of respect for the pathologist, finding him to be thorough and diligent but he knew that DI Fletcher had often found the man frustrating and cold.

'Your boss off doing more important things?' His smile took the sting out of the sarcasm, but Barratt still felt the need to jump to Kate's defence.

'We might have a link to another case. She's gone off to Sheffield to investigate,' he said, disclosing the surprising details of the email the boss had sent him just as he and O'Connor had arrived at the hospital.

'Ah, the lure of the big city. Shall we begin?' This last comment was directed at his assistant rather than to the two police officers. Barratt recognised the woman from previous PMs he'd attended. He was always struck by the contrast between her and her boss. Kailisa was short with dark hair and olive skin – his brown eyes shrewd but not unkind. The assistant was tall and slim with a helmet of bleached blonde hair cropped close to her head – a startling contrast with her dark skin. Whenever Barratt had needed to speak to her, her intense green eyes made him feel like he was a butterfly skewered on a pin. It wasn't an entirely unpleasant feeling.

The post-mortem on Peter Houghton was unremarkable and, in the absence of toxicology results, no cause of death was discovered. Kailisa was reasonably convinced that the man hadn't died solely from carbon monoxide poisoning but couldn't say for certain how close to death Houghton had been when the hose from the exhaust was placed in the car. Not prone to supposition, he offered no theories or speculation but simply recorded the facts.

'Well, that was tedious,' O'Connor said, tapping on the screen of his phone. 'I've emailed the key points to Kate. Coffee?'

Barratt would rather have gone over the findings himself, looking for anomalies, but there really hadn't been much to work with and caffeine seemed like a good way to fortify himself for Eleanor Houghton's PM. He allowed O'Connor to lead the way to the hospital canteen and didn't bother to argue when his colleague sent him to the counter – insisting that, as his junior, it was down to Barratt to buy the refreshments. Not that Barratt minded. There was only one rank between them, but O'Connor enjoyed the pretence of superiority and Barratt had no reason to deprive him of his fun.

'So, Kailisa's assistant?' O'Connor said with a grin. 'I can't tell if you fancy her or if you're scared of her.'

Barratt took a swig of his coffee and stared at the scuffed Formica tabletop. 'Me neither,' he admitted.

O'Connor laughed, a quick, sharp bark. 'Maybe you should find out which it is. Ask her if she wants a cup of coffee on her next break.' He was staring intently at Barratt over the rim of his mug, foam from his cappuccino caught in his moustache.

'Not while I'm working.'

'God, you're so bloody uptight,' O'Connor said, slamming his coffee down on the table hard enough to make Barratt flinch. 'It's a cup of coffee not dinner and back to yours. She might have some useful information for you. Use that as an excuse.'

'I don't even know her name,' Barratt admitted. 'Kailisa has never introduced us.'

'She's called Nicole,' O'Connor said with a smirk. 'I asked.'

'Oh, so she's one of your sloppy seconds?'

'No. I asked her name because I couldn't call her Kailisa's assistant when I was talking to her.'

Barratt wasn't convinced. 'Nicole what?'

'Sherwin, Sharratt, Shields? I can't remember. Cute accent though.'

Barratt thought for a second. He'd hardly heard the woman say two words in the lab. Had he picked up an accent? Obviously, O'Connor had managed a longer interaction with the woman, increasing Barratt's suspicions that she'd either gone out with O'Connor or she'd knocked him back.

'She's a Kiwi,' O'Connor said. 'South Island apparently. At least think about it, Matt. Maybe a date with a cute Kiwi might loosen you up a bit.'

Barratt picked up his coffee cup and stared into its depths. O'Connor was right in one way – it had been far too long since he'd been out with anybody. The bloody job just got in the way of everything and, if he was going to achieve his next life goal and make sergeant before he was thirty-five, he needed to focus on his work. 'I'll think about it,' he said.

'Yeah, right,' his colleague responded with a shake of his head. 'I won't be holding my breath.'

O'Connor's phone buzzed just as he was taking a last slug of his coffee. He glanced at the text message. 'They're ready for us again,' he told Barratt. 'Let's see if *Mrs* Houghton is a bit more informative than her husband.'

Kailisa had already started examining the body when O'Connor and Barratt returned to the viewing gallery. He glanced up as they took their seats, both leaning forward, eager not to miss anything.

'Welcome back, gentleman,' the pathologist said once they were settled. 'Act two has just started. External examination shows no obvious wounds or injuries so far. We have a vaccination scar on the upper left arm and a birthmark on the left calf. And we have initial toxicology results and bloods.'

'What do they tell us?' O'Connor asked as Kailisa stared at the screen.

'High levels of benzodiazepine and an opiate in both Mr and Mrs Houghton.'

'Prescribed?'

Kailisa shook his head. 'Unlikely at this dosage. And not in this combination. There are signs that some of the opiate had been broken down, suggesting it was consumed over the course of two, maybe three hours. I need to check the stomach contents of both to see if there's any residue, although Mr Houghton's stomach contained only a small amount of brown fluid suggesting he hadn't eaten anything in the hours leading up to his death.'

Barratt tapped the information into the email app on his phone, intending to send it to Kate as soon as he had all the relevant information. 'You said something about the combination of drugs?'

Kailisa looked up. 'It's very unlikely that a medical practitioner would prescribe benzodiazepines with an opiate. It's a potentially lethal combination. I can't say yet whether the drug was a sedative or something else, possibly Rohypnol. The most common opiate would be codeine or morphine.'

'Could either of them have been bought over the counter?'

'Not at this dosage. Codeine is the strongest pain killer a pharmacist can sell, and it must be less than twenty milligrams per dose. Anything more than that requires a prescription. I doubt anybody could be forced to take a handful of pills against their will.'

'And morphine?' O'Connor asked. The team had been involved in a case where a so-called mercy killing had been carried out using liquid morphine.

'Possibly. Morphine and diazepam are both available in liquid form.'

'Nothing else?'

'Alcohol. Both Mr and Mrs Houghton were over the legal driving limit. In England the limit is eight milligrams per 100 millilitres of blood. Mr Houghton had ninety-eight and Mrs Houghton had 107.'

Barratt included the figures in his email. 'Would this level of blood alcohol have had a negative effect when combined with the drugs?'

Kailisa smiled. 'We're getting into the realms of speculation, DC Barratt. At the moment I'd rather not comment.'

O'Connor stood up. 'But surely an elderly person with a few drinks and a hefty dose of a couple of drugs would struggle to stay conscious and awake? Could the killer have driven them to the dump site and just left them there, half-dead and let the carbon monoxide finish his work?'

'Speculation,' Kailisa repeated. 'I'd need to examine the results in much more detail in order to support or refute that hypothesis. Which I will do in due course.'

O'Connor sighed and sat back down.

Barratt could feel the frustration radiating from his pores as he rubbed his face with both hands. 'Look, Steve. It's something we can work with. I need to email Kate – she said the case in Sheffield involved diazepam. It's another possible link.'

'Hardly,' O'Connor responded. 'Half the population's on drugs for depression and anxiety and the other half just aren't paying attention.'

Barratt sighed, frustrated as he tried to focus on the autopsy. The pale flesh looked abandoned, marooned in the harsh light, the closed eyes and slack face somehow accusing. He was relieved when Kailisa called his assistant over to help him move the body onto its front.

'Another birthmark on the lower back,' Kailisa said, moving

the high-strength, digitally lit, magnifying glass up the body from the feet. 'Oh, what's this?'

Barratt stood up, squinting at the scene in front of him, trying to work out what Kailisa had noticed.

'We have a tattoo.' He gestured to Nicole, who'd picked up a large digital camera, and pointed out the design on Eleanor Houghton's shoulder. Standing back while his assistant took photographs from every imaginable angle, Kailisa looked at one of the computer monitors on the counter top which ran the length of the back wall of the lab. He frowned, strode over and clicked the mouse.

Barratt turned his attention back to the pathologist. 'What sort of tattoo?'

Kailisa muttered something inaudible to his assistant and the television screen in the gallery flickered into life showing a clear image of the tattoo on Eleanor Houghton's shoulder.

'What is that?' O'Connor asked, tilting his head from one side to the other. 'A tree?'

Like Julia's tattoo, the ink was faded, the outline blurred by time, but it was possible to make out a general shape. 'Can you enlarge it a bit?' said Barratt.

The image became slightly larger and marginally less clear.

'Is it a weapon of some sort – something medieval?'

'I think it's a labrys,' Nicole said.

'A what?' Barratt could hear the New Zealand accent clearly but couldn't make out the word.

'A labrys. It's a double-headed axe. Symbol of the Amazons.'

'I thought their symbol was a smiley arrow,' O'Connor joked but Nicole's mouth set in a straight line of disapproval. Barratt could see why Kailisa might have chosen to work with her.

'The Amazons were a race of warrior women,' she explained slowly and clearly as if she was telling a story to a child. 'The labrys was a symbol of their strength. It also has another connotation.' Nicole glanced at Kailisa who nodded for her to continue.

'In the seventies and eighties, it was adopted by lesbian feminists – especially separatists – for its associations with strong women.'

Barratt studied the image again. Another feminist symbol like the one Julia Sullivan had on her ankle. And, like Julia's, it looked old, possibly done by an amateur, and it was on a part of the body that wouldn't have often been visible. Something she wanted to keep hidden?

'How old is it? Is there any way to tell?'

Kailisa shook his head. 'It's not in an area that would be exposed to very much sunlight, so I'd expect it to keep some definition for many years. I may be able to use x-ray to see how deeply the ink penetrates the skin but that may not be of much use.'

'But it could be from the seventies or eighties?'

'It could.'

'Can I have a photo of the tattoo? I'll send it to Kate and Sam. It might help even if it's not the same as Julia's.'

'Already sent,' Kailisa said, nodding towards Nicole who was looking at a series of images on her monitor. 'It's very different from Mrs Sullivan's though.'

Barratt finished his email and tapped send. The blood results were useful, but the tattoo was a puzzle. What was a lesbian feminist symbol doing on the shoulder of an elderly, married woman?

15

'Hope *I* get to retire on a DCI's salary,' Hollis said as he turned in to the driveway of Olivia Thornbury's former home in Totley on the western outskirts of Sheffield. 'You'd not know you were still in the city if you lived out here.'

The area had a rural feel and Kate knew from the map on her phone that they were only a few minutes' drive from the edge of the Peak District. The lane that Olivia Thornbury had lived on was narrow with mature trees looming over the tarmac like bereaved relatives peering over the edge of an open coffin. It would have been oppressive but for the bright morning sunlight dappling the road with shifting shadows. The house itself was set back behind a dark hedge of leylandii, a wooden five-bar gate breaking up the deep-green foliage, opening onto a short gravel drive and a block-paved parking area. There were two cars parked – a white Mini and a dark-blue BMW – but still plenty of room for the Audi that Hollis had signed out of the car pool.

'It's not bad is it?' Kate said, taking in the double-fronted two-storey home with its bay windows and large oak front door. 'I reckon if you marry up a few ranks and never have kids you might be able to afford the top floor.'

Hollis grinned. 'Too much garden anyway. I prefer my flat: at least I don't have grass to cut.'

Kate rapped the heavy brass knocker against the door three times and stood back. Nothing. She tried again with the same result. Just as she was about to peer into one of the downstairs windows a figure appeared round the side of the house carrying a rake in one hand and a pair of shears in the other.

'Can I help you?' The woman looked as though she was in her late sixties or early seventies with a narrow, dark face and long grey hair tied back in a neat ponytail.

'DI Fletcher and DC Hollis from South Yorkshire Police.' Kate took a step forward holding out her ID.

The woman squinted, wrinkles forming deep nests around her brown eyes, before scrutinising Kate's face. She placed the head of the rake on the ground and slung her right hip outwards, using the handle like a pole to shift her weight to one side. 'Should I know you?' she asked. 'Were you one of Liv's colleagues?'

'No, I'm sorry, I never met her. Are you Sylvia Kerr?'

The woman's eyes gave a quick flick towards Hollis then back to Kate. 'You look like you're here on a death knock but you're a couple of months too late. What's this about?'

'We'd like to talk to Olivia's partner about her death. Would that be you? Are you Sylvia Kerr?'

The woman took a deep breath before offering the briefest of nods. 'I'm Sylvia. But I can't imagine you have anything useful to tell me. The case is closed as far as I know.'

There was anger in her tone. She wasn't happy with the investigation for some reason, Kate thought. Perhaps Cooper had been on to something. 'We're not here to tell you anything, Ms Kerr. We're here to ask you some questions – if you don't mind giving us half an hour of your time.' Kate could see that the woman was curious, but her grief was still raw, and her anger may have been the only emotion moving her forward. 'Honestly, I don't want to make things worse for you, but I'm involved with two cases similar to the death of your partner and you might be able to help.'

Sylvia gave Kate a sceptical sneer. 'A suicide? Why would somebody of your rank be investigating a suicide. What are you not telling me?'

Kate sighed. Obviously, years of living with a police officer had made Sylvia suspicious and cynical. She was just going to have to be honest. 'I'm sorry. I'm investigating two cases which aren't what they seem. Both look like suicide, but there are strong suggestions that they are in fact murders. One of my team found reference to Olivia's suicide note in our files and there are some similarities. I'm here to find out if there's a link. If Olivia's death wasn't suicide.'

'Liv,' the woman said, straightening and throwing the rake over her shoulder. 'If I'm going to talk to you, we need to get that straight. She was called Liv. Come round to the back garden.'

Sylvia led the way round the side of the house to a huge open space that was split into three different levels. The top was mainly decking and outdoor furniture, a summerhouse dominated the middle level, and the bottom was grass and raised beds.

The view was stunning. The garden dropped to open fields and the purple edge of the Peak District, with Lose Hill clearly visible in the far distance.

'Wow,' Kate said. 'I hadn't realised we were so high up.'

Sylvia smiled for the first time. 'It's quite a view. That's why we bought the house. Our bedroom looks out onto all that. We–' The woman's face crumpled as she struggled with the enormity of her bereavement, but she didn't give in to the wave of sorrow. With a visible physical effort, she straightened up, leant the rake against the wall of the house and continued. 'Can

I get you both a drink. Something cold perhaps? It's quite warm back here.'

Kate asked for water and Hollis followed her lead, allowing Sylvia the opportunity to get away from them for a few minutes and regain control of her emotions.

'Sit,' she said, pointing to a cluster of chairs encircling a cast-iron table. 'I'll only be a minute.'

Hollis sat down and leaned back, crossing his hands behind his head and stretching out his legs. 'Could get used to this,' he said.

'I've told you, work hard and marry up. In fact, marry *way* up. She'll need to be at least chief super to keep you in this style.'

'I think a lottery win's more likely.'

Kate didn't respond, allowing the warmth and the view to calm her as she mentally worked through a list of questions she needed to ask Sylvia Kerr. The woman was shrewd – she would see straight through any attempt to disguise Kate's real intent – and she was grieving. The direct approach was the only one likely to work.

'Here we go,' Sylvia said, stepping back out into the garden. She seemed much more composed as she placed a tray of drinks on the table and sat down opposite Hollis, who'd had the good sense to sit up properly and look attentive. 'Help yourselves.'

Kate reached for a glass and took a large gulp. The water was ice cold, refreshing. 'I'm so sorry to intrude like this,' she began. 'But when I saw the note that Liv had left, something started nagging at me. The wording was almost identical to the cases we're working. Are you convinced that Liv wrote that note?'

Sylvia shook her head. 'It's impossible to be certain. It was written in capital letters so there was no chance of recognising the handwriting. It was plausibly Liv's writing, but I honestly don't know. Part of me wants to say it wasn't, because then I don't have to accept that she killed herself and another part just wants to let it go and move on. Does that sound awful?'

'Not at all,' Kate said. Sudden death affected everybody differently and Kate wasn't about to judge this woman on the basis of a response that was just as valid as any other. 'Was there anything else that either confirmed suicide or made you suspicious that there was more to Liv's death? I read a statement from her sister which suggested that suicide was out of the question because Liv was raised Catholic.'

Sylvia smiled and took a sip of water, her eyes locked on Kate's over the rim of the glass. 'Catholic,' she said shaking her head. 'How likely is that? Do you know what the Catholic church's attitude is towards homosexuality? Liv had abandoned her childhood religion long before I met her and no, before you ask, I don't think she was reconsidering her position as she got older. We'd been together a long time, DI Fletcher. I may not know how or why Liv died but I certainly knew how she lived.'

Kate believed her. The woman had an inner calm and dignity which supported her words. Could Kate have said the same about her ex-husband, Garry? Did she truly know him? She doubted it very much. And Nick? Maybe one day, she hoped.

'How long had you been together?' Kate asked.

'Over thirty years. We met through mutual friends. I was a teacher reeling from the implications of Thatcher's Section 28 nonsense and Liv had just been promoted to detective sergeant. We just clicked despite the age difference and ended up moving in together later the same year. That was that really – Liv moved up the ranks and I ended up as the head of a large primary school here in Sheffield. I think Liv was a bit envious when I retired but she loved her job. We'd planned to travel after she finally gave it all up – India, South East Asia, Australia.' Sylvia sighed and shifted her gaze to the immense view. 'She was diagnosed with arthritis in her hip and lower spine, but I honestly didn't think she was devastated. Upset, yes. Worried, definitely. She loved to climb but she also enjoyed just being in the outdoors. She could still hike and cycle. We'd been looking at electric bikes the previous day.'

Kate thought about the picture Sylvia was painting of her partner. There was nothing to suggest depression or suicidal ideation. Then she remembered something from the PM.

'What about the diazepam? Why was she prescribed those if she wasn't depressed or anxious?'

'She told me they were for muscle spasms. She had a bit of sciatica as well as the arthritis, caused by spasms in her piriformis muscle.'

'Has her GP confirmed this?' Hollis asked, notebook and pencil in hand. It was a good question. If the drugs had been for something physical rather than psychological it suggested that Olivia Thornbury's state of mind might not have been as low as her actions suggested.

Sylvia shook her head. 'I honestly don't know. You'd have to check.'

Hollis made a note.

'Can I ask you about the morning of Liv's death?' Kate asked. 'I know it's painful, but we need to be thorough.'

Sylvia nodded, her expression eager rather than upset, as if she thought they might be able to unearth some new evidence.

'When did you realise Liv wasn't at home?'

'When I got up. I'm a heavy sleeper so I didn't hear her leave. It must have been around eight.'

'And her car was gone?'

'Yes. I didn't think too much of it. She'd been struggling with insomnia and pain, so she often went for a walk before breakfast. She said it helped to free up her joints.'

'Is her car one of the ones at the front of the house?'

'The BMW. Why?'

'Did you drive it back here or one of the police officers?'

'I did,' Sylvia said, frowning and running a hand through her hair, dislodging long strands from the ponytail. 'I had to take the spare key because Liv's was missing. I suppose it's amongst the rocks somewhere.'

Kate glanced at Hollis who raised his eyebrows slightly in acknowledgement. Similar to the Houghton case.

'What?' Sylvia asked. 'Is that strange? I just thought they'd dropped out of her pocket as she... as she fell.'

'What about the rope?' Kate asked. 'Was it one of Liv's?'

Sylvia shook her head. 'I don't know. I assume so. All the climbing stuff's in the garage but I haven't been able to face looking through it all.'

'But it was climbing rope?'

'Yes. Knotted around one of the boulders at the top of the edge.'

'Knotted?'

'I don't know. The police didn't give me specific details of the bloody knot. Liv knew what she was doing with ropes. If she'd wanted to make it secure, she'd have been able to.'

Sylvia Kerr was starting to get irate and Kate was acutely aware that the woman was still in the early stages of grief – anger was probably close to the surface of her emotions most of the time. Kate made a mental note to ask Cooper to access the scene photographs and forensics. If Liv hadn't fixed the rope, there may be a clue in the way it was knotted.

She stood up and Hollis followed her lead. 'I'm truly sorry for your loss,' she said. 'And I'm sorry we put you through this. If we do find a connection, and it's only an *if* at this stage, would you be happy for one of us to ask you more questions?'

Sylvia shook her head. 'I don't know. I don't see what good it would do, to be honest.'

Kate understood her sentiment. The connection between the three cases was tenuous at best and it was almost unbearably painful for Sylvia to speak about her partner's death. Their trip to Sheffield felt like a bit of a wild goose chase and Kate was very conscious that she'd promised Dan lunch if they didn't find a connection between Olivia Thornbury and the Houghton and Sullivan cases. It looked like the bacon butties were on her.

They didn't speak as Sylvia led the way back to the front of the house and the goodbyes were lukewarm and stilted.

'Hang on,' Hollis said, one leg in the car. 'What's that?' He nodded towards the BMW.

'What?' Kate couldn't see what he was looking at and Sylvia Kerr had turned towards the car looking puzzled.

'Was that from an accident?'

Sylvia took two steps towards the car and then shook her head. 'It was like that when I went to pick it up. I assumed somebody had knocked it after Liv parked up.'

She stepped back allowing Kate a clear view of the car. The mirror on the driver's side was completely shattered.

16

'You've got a broken mirror, similar notes and a couple of tattoos? Is that right?' Detective Chief Inspector Priya Das was making no attempt to keep the incredulity out of her voice or her shrewd brown eyes. 'And, based on these elements, you think the three cases are linked?'

Kate didn't embarrass easily but she was struggling to resist the urge to hang her head or clench her fists. She had a lot of respect for the DCI and had appreciated her support in the past. Das was a career copper but she was never blinkered or restrained by the politics of the job. Her small stature might have suggested weakness, but her immaculate tailoring and expertly applied make-up hid an almost forensic intellect. Not much got past Das and now, faced with the stark reality of the three cases Kate knew that the DCI would see the connections as tenuous at best. Kate felt that there was something there – she just didn't know how to convey that feeling to Das. She was glad that there was nobody on her team in the meeting to witness her humiliation.

'I just feel that there's something there...'

'Feel? I know we all go with our gut sometimes, Kate, but I'm just not seeing it. DCI Thornbury had no known connection with Eleanor Houghton or Julia Sullivan, and I don't think the tattoos are anywhere near good enough. I know a labrys is an odd choice for a seemingly heterosexual, elderly woman but who knows what she did in her past. Same for Sullivan. People change, Kate. I'm not the same person I was in my twenties – thank God – and I doubt you are.'

Das was right about that. Kate had floundered a bit after university and her father's death. She'd been quite anti-police during her teens but much of that was connected with the miners' strike and the opinions of her friends. If she were honest, she'd suffered more from the families of other miners calling her dad a scab because he was in a different union than she had from police or media perception of the industry. After a year of working in a pub in the evenings and a grocery shop at the weekend, Kate decided that she needed a career and the police force appeared to offer everything she wanted. She'd removed all but one of the piercings in her ears and let her short, platinum, bleached hair grow back to its natural blonde – relieved that she'd always resisted the lure of a tattoo – and, apart from the years when she was at home with her son, she'd fitted in and progressed.

'I think you'd be better off looking at *Peter* Houghton. In my experience cases like this are about money and his company made him a wealthy man. Perhaps he's connected to Julia's husband in some way. I don't want a respected police officer like Thornbury under investigation based on your hunch.'

Kate tried not to react to Das's comment about her experience. Kate was at least ten years older than her superior and had been doing the job since the DCI was a teenager. Instead, she gave a reluctant nod.

'I'll send O'Connor and Barrett back to the haulage yard,' she conceded. 'Cooper's still working on the Houghtons' finances. It looks like their solicitor is the executor of their wills so we should be able to find out who benefits from their deaths fairly quickly. We're still waiting on some tests from the Sullivan house.'

'And DCI Thornbury?'

Kate sighed. 'On the back burner.'

~

'We're not pursuing the Thornbury case,' Kate said to her assembled team. O'Connor smiled broadly but the others simply nodded. They understood the constraints that budgetary matters placed on investigations and they also knew that Das tended to favour Kate. If the DCI had told Kate to drop the case, there would have been a good reason.

'So, what now?' Barratt asked.

'We're going to have a good look at the haulage business. And we need to know who benefits from the deaths of Peter and Eleanor Houghton. I'm also curious about Eleanor's history. That tattoo doesn't tally with who she appears to be. If this isn't to do with the business, I don't want to risk overlooking something from her past. And we're still trying to link the Houghtons and the Sullivans.'

'I'll get on to the Houghtons' solicitor,' Cooper said. 'See what we can find out about the will. I'll also do a bit of digging into Eleanor's background – there might be something on social media. And I know there was a laptop taken from one of the bedrooms; I'll see if the contents have been accessed.'

Kate knew she could count on Sam Cooper's loyalty, but she also knew that the DC was inclined to dig deeper than the parameters she was set. The Thornbury element of the investigation wasn't dead until Cooper came up blank.

'Steve, Matt.' O'Connor and Barratt fixed their eyes on hers in anticipation. 'Back to Houghton Haulage in Thorpe. I want you to find out how the operation works, who's really in charge and who might be keeping secrets.'

The two men stood up and pushed their chairs under the table.

'What about me?' Hollis asked.

'You're still owed a day's leave. How about you take it while I go through some paperwork? Tomorrow we'll work through what these three have turned up.'

Hollis looked disappointed at being given the day off and Kate didn't blame him. He'd already gone to the effort of getting ready for work and driving into Doncaster from his flat in Bentley, but Kate didn't want to drag him into her plans for the morning. If she ran into trouble with Das it wasn't fair to have Hollis involved.

Adele Knowles answered the door with a bright smile. 'Detective Inspector Fletcher. Back again so soon?'

'Just a couple of follow-up questions,' Kate said, looking round to make sure the uniformed constable stationed at the gates of Peter Houghton's home hadn't recognised her. 'Could I come in?'

Adele held the front door open and ushered Kate into the hallway. 'That looked a bit cloak and dagger,' she commented. 'Not supposed to be here?'

She's observant, Kate thought. Which might not be a bad thing given the questions Kate had. She followed Adele through to the lounge where they'd spoken two days ago and took a seat opposite the picture window.

'Drink?' Adele asked.

Kate shook her head. 'I don't have much time. Just a couple of quick questions and then I'll be out of your hair.'

Adele sat on the edge of the sofa and leaned forward eagerly. 'I'm intrigued. The Houghtons' apparent suicide is the talk of the village, but I doubt I'll be able to help.'

Taking her phone out of her pocket, Kate scrolled to the image of Eleanor Houghton's tattoo and passed the device to Adele. 'Do you know what this is?'

The woman took the phone and studied the screen. 'It's a labrys. An Amazon axe.'

'What does it represent?'

'Strength, I suppose. It's a popular symbol with lesbians. Is that why you're asking me – as a representative of the LGBTQ community?'

Kate shook her head. 'Not exactly. Do you know anybody with a tattoo like this?'

'Nope. I've seen it on posters but never on flesh.' She passed the phone back to Kate. 'I don't see where you're going with this.'

Kate paused, trying to work out how to get the information she needed without giving too much away about the owner of the tattoo. Adele Knowles was bright; she'd start making connections as soon as Kate mentioned Eleanor Houghton but there was no other way to get the answers she needed.

'When we last spoke, you mentioned that Eleanor Houghton might have been frightened of her husband. Can you give me a specific example?'

Adele sighed and sat back. 'There were a couple of times I saw them coming home in the car and the way she got out to open the gates, she seemed mousy, scurrying around like she was in a hurry. As if she'd be in trouble if she wasn't quick enough. I know, it's not much. Oh, and there was a time when she was posting leaflets for some sort of church thing – not that I'd be interested – but she was going door to door in the village. He was doing the houses on the opposite side of the road. I opened the door before she could post her flyer to tell her not to bother and she was smiling, pleasant. She greeted me quite warmly and asked how I was. I was so surprised I spluttered something unintelligible and by the time I'd got my head around her change of attitude, *he'd* crossed the road and started dragging her away.'

In the absence of Hollis, Kate took out her notebook and jotted down the gist of Adele's account, underlining *dragging*. 'Physically dragging?'

'He grabbed her upper arm and pulled. Eleanor didn't have much choice other than to go with him.'

'And they were working for the church?'

Adele nodded. 'I think they were both involved with St Peter's in the village. As I said, I never went. I'm sure I'd have been seen as some sort of abomination if I'd rocked up one Sunday.'

Kate made a note of the name of the church. This wasn't getting the investigation much further but it was shedding light on the relationship between the Houghtons and adding to her feeling that there was more to that relationship than she'd first thought. She remembered the separate bedrooms in their house and wondered if she'd been wrong to dismiss their distance as solely due to their advancing age.

'I don't suppose you've heard of the Church of the Right Hand?'

Adele shook her head. 'I still don't get what that tattoo has to do with all this.' Adele's eyes suddenly widened. 'Unless...'

'It's hers. Eleanor's,' Kate confirmed.

'You think she had some sort of secret lesbian past?' The other woman's mouth hung open. 'I don't believe it.'

'I have no idea,' Kate admitted. 'I just got the impression

from our last conversation that you had a particular view of the Houghtons and I wondered if the tattoo would tie in with that.'

'Do you think Peter killed his wife and then himself? Is that it?'

'I really can't comment on an ongoing investigation.' The words were a formula to ward off nosey witnesses and journalists, but Adele Knowles was still in full flow.

'Because she was having an affair with a woman?'

'Ms Knowles,' Kate's voice was quiet but firm, 'this sort of speculation is not helpful. I genuinely can't tell you anything else and I'd rather you didn't share your speculation with anybody else.'

Adele nodded, contrite. 'Of course. I'm sorry – I just got a bit carried away. There's not much excitement in Turton. I was serious when I said I don't go in for local gossip, don't worry.'

The two women parted on the doorstep, Adele still trying to make up for her earlier ebullience and apologising for not being more helpful. Kate assured her that her insight might be of use, but her thoughts were elsewhere. She checked her phone before getting back into her Mini. A text from Sylvia Kerr.

We need to talk. I've had a look at Liv's climbing equipment.

17

O'Connor's mobile vibrated as he pressed the key fob to lock the car. Barratt watched as his colleague dug the phone out of the pocket of his leather jacket and used his thumbprint to open it to the main screen.

'Text from Cooper.' He read the contents then turned to Barratt with a grin.

'Guess who's going to inherit a controlling share in Houghton Haulage...'

Barratt shook his head. 'No idea but you look chuffed about it. Is it you?'

'Tony Sims. All that stuff about being treated like family and Peter being his mentor looks like it was true. Gives him a great motive for murder – this lot must be worth well into seven figures.'

Barratt looked at the row of trucks parked in the huge, fenced yard and the cluster of smaller lorries off to one side. Just this collection of vehicles would be worth a small fortune; combine that with the ones out on the road, the contracts and the good will and it was quite an inheritance.

'Do you think he knows?' Barratt asked over his shoulder as

he pushed open the door to reception.

O'Connor smiled. 'If he doesn't, he soon will. Have a good look at his reaction when I give him the news that *we* know.'

The woman behind the reception desk looked up as they entered.

'Maggie!' O'Connor greeted her like an old friend as he marched towards her, making Barratt cringe inwardly. It was one of his colleague's less endearing habits – and there were many – that he remembered names and used them to create a false sense of bonhomie.

Maggie Richardson gave them an obviously fake smile, her eyes wary, her hand hovering next to the telephone on her desk. 'What can I do for you gentlemen?'

'We'd like to speak to Mr Sims,' Barratt said. 'It's urgent.'

'I'm afraid that...'

O'Connor took a step forward, his smile widening. 'Don't finish that sentence, Maggie. We need to see Tony now. We have a lot of questions to ask him and I'm sure he'd rather answer them here than at Doncaster Police Station. If we have to go into his office and drag him out, I doubt he'll be very impressed with your skills as a receptionist.'

Eyes fixed on O'Connor, Maggie Richardson picked up the phone receiver and tapped on the keypad. She turned away as the call connected. Barratt couldn't make out what she was saying to her boss, but her posture suggested it wasn't positive.

'Go through,' she said, her expression blank as she turned back round. 'You know the way.'

Sims was sitting at his desk and didn't get up as Barratt and O'Connor entered his office. Instead, he scowled at them, pushing his chair back slightly so he could cross his legs. 'To what do I owe the honour of this intrusion? I'm very busy. I could do without interruptions.'

O'Connor pulled out a chair and sat down, leaving Barratt

lurking near the door. It was meant to confuse the man – two places to look; a two-pronged attack when the questions got intense.

'My colleague and I feel you were less than candid when we last spoke,' O'Connor began, leaning forward and grinning as though inviting Sims to a cosy chat. 'And now we think we know why.'

Sims paled but his expression remained defiant. He stared at O'Connor, his expression set, giving nothing away.

'You've inherited the company.'

Sims shook his head. 'That's not true.'

Barratt took an opportunity to wrong-foot him. 'You've inherited a controlling share. You can do what you want with it. Eleanor's nephew has a decent-sized chunk of shares, but you can easily deny him a say in whatever you decide to do. Might that be a good enough reason for murder?'

'Peter and Eleanor were murdered?'

Neither of the detectives answered the question.

Taking a deep breath, Sims placed his clenched fists on the desk as if he were struggling to stay in control of his emotions. Barratt half expected him to start banging them up and down like a frustrated toddler.

'Okay,' Sims admitted. 'It's true. But it doesn't change anything. I didn't kill Peter and Eleanor.'

'But it's handy to have them out of the way.' O'Connor turned the screw further. 'Nobody to argue when you want to make changes. Because you do want to make changes, don't you, Tony? We had a poke around when we were last here and we saw the new fleet. Plain white – no mention of Houghton's. What's the deal there then? None of the mechanics were willing to talk – ditto the drivers. And you practically jumped in your seat when I asked if there had been any arguments or disagreements with Peter Houghton.'

In truth they hadn't asked the mechanics or the drivers. Barratt had commented on the new smaller lorries, recently registered, but nobody seemed to think there was anything unusual about their addition to the fleet.

Sims stood up and wandered to the window that overlooked the yard where the vehicles were parked. He peered out and then turned back to O'Connor. 'They're mine. I wanted to incorporate them into the company fleet, but Peter wouldn't let me. I'm only telling you this because if you start digging, you'll see that they're registered in my name. I have absolutely nothing to hide – they're all above board – but I can't use them for company contracts. I've been looking at alternative European routes, post-Brexit, rather than using the French ports to the south of England. I think there's going to be a market for small European traders who want to export their goods further north, maybe even Scotland. Peter wasn't convinced and wouldn't invest. The best I could get him to agree to was that I could garage and service them here.'

Barratt studied the man as he spoke, assessing, gauging his tone and his expression. There was nothing to suggest he was lying.

'Why didn't Mr Houghton want to use the lorries?'

'They're small. Seven-and-a-half tonnes. He didn't think it was worth the diesel to take them over to the continent, but I wasn't planning to run them empty. There are a couple of local companies who're desperate to crack the European markets – one sells furniture, high-quality stuff and the other deals in plastics for the drinks industry. I've been taking their stock over one way and then we bring fruit and veg back the other. The vehicles are loaded with cargo for both trips – it makes good economic sense. We can't use the usual rigs because the British companies don't have huge volumes of product on a weekly basis – they'd be half full at best.'

There was an earnestness in his expression as he spoke, almost as if he were trying to persuade O'Connor and Barratt to invest in his scheme. This obviously meant a lot to the man, but something was puzzling Barratt.

'Where did you get the money? Eight new vehicles that size can't have been cheap.'

'I used some savings and borrowed the rest.'

'Borrowed?' O'Connor was quick to leap on the loan.

'From the bank. There's a paper trail. It's all legit.' Sims had raised his voice, his face reddening across his cheekbones as he allowed O'Connor to wind him up.

The DS simply smiled and nodded which only seemed to add to Sims's frustration. 'So now you'll be able to include your vehicles in the company fleet and, presumably, transfer the loan to Houghton's Haulage at a more preferential rate given the profile that Peter built up.'

Sims glared at O'Connor. 'You already know I'm not the only beneficiary,' he said. 'Eleanor's nephew has a lot to gain. If he decides to sell his shares, he'll be a very rich man.'

'And we'll be looking into that,' Barratt reassured Sims. 'But, as he was at his home in Australia on the night that the Houghtons died, it's unlikely he had anything to do with their deaths.'

Barratt folded his arms and leaned against the door jamb. They seemed to have reached an impasse. Sims didn't seem worried that they knew about his inheritance and they had no other information to present to him.

'Can we have a look at the new lorries?' O'Connor asked, his tone light. Barratt had no idea what he was thinking, this wasn't part of their plan and he didn't see what they might gain. Was the DS simply curious about haulage vehicles or had he spotted something that Barratt had missed?

Sims looked as puzzled as Barratt felt. 'What? Why?'

O'Connor shrugged and smiled. 'No reason really. Just curious. We had a look around last time we were here, but all the vehicles were locked. It might give us an insight into the type of operation you've introduced.'

Sims stood up, fists clenched by his sides, a muscle in his jaw flexing. 'No. You have no right to come here accusing me of all sorts. I've just lost my friend and mentor and you lot want to harass me into confessing to something I didn't do. For the last time, I didn't kill Peter and Eleanor Houghton and I've no idea who did. And if you want to poke around my yard get a bloody warrant. This conversation is over.'

O'Connor leapt to his feet and Sims stepped backwards as though expecting a blow but instead the detective leaned forwards and tilted his head slightly like a snake preparing to strike. Barratt tensed – his colleague was known for his short fuse – but was surprised when O'Connor simply whispered, 'You're right.'

Sims's eyebrows flew up in surprise, but Barratt knew O'Connor well. There was more to come.

'We should get a warrant,' O'Connor continued. 'I like to do things by the book.'

He winked at the man and turned to Barratt. 'Come on, Matt. Let's leave Mr Sims in peace. For now.'

1983

Anita's going to Spain for her holidays. It's not fair. We never go anywhere good like that. Dad's always too busy for holidays, so he says, so Mum gets the final say and she always brings me here. It's better in the summer. There are more children – some are my age, but a lot are much younger – so there's usually somebody to play with. And there's Taz. She's an adult but she likes to talk to the kids; she makes up really detailed stories, straight out of her head, and tells us rude jokes when the mums aren't listening. She's given me a nickname – Titch – it's because I'm only little, I think. She gives everybody nicknames. Our group is 'The Yorkies' because most of the women come from different parts of Yorkshire. Two live quite close to us but some of the others are from Leeds and there are a lot from Sheffield. There are other groups – a lot of the women are from Wales but I don't know if they have a nickname.

Taz is the only one who's explained to me why we're here and why it's important. When I ask Mum, she just says I wouldn't understand and to stand up straight when the policemen talk to me. But I do understand – thanks to Taz. She says that there are dangerous missiles behind the wire but they're not ours, not British. Our government – the men and women who run the country – have let the American army keep them here. They're very special and could blow up the whole world but other countries might want to attack us to get them for themselves.

These weapons are the most dangerous in the whole world and, if the Americans use them, there won't even be much of a world left, according to Taz. She says they were used in World War II and thousands of people died, and people are still dying because they've got some kind of poison in them.

The women don't want these missiles in England – they don't want these weapons anywhere on Earth because they're so scary – so they've said they'll stay here and make life difficult for the soldiers and the policemen until the Americans take the weapons away. I understand it all a lot better now, but I don't really see how we're going to make a difference. There are probably more than a thousand women here, but the people in government are bigger and stronger – and they're mostly men – and the Americans are stronger still.

Taz says it's not about strength though. She says it's about morality and when people see we're in the right they'll support us and get the weapons sent somewhere else. If that happens, will there be other camps, other women? Will it just carry on until there's nowhere else to put them and so they have to be destroyed? And how do you destroy bombs? You can't blow them up. That's the bit I find most confusing even when Taz explains it.

The other thing she says a lot is that there might not be a world left for me to grow up in. I hate it when she talks about that – it makes me feel funny in my tummy and I want to cry. There are big forests that help to keep us alive by making sure we can breathe but men are cutting them down so they can use the wood and then the land is left for houses or to feed cows. I don't really understand the thing with the cows – I like cows. Taz goes on a lot about pollution as well – pollution makes the rivers and the air dirty and it's not good for us. She says we're poisoning the planet and nobody cares. That can't be right though. Why would people deliberately poison the air that they breathe and the water that they drink? It doesn't make sense.

I like it better when Taz tells us stories. They're usually about girls who make the world better by saving animals or planting trees, stuff like that. It's always girls. She says that women are stronger than they know and that there's something called 'empowerment', but I don't know what that is yet.

Today we did something different – a new type of protest. A protest is a way of saying that you think something is wrong – Taz taught me that – but this protest didn't have any words. Lots of the women spread out, trying to surround the whole fence even though it's miles, and held mirrors up. If somebody had seen it from an aeroplane it would have looked like a massive eye, all lit up with the base as the pupil. I didn't understand what they were doing until I saw one of the soldiers come up to the fence and look at himself in the mirror. He was smiling at first, friendly, and he even said hello: then he saw the mirror and he changed. It was like there was something in his reflection that scared him or made him angry. Or maybe he saw how much he looked like a dangerous person and he felt like he had to act like his reflection. He swore at us and spat on the ground, but the woman just stood there, holding the mirror like a shield, waiting for him to turn round and leave.

I asked Taz about it later, but I didn't really understand her explanation. She said something about showing the men what they looked like – holding the mirror up to nature – and then she laughed and lit one of her funny-smelling cigarettes.

The best thing about being here in the summer is that we can stay up until it's dark and that's not till ten o' clock. When we're all sitting around a fire and the women are talking it feels like a proper holiday and I'm not jealous of Anita and her beach. It's like camping – sometimes we even roast marshmallows on sticks, but I don't like them much – they're too hot and sticky. The women in our group are like a little family. They all look out for each other and stick up for each other. Taz is good at making everybody feel wanted and welcome and she sometimes brings in what she calls 'stragglers' – women who've just arrived and haven't worked out where they want to be or who they want to be with.

Her most recent 'straggler', Sarah, is really nice – almost as nice as Taz. I hope she stays with us because most of the other women are old but Sarah's only a bit older than Taz. She doesn't treat me like a little kid and she answers all my questions when there's something I don't understand.

I've noticed that Mum's different here in the summer. She's more friendly with the others and she's not as strict with me. She talks about the future and how she wants a better world for me to grow up in. She believes in the same things as Taz, she just doesn't explain them as well. She knows about the missiles and the forests and the cows. Sometimes, when she's had some of Taz's home-made wine she gets a bit teary and tells me that she can't do it all – that it's up to me and my generation to make a change. We have to be the ones who make the men understand how to look after the planet and the people. I don't know how she expects me to do that yet, but she keeps trying to explain. I like Mum much better here than at home.

18

Sylvia Kerr opened the front door as soon as Kate and Hollis stepped out of the car. She'd either heard the crunch of tyres on gravel or, as Kate suspected, been watching for them to pull onto the driveway. The look the woman gave the two detectives was ambiguous, hard to read – there was relief there but something else, a darker emotion concealed in her eyes and the set of her lips. As she got closer Kate could read her expression more closely. Sylvia Kerr was furious.

'I can't pretend I'm happy to see you again,' Kerr snapped as she led them down the hallway of her home to the living room at the back. 'I don't want to have this conversation, but I need to find out the truth about what happened to Liv and you two are my best chance of doing that.'

Not exactly a vote of confidence, Kate thought, taking the seat she was directed to with a casual flick of Sylvia's hand.

'I need to get this off my chest,' Kerr said, sitting opposite Hollis, her back to the window, face obscured by shadows. 'If I don't, I'm afraid it will eat away at me and sully my memories of Liv.' The woman sighed and shifted slightly in her seat, tucking a stray strand of grey hair behind her ear. 'This isn't easy to admit and I'm so angry at her for putting me in this position, but I think Liv may have been seeing somebody else.'

'What makes you think that?' Kate asked. Having been married to somebody who treated infidelity like a game, she had some idea of how Sylvia might be feeling, but she'd only been married to Garry for fifteen years; this couple had been together for decades.

Kerr shook her head as if she couldn't quite believe what she was about to say. 'She'd changed. I thought it was retirement, that she was bored and struggling to adapt to not working. We laughed about her having so much time on her hands and I got her to start a few projects in the garden that she'd been promising to do for years but she seemed to get more distant the more time we spent together, if that makes sense?'

Kate nodded sympathetically. Nick had accused her of the same thing from time to time when she'd been preoccupied with a case – mental distance despite their physical proximity. It was probably part of all relationships, but she knew that the partners of police officers often complained about not being allowed into the lives of their significant others. If it had followed her into retirement, the distance did suggest that Liv had something else going on in her life.

'A few weeks before she died,' Sylvia went on, 'Liv told me that she'd heard from an old friend and that she was going to meet them for coffee. She was vague when I asked where she knew this person from, but I got the sense that it was a woman. She came back from that meeting even more preoccupied and that's when the early-morning walks started.'

'In the Peak District, where she was found?' Kate asked.

'That's where she said she was going. She was having trouble sleeping so sometimes she'd get up early and go out.'

'What was her state of mind when she came back?' Kate asked.

'Odd. Distracted. But then she'd seem to give herself a shake and throw herself into whatever we'd got planned for the day.'

'Did you ask her about these early-morning walks? Whether she'd seen anybody, met anybody?'

Sylvia smiled sadly. 'Of course, but when she said no what was I supposed to do? Ask her a lot of follow-up questions? Give her a multiple-choice quiz?'

The woman stood up and turned to the window, shoulders hunched, fists clenched. Kate glanced at Hollis who gave her a tiny shrug. There was little they could do except wait and allow Sylvia to tell the story in her own time.

'I'm not a suspicious person, especially where Liv's concerned.' Sylvia still had her back to them. 'We'd been together a long time and neither of us had been the perfect partner one hundred per cent of the time – who can be? But we trusted each other. If I messed up, I knew I could tell Liv and we could work through it. If she had been seeing somebody else, I would like to think she could have told me. Instead, she forced me to doubt her and to start looking for clues, slip-ups, inconsistencies. Do you know what happens when you start looking for things like that?'

She turned suddenly, glaring at Kate.

'You find them.'

Kate felt her cheeks flush. She remembered all too well the furtive checking of Garry's pockets, ringing him when he said he was out with friends to see if she could hear pub noise in the background and, much worse, the temptation to use ANPR cameras and CCTV to track his whereabouts. Thankfully, she'd realised that her job was worth more than her marriage to a cheat and she had never crossed that line, but the feelings of embarrassment and impotence remained not too far beneath the surface. She caught Sylvia's knowing look and hoped that

Hollis had the good sense to keep quiet. He didn't know much about her past and she didn't want him to ask.

'I was worried that I was turning into a stereotype. Questioning everything, doubting what I was told, what I saw for myself. And now I hate that I never asked. I never gave Liv the chance to explain herself, to put things right between us.'

Sylvia sat back down, leaning forward with her head in her hands. 'I never gave her the chance,' she said quietly. 'And then you two turned up and made me doubt the way she'd died. What if she had been seeing somebody and they'd killed her? What if this person from her past was somebody who'd borne a grudge for years and had finally paid her back for something? A criminal she arrested? A family member who blamed her for the incarceration of a loved one?'

She sat upright and looked directly at Kate. 'I'm sure there are people from your past who feel they owe you a violent end.'

The words were shocking, not least because they were said with such certainty. Kate saw Hollis shift in his seat as though unsure whether to intervene but there was no threat here, just a bald statement of fact. The job Kate did left her open to the possibility of retaliation.

'I'm sure there are,' she said. 'But I wouldn't meet any of them in the early hours of the morning, alone.'

Kerr nodded, conceding the point. It seemed unlikely that Liv would meet somebody she felt might be a threat, especially in a remote place at an early hour.

'But what if it was somebody who you didn't know was a threat? Somebody who you might think was a friend? Or somebody pretending a relationship that didn't exist at all?'

'Do you have somebody specific in mind?' Kate asked. Was that where they were being led – to the identity of Liv's murderer?

Sylvia's eyes drifted to the fireplace, unfocused. 'I'm sorry, I have no idea who Liv might have been meeting. It's a theory based on the suspicions of an old woman.'

'But...' Hollis said. Kate frowned at him to keep him quiet but she understood his frustration. Had they been called here for this – for Sylvia Kerr to vent her frustrations about the possible infidelity of her partner? There had to be something more. She'd mentioned the climbing equipment.

'You said in your text that you'd checked Liv's climbing equipment? Could we have a look, see what you found?'

'What's the point?' Kerr asked.

'The point is that you might feel differently about your partner if we can get to the truth about her death. However painful, it will give you certainty rather than those niggling doubts that never go away. I know about infidelity, Sylvia. I know how much it hurts but the not knowing is much worse, much more destructive.'

Hollis's eyes widened as Kate continued.

'My ex-husband was a cheat, and not a very good one. In the end *my* marriage wasn't worth saving but I think the memory of your relationship with Liv might be. Trust me, the truth is always better than the alternative.'

Sylvia Kerr nodded and got slowly to her feet as if the last few minutes had aged her. 'You present a compelling case, detective inspector. Follow me.'

She led them back down the hallway and through a door to the right. Passing through an immaculate kitchen with white cupboards and black marble worktops, Sylvia led them into a huge double garage. The wall opposite the internal door had been fitted with shelves to store tools and other household equipment.

'Over there.' She pointed to the corner furthest from the house where ropes and harnesses hung from hooks and shoes were shelved underneath. Carabiners and other metal objects that Kate couldn't name hung in their own area and two helmets nestled together next to a black fabric chalk bag.

'You've checked everything?' Kate asked, turning to Sylvia who was leaning against the kitchen door with her arms folded across her chest, elbows resting in opposite palms.

She nodded. 'Liv was scrupulous about her climbing equipment, obsessive. There's a list on the bench over there. I checked it and checked every piece of kit.'

She paused and threw her head back as tears filled her eyes. 'I can tell you with absolute certainty that rope that Liv was hanged with was not one of hers.'

19

O'Connor held the piece of paper up to the fading sunlight coming through the side window of his car and tried to memorise the registration numbers but there were too many and they weren't in sequence. He was going to have to do this the old-fashioned way, with a pen. Cooper hadn't asked a single question when he'd asked her to find him the index numbers of the small fleet of seven-and-a-half tonne trucks that Sims claimed to own. He knew that it wasn't because she wasn't curious, she just didn't want to be involved if the shit hit the fan with the boss. Fletcher had warned him off spending too much time investigating the haulage company, but she couldn't complain if he did it in his own time – she'd be seriously pissed off if she knew that he'd involved anybody else though, so he was glad that Cooper knew how to keep her trap shut.

He'd parked on a lane at the back of Houghton's yard, but he couldn't see all the vehicles from his car even though they were all parked up against the chain-link fencing. He needed to get out to do a thorough check. There was a night security guard in a tiny shed near the main gate. O'Connor knew this because he'd already spoken to the man, who'd seemed more interested in whatever he was watching on his tablet than in the safety of the yard. He showed little interest in O'Connor's fake report of a series of vehicle thefts in the area, simply saying he'd 'keep an eye out' for anybody who looked dodgy.

Dodgy. O'Connor smiled as he gently closed the car door behind him. It was a word that witnesses, and villains, often used to describe his own appearance. He was often 'that dodgy-looking copper with the tash' – hardly any of them remembered his name or his rank. Which suited O'Connor just fine. He'd spent enough time working in vice to know how to use his reputation to his advantage and even some of his colleagues thought he used questionable methods to get information. The irony was that he didn't. He was as straight as Barratt or Hollis, they just made assumptions and it served his purpose not to correct them. Even this recce was far from illegal and he had every right to ask Sam about the lorries as part of an ongoing investigation. It just wasn't part of his current brief and Fletcher would hand him his arse on a plate if she found out before he could deliver the result that he was sure would come. In time.

His shadow was long and lean as it flitted across the backs of the white lorries, each one precisely parked, lined up with the fence and equidistant from the next. O'Connor's list was too long for him to memorise but short enough for him to check the vehicles quickly. A count showed him that two of the eight were missing. He ran through the registration numbers and put pencil ticks next to the two that were absent from the line-up. Now all he had to do was find out where they were and where they'd been.

It was after midnight when O'Connor finally left his desk at Doncaster Central. He'd checked the ANPR data and pored over a couple of days of CCTV but he'd found what he wanted. Both vehicles had left the country via the ferry port on the River Tyne near Newcastle at 5pm. The departure point tallied with what

Sims had told them about hoping to exploit less busy routes to Europe. There was no indication of where the lorries took on their cargo – it could literally have been anywhere between Thorpe and Newcastle – and, obviously, there was no clue as to when they'd be back on British soil. All O'Connor could do was monitor the traffic cameras around the ferry port to see when the vehicles arrived and, possibly, where they went from there. It was a waiting game. Fortunately, O'Connor was good at waiting.

20

'We're now officially treating the three cases as connected.' Kate started the briefing with the key point from her morning meeting with Das. When presented with Sylvia Kerr's testimony the DCI had reluctantly agreed to revise her stance on the case and allow Kate's team to include Olivia Thornbury's death as an *official* part of the ongoing enquiry into the deaths of Peter and Eleanor Houghton and Julia Sullivan, with the proviso that there would be no statement to the press at this stage. It was a minor victory for Kate but a major step forward. With three cases came three lots of evidence and three opportunities for their killer to have made a mistake. It also meant that they could try to find witnesses to Olivia Thornbury's movements in the weeks leading up to her death. Kate wasn't sure how she could do that without involving the media, but she had to respect Das's wishes on that score.

'You managed to convince the DCI?' Barratt's eyes widened with surprise.

Kate nodded. 'We've got two similar factors in all three cases – the mirrors and the notes.'

She picked up a marker pen and strode over to the

whiteboard next to the window. 'Look,' she said, drawing a grid pattern and writing the names of the victims at the top of three columns. 'The Houghton case overlaps Sullivan because of the tattoos on the two women.' She wrote *tattoo* and ticked the appropriate columns.

'The Thornbury case, while there's a lack of tattoo, may suggest a link to Eleanor Houghton because her tattoo was a known lesbian symbol and Olivia Thornbury was gay.' She wrote the word in the appropriate square of the grid. On the next row down, she wrote *broken mirror* and ticked across all three victims followed by *note* with three more ticks. She added *diazepam* and ticked the Houghton and Thornbury columns and, as an afterthought added another column for Rohypnol.

'None of the victims had sought help for suicidal ideation. In fact, none of them were receiving any sort of counselling for mental health issues.' Kate paused, taking stock. 'We currently have no suspects and no motive for these murders beyond what's stated in the notes – *it's time to go* – whatever that means. The fact that only one case – Olivia Thornbury – was actually mistaken for a suicide suggests that the killer is not trying to hide the crimes but that the message may have been too subtle in the Thornbury case. I'm also convinced that Eleanor Houghton was the intended victim in the Turton murder – not her husband.'

'He did another one and made sure we'd know it was murder,' Barratt said. 'There's no point in sending a message if nobody understands it.'

'I just wish we knew what the message was,' Cooper muttered. Kate understood her frustration. Tasked with a trawl of CCTV and social media, Sam had been unable to find anything linking the three different cases. She'd found plenty of online information about Olivia Thornbury but it all seemed to relate to her career. Julia Sullivan was mainly mentioned in connection with her husband until her recent election to the local council.

'Can we add religion to the list?' Sam asked. 'We know about Sullivan, and the Houghtons attended their local church. Olivia Thornbury was raised Catholic. I know we discussed it before, but it is a potential overlap.'

Kate nodded. She wasn't convinced that this was the link, but it would be foolish to overlook it at such an early stage. She added it to the list and ticked the columns for the Houghtons and Sullivan then, after a second's thought, put a question mark in the Thornbury column.

'I know this is getting frustrating, but I think there are plenty of things to follow up. Barratt, O'Connor, I want you to interview the people that Olivia Thornbury climbed with. I got a list from her partner – there's a club in Broomhill that Olivia attended. Start there.'

Kate looked up in time to see O'Connor yawn.

'Am I keeping you awake, Steve?' she snapped. She knew that he wasn't completely convinced about the connection between these cases, but this was bordering on insolence. At least he had the good grace to look embarrassed.

'Late night,' he said. 'Honestly. Nothing to do with this.'

Kate believed him. If there was one thing she'd learned about O'Connor it was that he was generally straightforward in sharing his opinions. Sarcasm wasn't really his style when it came to commenting on cases. Downright defiance, yes, but at least he owned it when challenged.

'Sam. I've put in a request for a voluntary disclosure of the medical history of Olivia Thornbury and Julia Sullivan. We're waiting on the tox report on Julia. God knows what's holding it up, but it might help us to see if she was on any medication. I'm expecting to hear back from both their GPs this morning. Both bereaved spouses support the request so it should be straightforward. I'm still working on the Houghtons' doctor – I couldn't get hold of him yesterday, but I'll have another go later. I've also requested case notes from Olivia Thornbury's supposed suicide and from Julia Sullivan's car accident. All the paperwork is on file, but I wanted to see the physical evidence as well. If the courier arrives while I'm out, take the boxes and feel free to have a rummage.'

That was a lot to burden Cooper with, but Kate felt that they needed a breakthrough and she had a hunch that it might lie in the jobs that she'd allocated to the DC.

'Dan. I want to interview Sadie Sullivan to find out who her mother might have been having an affair with. If she can't give us a name, then we're back here helping Cooper. Everybody know what they're doing?'

Nods from her colleagues and then chairs began to shuffle as they got ready to leave.

'There are four murders here,' Kate said. 'The gap between the Houghtons and Julia Sullivan was only a couple of days. He or she could well be escalating. Let's put a stop to this, okay?'

This time the movements of her team were more purposeful, determined.

21

'And you'd never heard of her?' Hollis asked as he pressed the button next to the imposing front door of Sadie Sullivan's house on Doncaster's South Parade. Sandwiched between a veterinary practice and a solicitor's office, the Georgian house was separated from the busy road by a tiny strip of gravel and a low wall. It could easily have been mistaken for a doctor's surgery or an exclusive gallery, being rather grand for a private home.

'Not my kind of reading material,' Kate said. She'd looked Sadie's books up on the internet but none of the titles rang any bells – they had all been published after her son would have had an interest in such stories. 'Barbara Cartland's more my style.'

Hollis turned to her in surprise then grinned when he read her expression. 'I'd have had you down as a fan of the classics,' he said. '*Wuthering Heights* and all that Jane Austen stuff.'

Kate laughed. Given the pressures of the job, reading wasn't something she found much time for; she was much more likely to unwind with a pizza, a beer and a box set. She did know, however, that Hollis had a weakness for fantasy and horror novels. 'Did all that at uni,' she said. 'Now I'm more likely to read the bran flakes packet than the Brontës.'

'Well, somebody's buying books,' Hollis said with a nod towards the front door with its shiny black gloss paint. 'Most of these buildings are flats or offices, she must be doing well to have been able to afford this.'

Before Kate could respond, the door was opened, not by the servant in an Edwardian maid's uniform that Kate had imagined lurking in the below-stairs scullery, but by Sadie Sullivan herself.

'Detective Inspector Fletcher,' she said, pushing a pair of reading glasses up into her thick hair where they held a few stray wisps off her face. 'And?' She turned to Hollis expectantly.

'DC Dan Hollis,' he responded holding out his ID card.

'Has something happened? Have you found out who killed my mother?' The woman held onto the side of the door, barring entry into the house and seemed unlikely to invite them inside without prompting.

'If we could have a few moments of your time,' Kate said with a smile. 'I think it's best that we don't discuss the case on the doorstep.'

Sadie stepped back allowing Kate and Hollis to pass her. 'Straight ahead,' she said. 'I just need to save my work and I'll be with you.'

The tiled hallway led to an intimidatingly modern kitchen equipped with devices whose function Kate could only guess at. She took in the huge double fridge, the range cooker with six-ring hob and the island workspace that was almost the size of the entire kitchen in Kate's flat. The dark-red walls were half tiled in a black-and-white chessboard pattern, a series of brightly coloured, framed book covers adding a quirky touch to the otherwise austere finish. This wasn't what she'd expected, and she found herself wondering who Sadie shared the house with.

Hollis was craning his neck sideways, reading brand names on the stainless-steel coffee maker and microwave oven. Kate knew he was a self-proclaimed coffee snob and had his own state-of-the-art machine in his flat in Bentley.

'Impressed?' she whispered.

'Very. That coffee machine costs three times what I paid for mine. I hope she offers us a brew.'

'Of course,' Sadie said from the doorway. The glasses had been removed and her hair was neatly tied back. She was wearing a pale-blue vest top and navy capris which revealed her calves and bare feet. 'What's your "brew" of choice? Cappuccino? Latte? Macchiato?'

'Cappuccino please,' Hollis mumbled, his face flushed pink with embarrassment.

'DI Fletcher? You look like the complicated type. Let me guess... ristretto?'

Kate shook her head. 'Too strong for me. A latte would be good, thanks.'

After seating her guests at the breakfast bar which overlooked a small but immaculate patch of garden through a sash window, Sadie fussed with the drinks, spooning out beans and using a jug to measure exact quantities of milk. She placed Hollis's coffee in front of him with a flourish.

'Sugar's just there.' She pointed to a silver canister next to Hollis's elbow.

The latte took longer and then Sadie made herself an iced coffee which seemed an even more complicated procedure. Kate had the feeling that the woman wasn't used to visitors and was demonstrating the full range of the expensive machine.

'That's wonderful,' Hollis exclaimed, taking a sip of his drink. 'What beans do you use?'

'A local roaster,' Sadie said as she perched on a stool next to the island. 'Small batch. They call themselves Peak Perc – Sheffield based.'

'I've not heard of them,' Hollis said. 'I'll have to give them a try.'

Kate sipped her latte. It was good but she really couldn't tell the difference between one bean and another.

'Well, that's the small talk done,' Sadie said. 'What did you want to talk to me about?' She stared at Kate, amber eyes wide and expectant.

'We just need to follow up on a few issues raised by our conversation with you at your mother's house. Again, I'm so sorry for your loss and I completely understand if you find the circumstances of her death difficult to discuss but any information you can give us may help us to catch whoever did this to Julia.'

The woman's composure was impressive considering how recently she'd found her mother murdered. She nodded and took another sip of her coffee. 'Ask away. Anything to help.'

Hollis flipped open his notebook. 'Can we start with the night your mother didn't turn up for your appointment? You said you weren't really surprised, that you suspected she was having an affair?'

Sadie wrinkled her nose. 'Did I say that? I think I was in shock. Dad only moved out a few weeks ago and I think her *religion* might have forbidden that kind of thing.'

'You sound sceptical about her conversion. Did you not approve of her choice?'

Sadie snorted and took another sip of her drink. 'Choice? It was like she was on some kind of mission to be as offensive as possible to as many people. If that's religion, then you can keep it.'

'Offensive how?'

The sound of a glass being slammed down onto the marble worktop was shocking in the quiet kitchen. 'You must have read about her rants about refugees, about foreigners, about bloody Brexit? Christ, sometimes I was really embarrassed to admit I was related to her.'

'And yet you cared enough to go to her house in the early hours of the morning to check that she was okay...'

'She was my mother!'

Hollis didn't even flinch. Kate watched as he raised his mug to his lips, eyes fixed on his notes and then continued as though he was unaware of Sadie's raised voice.

'She had a car accident,' Hollis said. 'Your father says that's what brought about the change. Would you agree?'

Sadie rested her chin on one fist, her eyes becoming unfocused. 'Maybe. But you have to take everything he says with a couple of spoonfuls of salt. I think their marriage was struggling for years and her new views gave him the excuse he'd been looking for. You know he left on his birthday?'

Hollis nodded.

'Typical. He loves drama. When we're out people stare at him even if they don't realise who he is. He plays up to it, preening and raising his voice. Last month a woman thought he was Brian Blessed and he was insulted. Imagine that! Prick.'

Kate looked out of the window to hide the smile in her eyes as she remembered Hollis's comment when they'd visited the artist. It seemed that Sadie Sullivan had little time or patience for either of her parents. It was interesting background, but she needed to move the interview on to the night of the murder.

'You told me when we spoke before that you waited until it was light to go to your mother's house. Why was that? Why not just drive round there when you started to get anxious?'

'I don't drive.'

'At all?' Kate asked, surprised.

'No. I learnt as a teenager, but I decided that I didn't want to own a car. It's an environmental choice.'

'So how did you get to your mother's house? It's a hell of a walk.' Hollis was leaning forwards on his stool, obviously puzzled.

'I cycled. I have an electric bike. To be honest I'd rather have a normal bike, but I use it as my main form of transport and cycling on a standard bike would have me arriving hot and sweaty to important meetings. Not a good look. It's a compromise, I suppose.'

Unlike the house, Kate thought. The marble and gadgets seemed in stark contrast to Sadie's claim of a real concern for the environment. Some people were like that though. Kate had worked with a woman in Cumbria who was a stickler for recycling, anti-plastic and grew her own organic veg but when she left for work, she left a light and the radio on because she didn't like coming home to a dark, empty house.

'How long does it take to cycle to your mother's house?' she asked.

'Twenty-five minutes. There's an old railway track just past the racecourse which takes me most of the way. It's not lit though, hence the need to wait until it was light. I've got bike lights but I wouldn't feel safe on the track in the dark.' She ran a hand through her hair, pulling out the elastic tie that had been holding it in a ponytail, and drained her glass of coffee.

'When did your mother get her tattoo?' Kate asked, hoping the abrupt change of topic might help to focus Sadie's thoughts.

'When she was much younger,' Sadie said. 'Fancied herself as a feminist. She didn't show it to dad for months but, in the end, I think he quite liked it.' She smiled to herself, it was obviously a happy memory.

'Feminist but not a lesbian?'

'Ha! Hardly.'

'Not even when she was younger. A dalliance before she met your father.'

'As far as I know my mother was very heterosexual. I'm not so sure about my father however.' This thought seemed to amuse her, but Kate sensed that it might be some kind of family joke and let it pass.

Sadie fiddled with the hair elastic, wrapping it round two fingers then pulling them free before repeating the movement on the other hand.

'Can I ask you again about what happened when you got to your mother's house? You said you let yourself in with your own key, is that correct?'

'One of the joys of elderly parents,' Sadie said with a wry smile. 'Being constantly on call in case of falls or heart attacks. I'm sorry if I sound callous, I don't really think Mum's death has sunk in. I keep expecting her to ring or to pop round.' Her eyes welled with unshed tears and she blinked rapidly.

'Nobody else had a key. A neighbour maybe?'

'Only me and Dad.'

Kate nodded, watching as Hollis scribbled down this information.

'And you went straight upstairs?'

A nod. The woman's lower lip had a slight tremble.

'You didn't notice anything unusual? No sense that somebody else had been in the house, nothing out of place?'

'Not until I saw the broken mirror. I thought she might have had an accident. A fall. I heard a tap dripping in the bathroom, so I went in and I saw... I saw her in the bath.' Grabbing at Hollis's empty mug, Sadie stood up and went to the sink, keeping her back to Kate and Hollis as she ran the tap.

'I'm sorry,' Kate said. 'I understand how difficult this must be. Just a couple more questions. What was your first thought when you saw your mother in the bath?'

Sadie turned and looked at her as though she'd just spat in her face. 'My first thought? What sort of a question is that?'

'I'm just trying to get an impression of the scene,' Kate said, keeping her voice neutral.

'My first thought was that my mum was dead.'

'Did you think it was suicide?'

'I don't know. I could see the… the cuts in her wrists but it was like my brain couldn't make sense of it. I walked further into the room, trying to see her face, to see if she was still alive. I didn't want to touch her. Then I saw the wound in her neck. She couldn't have done that to herself, she just couldn't. I ran downstairs and called 999. I waited in the kitchen because I couldn't bear to look at her anymore.'

Sadie reached over and picked up her glass before fumbling with the catch on the dishwasher. She couldn't get it to open and she looked round helplessly as though she didn't quite know where she was or how she'd got there.

'Here, let me.' Hollis stood, opened the dishwasher door and pulled out the top tray, placing the glass neatly on a rack. He did the same with his own mug, but Kate shook her head, she hadn't finished.

'Sadie, can you think of anybody who might want to harm your mother? I don't mean in general – people who didn't like her politics – I mean a personal dislike. Did she have any specific enemies?'

'Only my father,' the woman said, leaning on the sink. She spluttered a shaky half-laugh. 'That's a joke by the way. He'd never hurt anybody. I really can't think of anyone.'

Kate drained her mug. It was time for the important question, the one that might indicate to a bright woman that her mother wasn't the only victim.

'Sadie, does the name Houghton mean anything to you. Peter Houghton or Eleanor Houghton?'

She nodded. 'He's the man with the lorry business. Is Eleanor his wife?'

'You don't know them personally. Did they have any connection with your mother?'

She just looked blank.

'What about Olivia Thornbury?'

'Doesn't ring a bell.'

Kate saw realisation shadow Sadie's face a half second before she exploded. 'Shit! Mum's not the first, is she? Whoever killed her has done this before!'

Kate glanced at Hollis who was hovering next to the sink as if uncertain what to do or where to be.

'Honestly, Sadie. We don't know. But you might be able to help us to find out.'

22

Medical records might as well have been written in a foreign language as far as Kate was concerned. She recognised the names of some common ailments and a range of drugs, but the language seemed designed to baffle and confuse. Olivia Thornbury's records showed that she'd been prescribed diazepam for muscle spasms, exactly as her partner had described. There was no mention of depression or anxiety and no suggestion that she'd been referred to local mental health services, either NHS or private. Scrolling back further through the PDF document that the GP had provided, Kate found the preliminary diagnosis of arthritis and the confirmatory X-ray and MRI scans.

She opened up Eleanor Houghton's file. Again, nothing especially surprising. Antibiotics for a chest infection the previous winter, diazepam for 'general anxiety' and painkillers for an arthritic knee but, again, no referral to any other service. Peter Houghton's records were even less helpful – it seemed he hardly ever visited his GP apart from a check-up every two years which revealed slightly elevated blood pressure and moderately high cholesterol both of which were treated with appropriate medication.

Kate looked up from her computer screen to check on her colleagues. Barratt and O'Connor were absent, still interviewing Liv Thornbury's climbing colleagues, she hoped. Cooper was poring over CCTV footage and Hollis was sitting with his feet up on his desk flicking through the contents of the slim cardboard folder which contained the report of Julia Sullivan's car accident. She'd given it a quick scan but left Dan to pick out the details and study the photographs, trusting him to find anything helpful.

An email pinged into her inbox. More detail from Julia Sullivan's post-mortem. The cuts to her throat and wrists were consistent with a slim shard of the mirror found at the scene. There were no cuts or abrasions to her fingers, indicating that she hadn't cut her own wrists or throat. Nothing that Kate hadn't expected. There was also evidence of a healed fracture to the side of her skull. Not recent.

Sighing heavily, Kate scrolled through the rest of the report but there was nothing to move them forwards. It seemed likely, in Kate's mind, that Julia had been drugged, probably using a spiked alcoholic drink and then, when she was drowsy and malleable, stripped and placed in the bath. She probably didn't have much idea what was happening to her – at least, that's what Kate hoped.

'Dan,' she called over to Hollis. 'Anything interesting?'

Hollis looked up and pinched the bridge of his nose with his finger and thumb, scrunching up his eyes. Kate had a suspicion that he needed reading glasses, but vanity was still winning the battle with practicality.

'Nope. Looks like a straightforward RTA. A delivery van pulled out of a side street on a green light, Julia Sullivan hadn't seen the red light ahead of her and carried on straight into its path. She was taken to the DRI; the other driver was unhurt but a bit shaken. Seems like driver error on Julia's part. No charges brought.' He looked back at the paper on top of the pile in the folder. 'There are no medical reports here, so I don't know the extent of her injuries.'

'Is it possible she had a head injury?' Kate asked. 'There's mention of a healed fracture in the PM report.'

Hollis removed a photograph from the pile and passed it to Kate. 'I'd be surprised if she hadn't. The driver's airbag deployed but even so...'

Kate studied the image of a badly damaged blue hatchback concertinaed up against the cab of a green van. The car looked like it had rammed straight into the side of the other vehicle with some force. 'Bloody hell,' she hissed. 'She was lucky to survive.'

Hence the religious fervour. She probably realised that she'd been incredibly fortunate and was looking for a reason. God fit the bill perfectly and Cora Greaves had been on hand for guidance and support. Kate checked her watch. It was nearly lunchtime. A good excuse for getting away from the frustrations of her computer.

'Sam, got anything?'

Cooper shook her head without turning round. 'Bugger all. I've been working on the traffic cameras closest to Julia Sullivan's house but there's nothing within half a mile. Thought I might see the same car going in both directions, maybe in the early hours but no joy.'

'Have a break. Eat. Coffee,' Kate instructed but she wasn't sure Sam would bother. Once she was deep in the digital world, Cooper tended to forget about trivialities such as food and drink.

'Dan and I are going out again.'

Hollis looked over at her, eyebrows raised. 'We are?'

'Yep. I can't ignore the religious link. I know it's unlikely, but I think we should head over to Turton to speak to Eleanor and Peter's vicar. He wasn't around last time I was there. Lunch is your shout,' she added with a smile.

She logged off from her computer and grabbed her handbag from the back of her chair.

St Peter's church occupied an elevated position overlooking much of the village of Turton. Built from solid-looking pale limestone it could be seen from most of the surrounding hamlets and no doubt the church bells could be heard for miles when it came time to summon the pious to worship. Kate had never been a churchgoer. Neither of her parents had been religious although her mum's funeral had been conducted in Thorpe parish church, much to her confusion. She and her sister Karen had agreed on a humanist service followed by a cremation for their father. It had seemed more honest somehow.

The vicarage was further down the hill, nestling in a small stand of trees and beech hedges, and was much more modern than the church. It resembled the red-brick semi-detached house that Kate had grown up in on the Crosslands Estate, 1950s optimism combined with the hangover of post-war frugality. Kate had rung the bell twice on her previous visit to the village but there had been nobody home.

'I was picturing something a bit more chocolate boxish,' Hollis said as he parked next to a twenty-year-old Fiat that looked like the rust was the only thing holding the bodywork together.

'Me too,' Kate said. Even though she'd grown up in the area and spent a lot of weekends cycling the backroads, she couldn't recall having seen Turton Vicarage before. 'Nice spot though.'

Hollis led the way across a mossy tarmac drive to the front door of the vicarage but, before he could knock, a voice came from behind them.

'Can I help you?'

Kate turned. The man who'd shouted was probably in his mid-fifties and his question seemed to have been genuine judging by his open expression and wide smile. Dressed in jeans and a T-shirt he didn't look much like Kate had imagined and the pair of golden Labradors straining at their leads added to the suggestion of a country landowner rather than a church minister.

'Reverend Kevin Preston?' Kate asked, taking a step forwards then hastily retreating as one of the retrievers lunged, huge pink tongue swinging in her direction.

'Down, Karla,' the man said but the dog didn't seem impressed by the command. The second one seemed to take it as encouragement and made its own bid to jump up at Kate.

'Inca! Down! Ignore them,' he said. 'They just want to lick everybody to death. I'm Kevin Preston. What can I do for you?'

Kate introduced herself and Hollis and explained that they were hoping for some background on the Houghtons.

'Bad do, that,' Preston said with typical Yorkshire understatement. 'I should have seen it coming.' He reined in both dogs and got them to sit at his feet. 'I had no idea that either of them felt so low.'

Clearly the man had taken the 'suicide' at face value and hadn't listened to any local gossip to the contrary.

'We'd just like to follow up. Get a sense of both of them, see if we can work out what happened.' Kate was deliberately vague, no point in putting the man on his guard by mentioning possible enemies at this stage.

'I was about to go up to the church. I need to do some preparation for a christening service at the weekend. I'm happy to talk to you both there. It's open, if you want to head up, I'll just give these two monsters a drink and meet you there.'

Ten minutes later Kate slipped into a pew, glad of the shady cool of the church interior. The walk had only taken five minutes, but the sun was high and there was little shade on the lane. Hollis sat on the opposite side of the aisle, looking as uncomfortably hot as Kate felt. The church interior was beautiful with a row of arches either side of a central nave leading to a chancel lit by three stained-glass windows. The wooden pews were a deep reddish-brown, burnished by the backs and bottoms of centuries of parishioners, and the altar, covered in a simple deep-blue cloth, was visible from all angles.

'What a lovely old building,' Kate said to the vicar as he pushed open the huge oak door and stepped inside.

Preston smiled. 'It is, isn't it? It's one of the oldest buildings in South Yorkshire, built on a Saxon shell. If you look, you'll see that the arches on the north aisle are different from those on the south.'

Kate followed his pointing finger. He was right. One side had rounded arches while, on the other, they rose to wishbone points. The difference between this and the small terraced house that was home to the Church of the Right Hand was stark.

'Eleanor Houghton used to do guided tours for the local primary schools. There's a lot of history here, masons' marks, a lepers' squint and some fascinating tomb markers in the chancel. She really enjoyed showing it all to the kiddies.'

'Did you know Eleanor and Peter well?' Kate asked.

'They were already churchgoers when I took over from my predecessor,' Preston said. 'I inherited his house and his flock when I took over ten years ago. Eleanor was one of the first to really make an effort to welcome me. She knocked on my door one afternoon with a Victoria sponge and a four-pack of chilled lager. I couldn't say no to that, could I?'

'Not really,' Kate said. She was surprised though. Nothing she'd heard about Eleanor Houghton suggested she was the type to enjoy an afternoon drinking session with a strange man.

She wondered what her husband had thought about the gesture.

'What about Peter? Was he as welcoming?'

'In his way,' Preston said. 'He was more reserved but a lot of people in the village tended to follow his lead, so I was relieved when he invited me round to dinner – Eleanor's suggestion I suppose.'

'Follow his lead, how?' Hollis asked.

Preston turned, frowning as though he'd forgotten that the DC was there. 'He was a wealthy man with some influence over parish matters. People often wanted to curry favour with him, keep on his good side. You'll have heard about him buying land around here?'

Hollis nodded.

'I think some villagers thought of him as a benevolent squire because he was well known in the Doncaster area.'

'I haven't seen any evidence of benevolence,' Hollis said.

Preston shrugged and began walking down the central aisle. 'I'm just explaining what people saw,' he said. 'To be honest, I knew Eleanor much better. I didn't have a lot to do with Peter apart from occasionally asking him for a donation. And then he always wanted to know what I'd done with the money – to make sure he'd got good value.'

There was a tension in the man's back and a clipped tone to his words which suggested to Kate that he hadn't liked Peter Houghton very much. She stood up and followed him towards the chancel, gesturing for Hollis to stay where he was.

'I take it you weren't a fan?' Kate said as Preston reached the altar. He turned and smiled. His face, lit in a dozen or more colours by the sun through the stained glass, was hard to read.

'It's not for me to pass comment,' he said. 'He came to church. Was sometimes generous with his donations. Kept himself to himself.'

'What about his wife. Was he strict with her?'

Preston hung his head and took a deep breath. 'You've obviously been speaking to people around the village. Gossip and speculation. Places like this thrive on it.'

'So, there's nothing to the suggestion that Peter kept Eleanor on a tight chain?'

The vicar picked imaginary specks of dust from the cloth covering the altar. 'She changed in the time that I knew her. Eleanor became more reserved, I suppose. She still made time for the children, still did the tours but she seemed worried.'

'Recently?'

Preston nodded. 'I think so. We spoke at length two weeks ago when she was helping with the flowers for a wedding. I got the sense that she was deeply troubled, but she wouldn't give me any details.'

'Was it Peter? Was he violent? Controlling?'

Preston shook his head. 'Nothing like that. It was to do with her past. She told me that she'd recently reconnected with somebody she knew years ago when she was a different person. That's how she described her past self – a different person.'

'Was she being blackmailed, do you think? Did they know something that might upset her relationship with Peter?'

'I don't think so,' Preston said, rearranging a handful of flowers in a glass vase. 'I tried to ask her about this person, where she knew them from, who they were but she clammed up.'

'Protecting her privacy,' Kate speculated.

'It wasn't that,' the vicar said. 'The last time I spoke to Eleanor Houghton I got the impression that she was genuinely frightened of somebody, but it wasn't Peter. It was someone from her past.'

23

Anna Cohen's mobile rang just as she was putting on her suit jacket. Glancing at the screen she finished shrugging on the second sleeve before picking up the device to take the call.

'I'm not at my desk,' she snapped, taking a step backwards as she closed her laptop. Simon was a stickler for the truth, from other people at least, and she felt the need to back up her statement by removing herself from the vicinity of her workspace.

'Anna, I can see you. You just stepped back so you wouldn't *technically* be lying to me.'

She turned to see his grinning face peering through the glass-top section of the office door, phone still to his ear.

'Fucking idiot,' she muttered as she hung up and marched towards her boss and former lover. She pulled open the door. 'What do you want? I've just finished for the day.'

Simon's grin widened. Anna could see that he was trying to wind her up, to bait her into losing her temper but she wouldn't let him win. Not this time.

'Ten minutes? I just need to go through the case notes on Jonah James.'

'No, you don't. I finished and submitted the notes yesterday. Why wait until knocking-off time to come and find me?'

Simon hung his head and peered up at her through strands of blond fringe. His expression was sheepish but his eyes were on the verge of laughter. 'I thought we might have a chat over a drink.'

So that was his game. He'd been trying to win her back for a few weeks now. After the first few acrimonious months he'd obviously realised what he'd been missing and had decided to up his game. Anna wasn't going to fall for it though. She'd been making discreet enquiries at other law firms and knew that there were positions coming up in Rotherham and Sheffield that offered better pay and the possibility of making partner before she retired. If she stayed here, she'd either never advance or, if she did, she'd never be able to shrug off the rumours that she'd only been promoted because she was sleeping with the boss.

It had been a huge mistake. Still reeling from a nasty divorce and a relocation to Doncaster, she'd fallen for Simon's seemingly effortless blend of professionalism and youthful good looks before she knew that he was a serial shagger and would chase anything in a skirt. She should have known. Simon was ten years younger than her and even though Anna knew she looked good for her age and she dressed to optimise her carefully groomed silver hair and trim figure, she hadn't been convinced that Simon wanted anything beyond the challenge of getting her into bed. She'd had plenty of offers throughout her life and hadn't been flattered by Simon's attentions to the point of forgetting all reason. He'd just turned out to be different from the man she thought he might be. Now though, he seemed to have become obsessed with her – ever since she'd dumped him – and she wasn't sure how to get rid of him.

'I need to get home, Simon,' Anna lied. 'I'm still not fully briefed on the Portman case and we both know that we don't need the publicity of another long battle.'

Simon's face went a shade paler. They'd still been sleeping together when a supposedly clear-cut case of entrapment had suddenly gone tits up and, in the long run, they'd been lucky to win. It wasn't even a case that Anna had wanted. As a defence lawyer she preferred to support the misused in society, to give them a fair hearing, but she'd allowed Simon to coax her into defending a man accused of sexual assault. It was a high-profile case and had attracted a lot of publicity. Over the course of their discussions, it had become clear that the defendant was innocent of the charges but that he was certainly guilty of similar crimes over a period of three or four years. They'd won but it had left a nasty taste and had deepened Anna's mistrust of her boss and her contempt for herself for being taken in by him.

'Look,' Simon said. 'I just want to clear the air between us, that's all. I didn't like the way things ended between us and I–'

'Simon,' Anna cut him off, unwilling to listen to any more of his bullshit. 'We had some fun and then I found out that you were seeing other women. It wasn't what I signed up for, so I ended it. It's not complicated and it's not an issue. I'm in a hurry because I want to get home and change. I'm meeting somebody for a drink later and I haven't seen them for years. I don't have time for this.'

He nodded and leaned against the wall of the corridor allowing Anna enough room to push past him. 'I just hope he's worth it,' he muttered as Anna pushed the button to summon the lift.

The lie had been a simple one because it had been based in truth. Anna had no plans to meet anybody *that* evening, but she did want to do some research and it was connected to her past. Earlier in the week she'd received an email to her work email address from an unknown sender that, when opened, claimed to be from somebody who'd known her over thirty years ago asking if she wanted to meet. Anna hadn't recognised the name, so she'd ignored the contact, dismissing it as a crank or an elaborate phishing scam. The second email contained a photograph that had changed her mind. That and the name.

She'd been using *Anna* since she'd graduated. Her full name, Anastasia, had always felt a bit pretentious and nobody could spell it properly so shortening it had seemed a good option at the start of her career. The name she'd used up to that point didn't suggest 'serious lawyer' and she'd never been able to imagine introducing herself to potential clients as Taz, so the change had been made.

Pouring another glass of Pinot Grigio, Anna stared again at the photograph. Grainy black and white suggested a newspaper cutting, the location unclear, but Anna knew exactly when and where it had been taken. Nobody who knew her now would have recognised the young woman in the image – face contorted with hatred as she pulled back her arm to throw a missile at a male police officer standing a few yards away – but Anna recognised her younger self clearly.

Greenham.

The word brought an onslaught of memories. Woodsmoke, cheap booze, pot and the constant, bone-numbing cold. The anger simmering under the surface of every interaction like the constant thrum of an engine in a waiting car. She'd spent eighteen months camped out on the perimeter of the base; eighteen months of hunger and frustration. But they'd also been eighteen months of camaraderie and fun.

The photograph was from a sit-in with a large group of police officers in the background. Anna recognised two of the women to her right and remembered that they'd left after the first winter to shouts of 'traitor'. She'd been so naïve then, so idealistic. A part of her was proud of the role she'd played in trying to build a better future, but another part was embarrassed by her former black-and-white views. Life had seemed so simple then. It was only after two years of study that she began to recognise the complexities and the nuances of modern life and international relations. She'd turned up for work hungover after Margaret Thatcher had resigned – who hadn't? – but she hadn't seen the fall of the woman as a victory for the downtrodden and deserted. Having lived through the fallout from 9/11 and now the Brexit debacle Anna had resigned herself to the stupidity and small-mindedness of politicians of all flavours and persuasions and accepted what she couldn't change while still trying to change what she couldn't accept. She hoped that, by now, she was wise enough to know the difference.

The message was short and contained no hint of threat, but Anna couldn't put a face to the name.

> Hi again Taz. I wonder if my last email got to you — perhaps you don't remember me so I thought this might bring back memories. I loved my time at Greenham Common and remember you very fondly. You taught me so much and I often think of your stories and explanations. You were my hero. Good times, eh? It would be great to catch up sometime.
>
> Love Titch

'Titch' suggested either a child or somebody quite small, but Anna had no recollection of anybody at Greenham with that nickname. There were a lot of children around and Anna probably called most of them Titch at one time or another. Some came and went over the course of the year – their presence at the base dictated by school holidays – some younger ones were there all the time. It could have been one of the women – a lot were known only by nicknames in order to protect their identity if any of their friends were arrested and questioned about their associates.

Anna looked at the photograph again. There were three other women and one looked quite small – was that Titch? She had no idea, but she did have some thoughts about where she might look for clues.

The loft had been one of the reasons that Anna had bought the house. After her divorce, she'd needed to downsize from their five-bedroom Victorian terrace in a bright, leafy square in Lincoln but she had a lot of clutter still to sort through and the loft space in her current house was the perfect place to store it. The fixed sliding ladder that dropped down automatically when she opened the hatch on the landing had been a bonus.

The boxes and bags stacked around the edges of the space and hulked against the underside of the eaves contained the remains of Anna's possessions from her previous lives. They were still waiting to be sorted into junk and treasure, but she'd not got around to the final declutter. Hauling herself onto the boarded floor of the loft Anna sat hunched and looked around. She didn't subscribe to the idea that if something wasn't valuable or practical it should be thrown out – there were years of memories in these boxes and everything meant something. Didn't it?

She crab-crawled across to the far wall where her semi butted up against next door, and scanned the banana boxes and old suitcases. She remembered that most of her teenage pictures were in a suitcase, but she wasn't sure which one. Only one way to find out.

Dragging the first piece of luggage towards her she flicked the catches and lifted the lid. School books. A whole case full of exercise books and folders from her O-level studies. Anna closed the lid and tried the next suitcase – more old books. She struck lucky on her fifth try. A hard-sided, wheeled case contained dozens of packets of photographs stored with no thought to chronology or geography.

'Gonna take ages,' Anna muttered to herself as she thumbed her way through the first packet – university parties – and placed them on the floor behind her.

The Greenham Common photographs were lumped in with some from a family holiday when she'd been sixteen. Shy teenage poses in her one-piece swimming costume gave way to a wire fence and piles of blankets.

'Gotcha!'

Two more packets also looked promising and she settled herself more comfortably on the hard boards to have a closer look.

Simply handling the photographs was an act of nostalgia, a form of archaeology. She was used to quickly flicking through images on the screen of her phone or on her iPad. Handling the slippery card forced her to slow down; to look more closely.

The first images from Greenham looked like she'd been in an arty, experimental phase. Blurry shots through the artificial border of the diamonds of the wire fence focusing on one guard or a single stalk of grass. Then there were group shots. Women in makeshift shelters, women in circles, women in pain. It had felt natural at the time, being in an all-female society, but the photographs highlighted how unusual the camp had been. Some of the pictures were well composed – one or two children of indeterminate age and gender huddled against the fence while a policeman towered over them was shocking – others were little more than snapshots. As she scoured the faces Anna remembered a few names. There was Eleanor, one of the earliest protesters who seemed to do a lot of the cooking. She saw Sarah, her first serious crush, then two small boys who were obviously twins. One of them had been called Riley but she couldn't remember the name of the other one – Titch?

Half an hour later she was no closer to discovering the identity of her mystery correspondent and desperate for another glass of wine. With the nostalgia had come a nagging feeling that her life hadn't turned out as she'd intended and that Taz wouldn't have been especially impressed by the woman she'd become. Would Titch still see her as a hero? Or a failure, a sell-out?

'One way to find out,' Anna murmured to herself as she dropped one leg over the edge of the loft hatch and felt for the first rung of the ladder. A glass of wine for Dutch courage and then she'd respond to the message and arrange a meeting to see what sort of person Titch had grown into.

1983

Dad wasn't happy that Mum wanted to bring me here just for the weekend. He says it's too far to go for one night and I think he might be right. It took ages to get here yesterday because we have to come by train and bus now that there are no more van pickups, and when we arrived there was nobody here that I knew. A lot of the women were away at another site. I think that's why we had to come, to keep up the numbers. But Mum says some of them have given up the fight and gone back to their husbands and their careers. Her face scrunches up when she says stuff like that as though those women taste sour in her mouth, like a lemon.

Winter's back at the camp like an unwanted visitor that the women have to accept even though they don't like the way he makes them feel. I can see him in their eyes and the way they move as if they're all old women, shuffling and bowing down like they have no choice but to worship the cold. Mum says that they didn't expect to be here for so long, that another winter isn't what they planned for, but they can't give up now – they have to see this through and make sure that the missiles are taken away.

I don't really understand that. I asked Mum but she just smiled – I don't think she knows either, but she pretends that everything will work out for the best.

Taz turned up this morning. She's moved her bender – that's what the funny shelters are called – further round the perimeter. Mum didn't seem very happy to see her, but she gave her a hug even though her eyes were cold. It was better after Taz arrived. She took me to see where she's been staying and it was really nice even though it's on a windier part of the fence, high up with a view over the silos. It was Taz who taught me that word – it's where the missiles are kept – it sounds sad, like they don't want to be here. *Sigh low.*

The police arrived on Sunday morning. Lots of them. One of the leaders of the police told us all to pack up and go home but the women stayed where they were, some padlocked themselves to the fence just to be certain that they couldn't be dragged away, and then they all started keening. I don't like the noise. It gets in my mind and makes me want to scream. Perhaps that's what it does to the police as well because they eventually went away. Taz laughed and called them pigs. She says they like the power they have over us more than they care about the law. She says they're not really bothered about the base, but they like to come and frighten us just for the sake of it.

We had a bit of a panic when Sarah disappeared. One minute she was chatting to Mum and the next minute she'd gone – just as the police arrived. I wondered if they'd arrested her and taken her away, but she came back as soon as the police had gone. She didn't say where she'd been, but me and Taz thought that she looked a bit more scared than usual.

I hate the police.

After they'd gone, I saw two women putting their things into bags and taking their tent down. Taz ran over and begged them to stay but they didn't listen and then an old red van turned up and they got in with Taz shouting 'traitors!' at them. Traitors are people who let you down, who side with the enemy. That's what Taz says. She says that, when she's older, she'll only ever help people who care about the future and the planet. She's going to university next year to learn to help those people.

24

Checking his watch yet again, O'Connor was still trying to get his brain to accept the time. Driving just over 100 miles north made a surprising difference to the daylight at this time of year. His watch was telling him that it should be dark by now, but his senses were telling him something different, something he hadn't planned for. It wouldn't be so easy to follow the unmarked Houghtons' lorry in daylight.

He'd spent a few hours trying to piece together the routes taken by Sims's 'special' fleet and was fairly convinced that he was safe enough to start the tail from a convenient lay-by about five miles west of Newcastle on the A69. The two lorries he'd tracked on CCTV and ANPR cameras had both taken that route, but he lost them after Hexham which suggested that they'd probably turned off north or south on the A68 either heading for the Scottish border or deep into the Pennines.

The ferry from Amsterdam docked at 8.30pm and the lorries had reached O'Connor's current location by 9.30. He'd been in position for nearly an hour watching as the traffic flow increased, HGVs and motorhomes forming the bulk of the road users – holidaymakers from Europe heading to the Lakes and

Ireland, goods heading the same way, out to the Cumbrian coast, Scotland and Northern Ireland. A good handful of cars with Dutch plates passed, sticking assiduously to the speed limit as they presumably adapted to driving on the left.

And then he spotted it. A white seven-and-a-half-tonne lorry. He clocked the index number as it passed doing just under sixty miles an hour. It was one of Sims's.

'Gotcha!' he hissed as he turned the ignition key and slipped his Volvo into gear.

He kept two cars between himself and the lorry, dropping his speed where necessary, as the road curved gently to the north west, the setting sun temporarily blinding before another curve sent the dazzling rays further to O'Connor's right. He groped around for his sunglasses and flipped the visor down, narrowing his eyes as the light hit the roof of a car on the opposite carriageway and leapt through his windscreen.

The roundabout for the A68 south slowed progress and O'Connor watched closely as the lorry decelerated, anticipating a left turn but, instead, it continued straight ahead towards Hexham and Carlisle. At the next junction he was about 200 yards behind the lorry with only a single car between them allowing him a clear view as Sims's vehicle turned off the A69 onto the A68, heading north.

'Och aye,' O'Connor muttered to himself as they joined the road to the Scottish border. His presumption was short-lived, however, as he saw the lorry indicate left again following signs for Hadrian's Wall and Chollerford. The sun had dipped below the horizon and the sky was a deep blue as O'Connor continued his pursuit west and then north again deeper into Northumberland.

'Where the fuck are you going?' he muttered at yet another left turn just outside Bellingham. The road narrowed and O'Connor found he had to hang back but, even so, he kept catching up to the lorry on awkward bends. In the end the driver seemed aware of his presence and pulled into a lay-by, politely allowing O'Connor to overtake.

'Bugger!' O'Connor cursed, trying to negotiate the lane and rethink his strategy. It was dark now and his car was mid-grey and fairly anonymous. Would the driver of the lorry recognise it again if it suddenly reappeared in his rear-view mirror? O'Connor hoped not. He drove for a few more miles then turned into a farm lane and knocked his lights off. A minute later he watched in his rear-view mirror as the lorry passed his hiding place. He counted to ten, did a dodgy three-point-turn and resumed his pursuit.

Trees started to close in to the left of the road and O'Connor could make out the black shape of Kielder Water to the right. The lorry's rear lights appeared and disappeared as the driver followed the bends of the smooth road next to the reservoir, O'Connor keeping at least a quarter of a mile back. Suddenly the lights got brighter as the driver braked and turned off to the left. O'Connor slowed his speed and crawled the last few yards to the turning before driving past and pulling up in a lay-by further along the road. He opened the driver's door cursing as the interior light came on, and eased himself out, closing the door behind him as quietly as he could manage.

A huge moon had appeared over the tops of the trees and it wasn't difficult to see the road or the dark entrance to the turning the lorry had taken. O'Connor had no idea if it was a car park or one of the forest tracks that he knew were popular with mountain bikers and walkers. If it was the latter, then the lorry was as good as lost to him – the tracks went on for miles. O'Connor had spent a team-building weekend with some colleagues from his previous posting in a cabin on the lakeshore and they'd hired bikes for the day, ending up mostly lost and frustrated by the dense forest.

Keeping to the grass verge to mask the sound of his footsteps he crept closer to the turning, stopping suddenly when he saw the lights of the lorry just a few yards from the road. He crouched down and inched forward like a clumsy Cossack dancer trying not to fall flat on his face.

The driver's door of the lorry was open, and the driver was fiddling with the lock on the rear doors. He climbed inside and started to remove boxes, stacking them on the hydraulic platform that folded down at the back of the lorry for easy unloading. Instead of lowering them to the ground he left them in a neat pile and disappeared further into the interior of the storage area.

A minute later he was back but he wasn't alone. As he jumped down three men followed him, each one clutching a water bottle. In the silence of the night, O'Connor could hear them breathing heavily as they eased themselves down to the ground and looked round at their location. One split away from the other two and approached the driver. O'Connor couldn't hear what was being said but the tone was angry. The driver simply shook his head, locked the lorry and walked back to the cab. As he climbed inside, the other two men started shouting but he ignored them, put the vehicle in gear and drove back to the road.

O'Connor just managed to duck out of sight of the sweep of the headlights, throwing himself into the gap between a pair of gorse bushes, cursing under his breath. He counted to ten and then struggled to his feet, ripping his shirt on the thorny branches as he pulled free. His first thought was to follow the lorry, but he needed to find out who the passengers were and what they'd been promised. He had no doubt that they had been smuggled into the country and their testimony would help him to build a case against Sims and the driver of the lorry if he could get them to tell him exactly what had happened.

Stumbling along the grass verge, trying not to think about what he might be treading in, O'Connor jogged into the parking area. He couldn't arrest the three men, not until he knew for certain that they were illegal entrants to the country, but he could help them, get them to a town, to a bed. If he could persuade them to come with him.

The car park was deserted. O'Connor had no idea what the men had said to the driver, but they sounded like they hadn't expected to be dumped in the middle of nowhere. They must have set off on foot, hoping to stumble upon civilisation by luck. He considered shouting out to them but what could he say? They'd already been betrayed once. If they thought he was the driver why would they come back? And if they knew he was the police they'd only run faster and further.

'Fuck it!' O'Connor cursed, turning back the way he'd come. There was nothing more he could do here. As he made his way back to the car, he took comfort from one thought – he'd been right about Sims.

25

'Bugger!' Ian Dalglish cursed as the car in front slowed. He could see brake lights ahead – three lanes of traffic grinding to a halt. *There must be road works,* Dalglish thought. Why else would there be delays at half past one in the morning? Inching forwards he considered ringing Eileen, his wife, to let her know that he was delayed but he'd probably wake her up and he didn't want to have to face her wrath as soon as he got home. She'd be angry enough anyway.

He hadn't expected to be so late. His brother's stag party was supposed to have been a tame affair, just a curry and a few beers – but not for Dalglish as the designated driver. What he hadn't anticipated was just how drunk Greg would get and just how little regard his friends had for his safety. He'd had to drive Greg back to his fiancée's flat after he'd been abandoned in a Portaloo in Sheffield city centre. At least he'd managed to stop the so-called friends from tipping the plastic toilet over and soaking his brother in sewage.

It had taken an hour to persuade Greg to go to bed and another twenty minutes to explain and apologise to his fiancée who seemed to blame Ian for the whole sorry mess. And now here he was crawling along in the slow lane of the M18 somewhere south of Doncaster.

Consulting the satnav didn't help as it showed there wasn't a junction for at least eight miles, so he'd have to sit it out until then. He tapped the screen again and consulted the list of radio stations. If he was going to be stuck at least he could find some decent music. He scrolled down to a rock station and turned up the volume. Just as he put his hand back on the steering wheel, the glow of brake lights started to fade and the red pinpricks in the distance disappeared. Whatever had been causing the hold-up seemed to have loosened its grip on the snake of traffic.

'Thank fuck.' Dalglish sighed, increasing the pressure on the accelerator.

Two minutes later and the traffic was flowing smoothly allowing him to speed up to eighty miles an hour. He adjusted the volume on the stereo, turning it down to help him to concentrate on the galaxy of cats' eyes guiding him along the motorway.

Something ahead and above caught his attention, his eyes automatically drawn to the dark horizontal line of a bridge ahead. Was there a person there? Or an animal. Going too fast to make any sense of the movement, Dalglish gasped as the blur solidified into the shape of a person teetering on the wrong side of the bridge's railings. He yelled and slammed his foot down hard on the brake, steering to the left through the vibrations of the raised markings on the hard shoulder, coming to a stop under the bridge.

'Jesus,' he whispered to himself as he leapt out of the car and ran back along the hard shoulder to where he'd seen the person falling. Other cars were slowing down, the traffic splitting to the left and right to avoid the shape in the road. Three cars were lined up in the slow lane and he could see the glow of a mobile phone in one as somebody called for help. Hazard warning lights surrounded him as he stepped into the middle lane, protected by a line of four or five cars, and made his way to the person lying on the tarmac.

He knew not to do more than a basic check for breath and a pulse – moving an injured person could be fatal – but he couldn't help but push a stray strand of hair back from the face for a clearer view. A woman. She looked to be in her late forties or early fifties, the side of her face that he could see was expertly made-up and he could smell her perfume over the exhaust fumes of the surrounding vehicles. Dalglish didn't know much about women's fashion but her clothes looked expensive – this wasn't somebody who'd hit rock bottom, she looked more like she'd been for a night out with friends, or a boyfriend.

Had she been alone? Dalglish stood up and closed his eyes, trying to remember what he'd seen in the few seconds before the woman had fallen from the bridge. Had the movement been a struggle between two people or was it just one woman climbing the railings? He didn't know. He couldn't remember.

A distant siren made him open his eyes again. The emergency services were on the way.

He stared down at the broken mess on the road. It looked like help was going to be too late for this woman.

26

'Julia Sullivan suffered a traumatic injury to the skull from the car crash,' Cooper said as soon as Kate set foot in the incident room. 'That must be the healed fracture found at the PM. It's in her hospital notes but it wasn't covered in the information from her GP.'

Kate removed her suit jacket, draping it across her chair, and settled in front of her computer. It was too early and she hadn't had enough caffeine to be able to see where Cooper was going with her comment. She looked at the DC and made a 'come here' gesture with the fingers of one hand while using the other to swipe her ID through the card reader that would let her into the computer system.

Cooper smiled. 'Too early for conversation? Okay. Here's what I've been thinking. What if Julia Sullivan's head injury caused her personality to change? It's well documented that people who suffer from traumatic brain injuries often seem different. It might explain her religious conversion and her radically altered political views.'

'It might,' Kate agreed. She'd come to a similar conclusion herself while researching the Church of the Right Hand but she hadn't seen anything criminal in their activities. She typed in her email password. 'But how is it relevant?'

'We can't find a link between the three victims,' Cooper said. 'But they've all been in the local press. The Houghtons because of Peter's environmental scraps with various bodies, Julia Sullivan and her odious views and Liv Thornbury was in the *Sheffield Star* a couple of times when she was coming up to retirement. There are at least two 'profile' pieces on her. We've been told that all three may have met with somebody unknown to their family or friends. What if that somebody has been checking the local press and biding his time?'

'I still don't see–'

'Change,' Cooper said. 'They've all changed. Liv retired, Julia went very right wing and Eleanor got married to an environmental vandal. The changes in their lives were very public and might have drawn the attention of our killer.'

Kate sighed. 'Sam, this feels very tenuous. If the killer knew these women in the past it wouldn't have been difficult for him, or her, to find them.'

'I know that. But why now? What if he saw an article about Liv's retirement and it prompted him to look up other people he knew...'

'You're missing the obvious here, Cooper. If the killer knew these women then there must be a link. If nothing else, the killer is the link. Who did they all know in the past?'

It was Cooper's turn to sigh heavily. 'There's something here, I can feel it. I just can't put my finger on what it is that's bugging me.'

Kate opened her email account and scanned through the latest communications. 'We've got some forensics back on the Houghtons' house,' she said, clicking on the title of the message. It wasn't good news. Analysis of the contents of the outside dustbin was inconclusive. The fibres and debris were contaminated with dust and grime from the inside of the bin and it could easily be argued that the dustbin might have been mixed up with that of another house at some point. The hairs were awaiting DNA analysis, but Kate knew that unless the owner was on the database, they'd be useless unless a viable suspect was found. No fingerprints on door handles or the gin bottle – not even those of Peter or Eleanor Houghton, confirming Hollis's suspicion that the killer would have wiped everything clean – and no DNA from the washing-up gloves. The car was also clean. The only prints on the door handles belonged to Cain Powell and there was nothing on the steering wheel, the tubing or the tape that had been used to secure it to the rear window. There was no similar tubing or tape in the Houghtons' house or garage suggesting that the killer had been prepared.

'Bollocks,' Kate hissed.

'Problem?' Cooper's blonde head popped up like a meerkat from behind her computer monitor.

'Forensics on the house in Turton. Nothing. Not a fucking thing!'

Cooper flinched at Kate's outburst. 'Looks like somebody knew what they were doing. I bet the Sullivan house is the same.'

'Probably. The SOCOs were already there when Dan and I arrived so it was difficult to see if any cleaning had been done. If there's anything I'm sure they'll find it.'

'Find what?' O'Connor rolled up his shirtsleeves as he strode to his desk. 'Lost something?'

'And a good morning to you, too, Steve,' Kate sniped.

O'Connor gave her a lopsided grin and tugged an imagined forelock. 'Sorry, boss. How are you this fine morning?'

'Crap,' Kate said. 'Why do you look so chipper, or shouldn't I ask?'

O'Connor sat down and pulled his chair tighter in to his desk before swiping his ID and logging on, all the time with a maddening smile plastered across his face.

'He's up to something,' Cooper said. 'I know that look.'

'I am most definitely up to something,' O'Connor admitted, turning his chair round to face Kate. 'Remember when I said that there was something not right about Houghton Haulage?'

Kate nodded, wary. She thought O'Connor's maverick tendencies might have been curbed after she'd sent him off on a couple of menial errands, but it seemed he was still on top form.

'Well, I took it upon myself to investigate further and–'

'Steve, I told you to leave it alone.'

'It was all in my own time,' he said. 'I've been tracking the unmarked lorries that Sims bought, and I've found out why he was so cagey when me and Matt last paid him a visit. He's involved in people trafficking.'

'I don't...' Kate began but O'Connor spoke over her, giving an account of tailing one of Sims's vehicles through the wilds of Northumberland the previous night. She listened, incredulous, as he described seeing three men get out of the back of the lorry in Kielder Forest before being abandoned by the driver.

'And you know for certain that Sims is involved?' she asked, her mind spinning as she tried to work out what to do next. She'd need to liaise with Border Force and Northumbria Police and get a warrant to search the vehicles at Houghton Haulage. And she needed to apologise to her detective sergeant.

'He told me and Matt that he owned the fleet of seven-and-a-half-tonne trucks. They're part of his pet project which he claims is about exploiting different ferry routes post-Brexit. Looks to me like it's more about exploiting desperate people with nowhere else to turn.'

'Wow,' Cooper interjected. 'Growing a social conscience, Steve?'

O'Connor ignored her. 'If we search the trucks and find that they've all got some sort of hidden compartment then Sims has got a lot of explaining to do. If we can get Northumbria Police to do what I did and follow one of them then he won't have a leg to stand on. It'll be his word against the driver's, but I'll bet there's a paper trail.'

Kate grinned. 'I'm sorry, Steve. You were right. This is your case so how do you want to play it? Do you want to be part of the search team or do you want to be the one to collar the driver?'

'Both,' O'Connor admitted.

'Okay, well, that won't work. Look, I'll let the DCI know what's going on and tell her that you're running the case. You're a DS with a lot of experience, I doubt she'll argue. You'll need to contact Border Force and find somebody in Northumbria Police to work with. This is going to take a lot of your time, but you deserve the credit.'

O'Connor nodded. 'Appreciate your support, Kate,' he mumbled, uncomfortable with the praise but not, she suspected, the responsibility.

'And I want to know immediately if there's any link to Houghton Haulage and the murders of Julia Sullivan and Liv Thornbury. The trafficking and the murders are to be kept separate for now but, if you find anything, however insignificant you think it might be, you're to tell me immediately. Clear?'

'Crystal.'

'Great work, Steve.'

Kate continued trawling through her email. It always amazed her that she could log off at six or seven in the evening with an empty inbox and, twelve hours later, log on to at least a dozen messages, most of them sent by colleagues at odd hours. After the disappointment of the forensics report she wasn't especially buoyed by the fifth email in the list.

'Got phone records for Liv Thornbury and Julia Sullivan,'

she told Cooper. 'Nothing for the Houghtons yet. I'll send you a copy and get them to Julia Sullivan's family and Sylvia Kerr. They might be able to help us eliminate some numbers.'

Trawling through phone records was tedious work but, with Cooper's eye for detail, it had proved crucial on past cases. They needed to find and call any numbers not known to the family and to see if the same number appeared on both sets of records – the former could be farmed out to civilian admin staff, but Cooper's were the only eyes Kate trusted for the latter task.

Emails checked, Kate slipped her jacket back on and stood up. 'Briefing in ten,' she announced. 'I'm off to get coffee.' She didn't bother asking what Cooper and O'Connor might want, she knew their preferences well enough after working with them both for so long and she often supplied the coffee for morning briefing, especially when she had very little to report. It seemed to help soften the blow when she had nothing else to offer.

She'd just started up the second flight of stairs to the canteen on the top floor of the building when her phone rang.

'DI Fletcher.'

Silence.

'DI Kate Fletcher speaking.'

'Sorry,' the person at the other end of the line said. 'I dialled then wasn't sure whether I'd done the right thing. It's Sylvia Kerr, Liv Thornbury's partner. I was going through Liv's laptop and I found something that I think you might want to see.'

27

'What am I looking at?' Kate asked as Sylvia Kerr pushed the laptop across the table towards her. The woman had offered to come into Doncaster Central as she had an appointment in the town later that day and Kate had wanted to see the laptop not just the email. She'd commandeered an interview room where they wouldn't be disturbed.

'It's Liv,' Sylvia said.

Kate studied the grainy black-and-white image of two distinct groups of people in an apparent stand-off. The police officers were all standing while the women were lying or sitting down in front of them. Behind the police was a chain-link fence topped with two rows of barbed wire.

'Which one? All the coppers look like men to me.'

'Not the policemen. Look at the women.'

Kate put on her reading glasses and leaned in towards the screen. The women's faces came into much sharper focus. Most were smiling or laughing – one had her mouth open wide and appeared to be yelling something – none looked angry or upset. They all wore coats and jumpers and at least a dozen were sporting woolly hats and fingerless gloves; others had headscarves tightly fastened beneath their chins.

'Where is this? And when?' Kate asked, unable to make out anybody resembling the image she had seen of Olivia Thornbury.

'It's Greenham Common. Early eighties I'd imagine. That's Liv.'

Sylvia pointed to a young woman sprawled on the ground at the front of the picture. Her dark hair was sticking out from under a woollen hat and her hands were linked behind her head as though she was about to take a nap. She was grinning at somebody out of shot. There was nothing of the well-respected DCI in the face of this protester – not as far as Kate could see.

'I wouldn't have recognised her,' Kate admitted. 'How old would she have been?'

'Twenty-three or four. It's before I knew her. I could see straight away that it's her. It's her smile.'

'What was she doing there? Did she ever talk about it?'

Sylvia shook her head. 'I had no idea she'd been there.'

'Well, we all do things when we're younger that we feel embarrassed about. It doesn't really sit comfortably, being a police officer and a former protester. Perhaps that's why she didn't talk about it. Joining the force may have changed her perspective.'

Sylvia stared at Kate as though she'd just said something really stupid and Kate wondered what the hell she was missing.

'Liv joined the police force after her A-levels. She'd have been a serving officer for over five years when this photograph was taken. She'd never expressed any sympathy with the Greenham women, at least not to me, so what the hell was she doing there?'

Kate looked at the photograph again. It had been sent as an attachment on a blank email. The title was 'Remember this?'

The sender called themselves 'titch_1983' and he or she had used a web-based email service which would make the owner of the email address almost impossible to trace.

'Are there any more messages from this sender?'

Liv leaned over and tapped the keyboard. 'I found this in the 'deleted folder'.'

The message was from the same sender and contained a series of numbers.

'It's a mobile number,' Kate said.

'I know,' Sylvia said. 'I rang it.'

'And?'

'Nothing. The number's disconnected.'

Kate picked up her phone and rang the number. The recorded message told her that it was not in service, so she texted the digits to Cooper to check against Liv Thornbury's phone records. This was their best lead so far. If Liv had been contacting this person, it was possible that they were connected with her death. But what was the link to Greenham Common? Kate had a suspicion, but it wasn't going to be a comfortable conversation to have with Liv's partner.

'Have you heard of the SIS?' she began.

Sylvia shook her head. 'Nope.'

'It was an undercover Met Police unit.'

'Liv trained at Hendon. She started her career in the Met.'

Kate digested this information. It tied in with her suspicions and the timing made perfect sense.

'The SIS was the Specialist Infiltration Squad. It was set up by Special Branch in the sixties to destabilise supposed left-wing groups, CND, anti-war protesters, that sort of thing.'

Sylvia's eyes narrowed as she kept them fixed on Kate's face.

'It was disbanded about ten years ago.' What Kate didn't add was that some of the undercover officers were alleged to have engaged in illegal activities. 'There were probably members of

SIS at Greenham in the eighties. They would have blended in, lived and protested with the women.'

Sylvia Kerr shook her head. 'No. Not Liv. She was a feminist. She wouldn't have done anything like that. She hated deception.'

Inhaling deeply, Kate continued. 'If she was young and ambitious it would have been a golden opportunity to make her mark. If she'd delivered anything useful to the squad she'd have been in line for promotion, may have even been able to pick her next job in any force that she fancied.'

'She'd just moved to South Yorkshire when we met. She said she'd had enough of London and wanted somewhere she could go climbing at the weekends. It was towards the end of 1986 and she'd just been promoted to detective sergeant.'

'In her mid-twenties? That's quite a meteoric rise,' Kate said. She'd not been made a DS until she was in her early forties and O'Connor, her own DS, had been at the same rank since his mid-thirties.

'I just thought she was good at her job.'

It would probably be very difficult to find out if Liv Thornbury had been involved in the SIS. Since the unit had been disbanded there had been a lot of adverse publicity which had spilled over to other areas of undercover work and several high-profile convictions of former police officers. There seemed little point in dragging DCI Thornbury's name through the mud based on Kate's hunch, but it did suggest a motive for Liv's murder. Her retirement had been covered in the local press, along with her photograph, and it was possible that somebody she knew at Greenham might have recognised her. Had she been instrumental in a previous arrest or conviction of the killer? Could it be somebody bearing a thirty-year grudge who'd finally enacted revenge on her betrayer? It was plausible except for one thing – what had

Eleanor Houghton and Julia Sullivan done to piss off their murderer?

The photograph showed around fifty women. Were Eleanor and Julia among them? Kate tried to enlarge the image on the laptop screen, but it started to blur after a couple of key taps and the faces of the women melded into each other.

'I'm going to need a copy of this,' Kate said. 'And I'd like to keep the laptop for a while if that's okay? I want to get digital forensics onto it – see if there's anything else there.'

What she didn't include was that she'd give Cooper first bash at the hard drive.

'That's fine,' Sylvia said, sitting back in her seat and smoothing down a few strands of unruly grey hair. 'If it helps you find out what really happened to Liv you can have it for as long as you want.'

'I'd also like to give you a copy of Liv's phone records – I'd like you to see if there are any unfamiliar numbers.'

Sylvia nodded. 'I'll have a look but without her mobile phone I'm not sure how much help I'll be. Who remembers phone numbers these days?'

She was right. Most people could barely remember their own number and relied on their contacts folder in their phone to store information about others.

'You've given us a lot of helpful information, Sylvia,' Kate said, pushing her chair back from the desk and hoping to wind up the interview. 'I'm sure we'll be able to...'

A knock on the door cut short her intentionally anodyne statement and Barratt burst into the room without waiting for permission to enter.

'Matt, I said I wasn't to be disturbed,' Kate snapped but Barratt ignored her admonishment.

'There's been another one,' he said. Kate shook her head and stared pointedly at Sylvia Kerr. She didn't want the woman hearing anything inappropriate about the case. Barratt took the hint and backed away into the corridor, Kate following after quickly excusing herself.

'What the hell, Matt? This had better be important.'

'It is. There's been another supposed suicide. Similar note and everything. This one looks like she was pushed from a motorway bridge in the early hours of this morning just south of Doncaster.'

'Oh shit.' Kate sighed. 'He's escalating.'

'That's not the big news,' Barratt said. 'This woman's still alive.'

28

Looking down at the woman's ruined face, Kate questioned her decision to come to the hospital. There was nothing to be gained from standing over the bed listening to the rush of the ventilator and the beep of the heart monitor. But she had to see. And, if the woman were to gain consciousness, Kate needed to know. The woman's head was swathed in bandages and the small patches of uncovered flesh were angry shades of purple and blue. She was slim, her body almost lost under the white sheet that covered her legs and torso, only her arms were exposed – each one connected to a tube.

Anastasia Cohen.

She'd been followed in her plummet from the bridge by a plume of business cards which had scattered across the carriageway like oddly angular snowflakes.

A nurse came in, ignoring Kate, and checked the level of the fluid dripping into Anastasia's right arm. She looked at the monitor above the bed, scribbled on the top sheet of the notes that were hanging on a hook at the foot of the bed and left without saying a word.

The SOCOs had found a note in her handbag which had

been tied to the railings of the bridge. Two lines which, to anybody unfamiliar with the other cases, would have suggested suicide.

> *Life has been good.*
>> *It's time to go.*

It was chillingly similar to the other three, printed on A4 paper and folded once, and felt like a taunt, a challenge. Also in the handbag was a make-up bag which contained a lipstick, a dried-up tube of mascara, foundation and a small mirror – cracked across the middle. The killer was teasing them, daring them to catch him.

'Any change?' Hollis asked as Kate stepped into the corridor, gently closing the door to the ICU behind her. She shook her head.

'It's the same killer, isn't it?'

'I think so. The note's the same.' She didn't know what else to say. Somehow it was easier to deal with a dead body; that was done, over. This felt like a state of limbo. The woman might live or she might die and, if she lived, she might be disabled or brain-damaged. There was nothing to be learned until the woman was woken from her induced coma and it felt ghoulish to be hanging around. Now she'd seen the wreckage of the person attached to the name Anastasia Cohen, Kate felt a deep sense of sadness and anger. She was going to catch the bastard who'd done this. There was no sign of Anastasia's car at the scene and, so far, nobody had been able to locate the vehicle. It seemed likely that the killer had driven it away and that might be his biggest mistake to date. Kate texted Cooper to ask her to check CCTV.

'Come on,' she said to Hollis. 'We need to put a stop to this.

Text Matt, he needs to hear what I have to say. I've got some new information that I need to share.'

'And Steve?' Hollis asked, thumb poised over the send button on his phone.

'No. Steve's got other fish to fry.'

Hollis stopped walking. 'What? You've kicked him off the case? I know he's been a bit too focused on Houghton Haulage, but don't you think...?'

Kate held up a hand, stopping him mid-flow. 'Steve's dug up something very interesting and I'm going to let him run with it.'

'Care to share?' Hollis asked.

'It's Steve's thing. I'll let him tell you. It's going to keep him busy, so I need you and Sam and Matt even more focused.'

Hollis clicked his heels together and saluted. 'Yes boss.'

Kate smiled and shook her head. If there was one thing she could rely on Hollis for, it was to keep the mood light.

Priya Das was waiting in the meeting room with Cooper and Barratt, her eyebrows raised in a question and her arms folded across her chest. 'I thought I'd sit in,' she said. 'DC Cooper tells me that you've got a promising lead from Olivia Thornbury's partner.'

Cooper shot Kate an apologetic look and then fixed her eyes on the screen of her laptop.

'It's hardly a promising lead,' Kate said, taking off her suit jacket and resisting the urge to fan her armpits. The heat in the room was stifling, somebody had forgotten to switch on the air con. 'Can we get some air in here,' she said, stalking over to the controls on the wall next to the whiteboard. She tapped to increase the airflow and then saw that the temperature was already well below the outside temperature. Just what she needed. A bloody hot flush at the start of an important briefing. A friend had once gleefully recounted stripping to her vest top in a business meeting in response to an unexpected temperature surge, much to the bemusement of those present. Kate wondered what her colleagues would do if she slipped off her blouse and stood there in her bra. Probably pretend not to notice.

'Okay,' Kate said, pulling out a chair and plonking herself down. 'Sylvia Kerr found an interesting email on Olivia Thornbury's computer. It contained an image of a protest at Greenham Common probably in 1984 or 1985.'

She nodded at Cooper who projected the image onto the screen at the front of the room. Das studied it, frowning, then pulled out the chair next to Kate and sat down, eyes still fixed on the screen.

'One of the women in this photograph is DCI Thornbury.'

Cooper tapped the trackpad and a yellow circle appeared round the face of one of the women towards the front of the crowd. 'This is before she met her partner but, significantly, after she joined the Met.'

She heard Das inhale sharply. The woman was very quick on the uptake. 'She was undercover?' Das asked. 'That was highly unusual for a female officer in the eighties.'

'I think she might have been with the SIS.'

Blank looks from her three younger colleagues prompted Kate to explain about the secretive group of Special Branch officers despite Das's obvious discomfort. Kate knew that a lot of senior coppers weren't happy with the adverse publicity generated by the SIS over the years.

'So, you think one of the women from Greenham Common recognised her and killed her as revenge for... for what?' Das seemed genuinely puzzled.

'I don't know,' Kate admitted. 'Perhaps she just saw

Thornbury as a traitor. Perhaps she was taken in by the DCI and felt cheated. Or it might be somebody who was a police officer there and Thornbury knew something incriminating, or vice versa. I'm not ruling anything out.'

Barratt looked sceptical. He was fiddling with the knot in his tie as though he wanted to say something but whatever he had to offer was making him nervous.

'Out with it, Matt,' Kate prompted. 'I can see you've got something to say.'

'If Olivia Thornbury was killed by somebody who recognised her from thirty-odd years ago surely it must be for more than feeling cheated. That's a bit of an extreme reaction to finding out that somebody you knew a long time ago wasn't who she claimed to be. And what does it have to do with the other two women?'

'Three,' Cooper reminded him. 'There's Anastasia Cohen as well. I've done a social media trawl. None of these women were friends on any of the obvious platforms. In fact, Cohen and Sullivan are the only ones with any social media presence. Both have Twitter and Facebook. Cohen uses Anna rather than her full name.'

'She's the youngest,' Das said. 'The others were in their sixties and early seventies – the age group least likely to be computer literate. Julia Sullivan would have needed to use social media for her political work.'

'Thornbury would have used tech in her job,' Hollis said.

'Yes. But she was a senior police officer. How many of you have Instagram accounts or anything similar?' Das was right. Most police officers understood the dangers associated with social media all too well and tended to steer clear. Kate had set up a Facebook account in her maiden name for a recent case but had deleted it as soon as it wasn't of any further use and she suspected that Cooper had more than one account but doubted that they were in her own name.

'How old would each of our victims have been when Thornbury was at Greenham?' Das asked. All heads turned to Cooper – the keeper of statistics.

'Anastasia Cohen would have been around twenty, Eleanor Houghton would have been in her mid-to-late-thirties and Julia Sullivan would have been in her early-to-mid-thirties. They could have all been there at the same time and they could easily have known each other, but how do we prove it?'

'We can ask Lincoln Sullivan about his wife,' Hollis suggested. 'He'd remember if she spent time there. Maybe Eleanor Houghton's nephew might know something. Anastasia Cohen's ex-husband? It's got to be worth a try.'

Kate thought about the tattoos; nothing like them had been found on Anastasia Cohen but, if she'd been younger than the others, if the artist was one of the women at the camp, she may have been reluctant to mark somebody so young for life. Or maybe Anastasia just didn't like tattoos.

'I think we need to find out more about what Thornbury was doing at Greenham,' Kate said, watching as Das shifted in her seat. She'd been reluctant to dig up the former DCI's past but the attack on Anastasia Cohen had convinced her that they needed as much background as they could get. She knew it wouldn't be easy as she was fairly convinced that the documents she needed were deeply buried in a Special Branch vault somewhere, but there seemed no other course of action. If they could find out what Thornbury's brief was and possibly access her reports, they might be closer to working out who she'd pissed off and why.

'I'll see what I can do,' Das said in a tone which suggested she didn't expect to be able to do very much. Kate knew she'd try though. The DCI could be relied upon to follow through if she thought a task was worthwhile and finding out about Olivia

Thornbury's time at Greenham seemed to be important to this case.

'Right, Sam. Have a look at Liv Thornbury's laptop and see if you can find anything else from the person who sent the photograph. There's also an email with a phone number. It's disconnected but I want you to scan the records of the Houghtons and Julia Sullivan – see if it shows up there. And, see if you can put me in touch with anybody who was at Greenham Common between 1983 and 1986 – I want to get more of an idea of what the relationships between the women and the police were like. Matt–'

'I can put you in touch with somebody,' Barratt said, not waiting to see which jobs he'd be allocated. 'My auntie was there. Get her piss–' He glanced at Das. 'Drunk, and she won't shut up about it. Solidarity, women against the world, sisterhood, that sort of thing.'

'Do you think she'd be willing to talk to one of us?'

Barratt grinned. 'She's not a big fan of the police but she does love her nephew so I'm sure it can be arranged.' He flinched and frowned at Hollis who'd obviously just kicked him under the table.

'Favourite nephew,' Hollis teased. 'Does she buy you sweeties for your birthday?'

Barratt opened his mouth to reply but Das held out a hand, palm facing the squabbling DCs. 'Enough. We need to find out if the other three women might have encountered Olivia Thornbury at Greenham Common. I suggest Barratt talks to Julia Sullivan's husband and to Eleanor Houghton's nephew.'

Kate nodded; she'd been about to assign those jobs to him herself. 'And see if you can get next-of-kin details for Anastasia Cohen,' she added. 'We need to talk to somebody who knows her well and might know about her past.'

'Wouldn't it be better if I came with you to my auntie's house?' Barratt asked.

Kate shook her head. She'd rather the woman wasn't distracted by the presence of her 'favourite nephew' and she also didn't want her to feel she needed to filter or censor any information. 'Thanks, Matt, but I'd rather you set up a meeting and then stepped back. To be honest, you might be a distraction. I'll take Dan.'

If he was disappointed, Barratt hid it well as he took out his phone and tapped the screen. 'You might be right,' he admitted. 'I've texted you her number. Her name's Bev Padley. She's retired so she's usually around in the daytime.'

Kate smiled her thanks and stood up. 'I'll check in before the end of the day, see where we're all at.'

Her colleagues nodded, a little too enthusiastically which, Kate realised, was for the benefit of the DCI. It didn't hurt to seem eager and she wouldn't normally have mentioned checking in – it was taken as read after every briefing – but she wanted Das to know that she was organised and in control. She thought she'd got away with it as her team filed out and she shrugged on her suit jacket, dreading the heat of the car park. She'd slipped her phone into her pocket and closed her laptop before realising that Das wasn't leaving. Not a good sign. Before she could ask if the DCI had any questions, Das scowled at her. 'I'd like a word now we're alone.'

1983

We were packing to go home when the men arrived; only four of them but they moved together like an eight-legged beast. Their faces were beastly too – beards hiding their lips and shaggy hair in their eyes. If they had been wearing animal skins, we might have thought they were cavemen.

Taz told me that there had been trouble in one of the villages near the base – some of the people who lived there didn't like women from the camp going to the pub because they thought the police would come and there'd be trouble. Taz said that she thought some of the locals were the ones who rang the police just to get rid of the women. She said that most people don't really agree with what the camp women want and, even the ones who do, don't have the courage of their convictions. I'm not sure what that means, but I think it's like putting your money where your mouth is.

The men started shouting as soon as they got near the small group of women who usually stand next to the gate, calling them bitches and dykes – I know what both of these mean now thanks to Taz – but the women didn't say anything back. They just huddled a bit closer together, linking arms as though they were making their own fence. Then one of the men took a knife out of his pocket and started waving it around. The others backed away from him like they didn't want anything to do with the knife, but he kept shouting and lunging at the women.

Mum tried to cover my ears so I couldn't hear the swear words, but I shrugged her off. I've heard much worse from some of the other women and I know what most of the words mean. The only one I hadn't heard the women use was 'cunt', but I know that one from some of the boys at school. It's not a word that girls and women like to use – it's a man's swear.

Other women came running from other parts of the camp – whenever anything happens it gets passed along the fence like Chinese whispers – and started to challenge the men. The three who didn't have knives looked a bit sorry for themselves and started to walk away but their friend started to call *them* names as well. Then he turned round, really fast, and grabbed Sarah by the neck, holding her against him like a shield with the knife at her throat. There was a big gasp from the women. Sarah looked terrified but then Taz stepped forwards, right up to the man. I couldn't hear everything she said because she lowered her voice and spoke straight into his face, but I saw him go red and shake his head. I heard her say something about the police and five minutes and I wondered if she'd sent somebody to the phone box near the village to call 999.

As suddenly as he'd grabbed her, the man let Sarah go and put the knife back in his pocket. He pushed Taz out of the way and jogged towards his friends who'd been watching from further back. All four of them yelled and stuck two fingers up and then they just turned round and walked away. Mum pulled me into a tight hug, but I pulled away and ran over to Taz who had her arm round Sarah.

'What happened?' I asked, but Taz just carried on whispering something to keep her friend calm.

'Taz? What did that man want?'

She looked up at me suddenly, her eyes like car headlights in the dark – piercing and angry. 'He wanted to hurt Sarah, and the rest of us, in the worst way a man can hurt a woman. He was going to take her somewhere with his friends and use her to teach us all a lesson.'

I didn't understand but I knew it was bad when Sarah started to cry.

'We need to stick together,' Taz said. 'All of us. The police won't help us and the soldiers in there are as bad as the men out here.' She carried on, her voice getting louder and shakier.

I wanted to hear what she was saying but this time Mum covered my ears and steered me away to our tent so I could carry on packing. I didn't really want to go home. We'd had fun today and lots of the women were laughing and joking. We'd had a picnic. It was a bit strange, but it was kind of silly. Some of the women dressed up as teddy bears and used big ladders to climb over the fence singing daft songs as they went. Me and Mum sat outside the fence on a blanket and ate our sandwiches – Mum said it wasn't safe for me to climb over – but it was too cold, and the bread tasted of nothing. I suppose it'll be nice to be back in our warm house again.

29

Still smarting from Das's dressing down, Kate jabbed at the car's air con, desperate for something cooler than the lukewarm draught that was trickling from the ventilation system.

'What the hell's wrong with the air in this car?' she said, twisting one of the dials all the way into the blue and tapping the grille next to the passenger window.

'Give it time,' Hollis said. 'We've only been driving for a minute.' If he thought she was behaving as irrationally as she felt, he gave no sign, probably assuming that she was in a foul mood because of whatever Das had said. Hollis had been the last one out of the briefing room and Kate was convinced he had overheard Das asking for a word. Thankfully, he wouldn't have heard the DCI accuse Kate of allowing one of her team to 'go rogue' and follow his own investigation. She had been slightly mollified when Kate explained that she'd had absolutely no knowledge of O'Connor's nocturnal activities, yet she thought he'd done excellent work and this could be a big coup for all of them, but Das had warned Kate that she needed to keep a tighter rein.

The air con finally kicked in and Kate began to relax. O'Connor's investigation would yield results – she was sure of it – and when it did, she would make certain that Das congratulated him. He might even be encouraged to go for promotion which was no bad thing. Despite some of his less appealing characteristics, Kate thought O'Connor was ready to run a team.

'Have you thought about taking your sergeant's exam?' Kate asked as Hollis pulled onto the A1.

'Where did that come from?'

'Just thinking. It can't hurt to give it a try.'

'What about Matt?'

Barratt had been a DC longer than Hollis and he was certainly ambitious. Kate felt though, that Hollis needed a push. He was not the kind to put himself forward even though his work was excellent and he was a diligent detective.

'I'm talking about you, not Matt. You could do it, Dan. Give it some thought?'

He gave her a non-committal shrug and changed lanes, his attention fixed on the rear-view mirror.

'Your choice,' she said. 'But I wouldn't have suggested it if I didn't think you were capable.'

The subject seemed to be closed as they turned off the busy motorway and drove the couple of miles of A-road into the village of Hickleton.

'I don't think I've ever been here,' Hollis said, looking round at cream stone houses glowing gold in the early afternoon sun. 'I wonder why this case keeps bringing us to the poshest spots in South Yorkshire.'

'It's not as posh as it used to be. Hickleton Hall used to be owned by the Earl of Halifax. The village grew up to serve the hall so a lot of these properties would have been rented out to commoners like us.'

'Thanks for the potted history,' Hollis said with a grin. Kate smiled back. She'd done a project on local stately homes when she'd been in junior school and remembered learning about the village.

'I suppose where there's money there's murder,' Kate quipped as they pulled up outside a small bungalow in a quiet cul-de-sac. The houses were set back from the road and each had a well-tended front garden suggesting that the occupants of most of the homes were probably retired. Kate thought about the garden in her new house. Would she ever have time to keep it tidy?

'Kettle's on,' Bev Padley said from her open door as soon as Kate stepped out of the car. 'I was looking out for you.' A tiny woman with a halo of grey hair and a face as brown and wrinkled as chamois leather, Barratt's aunt bore little resemblance to her nephew. She wore cut-off dungarees exposing skinny legs that were as brown as her face. Her blue eyes were alert and intelligent, on either side of a hooked nose that *was* familiar.

Kate extended her hand. 'DI Kate Fletcher. This is DC Dan Hollis.'

'Lovely to meet you both. I've heard a lot about *you*,' she said, giving Kate's hand a hard squeeze. 'Our Matty's always telling me what a good boss you are.'

She saw Hollis's lips twitch as he tried to contain a smile. Barratt was going to be on the receiving end of some serious tormenting about his aunt's diminutive nickname for him when they got back to Doncaster Central.

'Come on through,' Bev said. 'There's a good patch of shade in the back garden, it'll be a lot cooler than sitting indoors.'

Kate followed the woman down a short, gloomy hallway, into a tiny kitchen and out through a stable-type door into the back garden. Their host wasn't wrong. The garden was an oasis of cool and shade with tall, leafy plants that Kate couldn't name casting shadows on the red-brick patio.

'This is lovely,' she said, taking in the colours of the flowers and the range of foliage.

'My pride and joy,' Bev said. 'My late husband was always telling me I spent too much time out here – he didn't realise it was to get away from him. Poor bugger. Drinks? Tea, coffee, a cold drink?'

Hollis asked for tea, he'd obviously not been impressed with whatever coffee-making facilities he'd spied in the kitchen; Kate asked for iced water. Despite the shade she was struggling with the sluggish, warm air on her face and neck and she used Bev's brief absence in the kitchen to take off her jacket and find a slight breeze coming through the back gate.

Drinks passed round, Bev sat opposite Kate and smiled. 'You want to talk to me about Greenham Common? It's such a long time ago, I'm sure anything I did back then isn't something that I can be arrested for now.'

'It's background for a case we're working,' Kate explained, sipping her water gratefully. 'I can guarantee you won't be arrested.'

Bev leaned back in her chair and crossed her arms. 'Background?'

'I want to know what it was like. How it was organised. How you all lived.'

'Organised. That's a laugh. There wasn't much organisation – it was more like Chinese whispers. One group came up with an idea and it got passed all round the perimeter fence. Did you know we had 50,000 women there at one point? Stretched out along the fence holding hands. It must have been quite a sight.' She smiled, obviously getting lost in her memories.

'Were you there for a long time?' Hollis asked.

'I first went in '81 but I didn't stay. Some friends were going down to support one of the early demonstrations and I tagged along. There were about three dozen women chained to the fence at that point. We gave them food and chatted to them for a bit and then came home. I went back at the end of the following year and decided to stay. It was a women-only space by then. The protest had grown from those few women to 30,000. That was the first Embrace the Base protest. The next one was even bigger.'

There was a sense of pride in Bev's account. She obviously felt that she'd been a part of something important. Kate could barely remember the Greenham Common protests. She'd been in her teens when the camp had first appeared on the news and the women had been dismissed as 'loony lefties' and 'lesbian fanatics'. The woman in front of her didn't seem to fit in either category.

'I was there when the first missiles arrived,' Bev continued. 'Word went round that we were going to break through the fence and confront the soldiers. They were British. The American military tended to stay well away from the fence – left it to the squaddies, and the police, of course.'

Bev obviously saw something in Kate's face as she spat the word 'police' because she held up a hand in apology. 'I'm sorry but you have to understand that the police and the military were representatives of everything we were against. Politics, patriarchy and violence. They used to come in the night and drag us out of the benders to evict us. Some women were followed into the bushes when they went for a wee. It was intimidating.'

'But you still broke into the base and stood up to them?'

'We dressed up as teddy bears and climbed the fence.'

'What?' Hollis spluttered. 'Why?'

'We knew that we'd been getting a lot of negative press attention so the idea was that the newspapers would take pictures of police officers and soldiers arresting and pointing guns at teddy bears. It was meant to be absurd – to show the public that we were harmless.'

Hollis shook his head. 'That's mad.'

Bev grinned at him. 'It worked. It made the authorities look daft, like they were overreacting. We did another one. Reflect the Base. We wanted the police and soldiers to take a long hard look at themselves, so we surrounded the fence and held up mirrors.'

Kate saw Hollis sit up straighter. He'd obviously had the same thought. *Mirrors?*

'Tell me about that,' she said. 'How did it work?'

The wrinkles around Bev's eyes deepened with amusement. 'We all lined up around the fence, facing inwards and held up a mirror. There were thousands of us. God knows where all the mirrors came from. It was symbolic – we were trying to show the people inside what they looked like to outsiders like us. To make them examine their motives.'

'How did they react?' Kate asked.

It really freaked some of them out. Especially when we started keening. You know...' She threw her head back, closed her eyes and let out a high-pitched wail. Hollis bit his lip and Kate could see he was trying not to laugh. She needed to get the woman back on track.

'What was the atmosphere like?' Kate asked. 'Did the women get along with each other? Were there factions or disagreements?'

Bev stopped wailing and frowned, her eyes drifting to a point over Kate's shoulder. 'Not factions exactly,' she said. 'We were all there for the same reason. There were groups though. Each gate had its own group – they were named after colours of the rainbow – and there were groups of women who had things in common; usually they were from the same area of the country or they were into the same thing; religion, Wicca, smoking dope.

There was a group from Kent who were rumoured to be the most confrontational while the Yorkshire lasses supposedly got the best food parcels. Nonsense, of course, but it made the days and hours pass. There were some women who were political – left of centre, of course – but they didn't do much in the way of conversion. We were a society, and in any society you get diversity. Some women were middle class, some came from very poor backgrounds. We had teachers mixing with cleaners, lawyers with laundry workers. The mud and the cold were great levellers. All ages as well. Some women brought their kids, some even brought their grandkids. But no husbands.'

'I suppose that's why the media portrayed the protesters as loony lesbians,' Kate said.

'Oh, there were a fair few loony lesbians, and non-loony ones as well. And a few part-time ones,' she added with a lewd wink. 'Nothing wrong with a bit of company on a cold night.'

'Do you keep in touch with any of the women?' Kate asked.

Bev shook her head. 'It wasn't so easy in those days. We couldn't just swap mobile numbers or friend each other on Facebook. I had a couple of addresses and phone numbers, but people move around and we just lost touch.'

Kate asked if Bev remembered Julia Sullivan, or Anastasia Cohen or a woman called Eleanor but none of the names were familiar. She tried showing her photographs of each of the women but her reply was still negative. Then she flicked to a recent picture of Olivia Thornbury and passed her mobile phone back to Bev.

'Oh! That's a familiar face. I shared a bender with her for about a week when she first got to Greenham. She was a bit lost so a couple of us showed her the ropes. She hasn't changed much. Hair's grey but her eyes are the same.'

Kate's heart rate picked up. Here was something concrete – finally. Liv Thornbury *had* been active at Greenham Common. 'I don't suppose you remember her name, or the names of any of her friends?'

'She was called Sarah. No idea what her surname was. She was friendly with a young girl – only about eighteen or nineteen – funny name she had. What was it...?' She closed her eyes, deep in thought. 'Nope. It's not going to come. Nice kid though.'

Kate drained her glass. 'I really appreciate you talking to us,' she said. 'It's a big help.'

She stood up and Hollis followed her lead, allowing Bev no option but to show them out. Just as Kate closed the car door the woman tapped frantically on the window. Kate pressed the button to lower it slightly, reluctant to allow too much warm air into the vehicle.

'Taz. The girl that Sarah was friendly with was called Taz. I always thought it was short for something but buggered if I could work out what.'

30

'I've got Thornbury's reports from Greenham,' Cooper said as soon as Kate stepped into the office. She'd sent Hollis up to the canteen for coffee and had hoped for a quiet few minutes to respond to a series of texts from Barratt as well as an email from Das about O'Connor.

'Das came through? That was quick. She must have known exactly the right strings to pull.'

Cooper's lack of response prompted Kate to look up. The DC's head was lowered over her keyboard but her blonde hair did little to cover her flaming cheeks.

'Sam! What did you do?'

Cooper squinted up at Kate as if in anticipation of a hard slap. 'I contacted a friend who has a friend in–'

Kate held up her hand. 'No. Don't tell me. If Das finds out I want to be able to tell her honestly that I didn't know.'

'I've not done anything wrong,' Cooper said defensively. 'I just know it can take ages to get historic files, especially if they're sensitive. I cut a few corners, that's all. It's just background anyway – I doubt there'll be anything of evidentiary value after all this time, but they might tell us who Thornbury was friendly with at Greenham. If there is anything then, if *I* could get hold of them Das will be able to. I'm speeding things up, that's all.'

Kate knew that, technically, Cooper was right. There was no reason why they shouldn't access Liv Thornbury's files as part of an active murder investigation but, if the timeline were to be called into question, they might be on tricky ground. 'Have you looked through them yet?' Kate asked.

'No. I thought I'd best wait for you. I'm happy to give them a quick scan if you...?'

'No. Email them to me and I'll have a read. Anything on the phone records?'

Cooper shook her head. 'Bugger all. The number that appeared on Liv Thornbury's email is on her records. She rang it six times and received calls from it on three occasions. It's not on Julia Sullivan's phone records and I've had a look at Peter and Eleanor Houghton's calls – nothing there either. Eleanor did have five calls from the same number four times in the days before she died. It's not in her earlier phone records so it's a new contact. I've tried ringing but it doesn't connect. There's nothing on the laptop that was found at the bungalow so the killer must have been contacting her by phone rather than email. Unless she had a device or an account we don't know about. I've also been looking at camera footage to try to find Anna's car for the last hour. Nothing so far.'

Burner phones then, Kate thought. Bought anonymously and no doubt in a skip somewhere by now. It didn't help but it was another sign that their killer was a careful planner which would make them more difficult to catch. If he or she had been active at Greenham Common in the early 1980s, that would put them in their mid-fifties or older – assuming that they'd been aged between eighteen and thirty at the time. Olivia Thornbury may have been the first victim because there may have been a genuine sense of grievance that Thornbury had been an undercover police officer; but what had the other victims done to deserve their fate?

Kate picked up her mobile phone and scanned through Barratt's texts. He'd been unable to get in touch with either Lincoln or Sadie Sullivan, and Eleanor Houghton's nephew had no idea what his auntie had been doing in the eighties but thought it unlikely that she'd been a protester at Greenham. There was one useful aside from the conversation – the nephew gave them his aunt's maiden name – Eldridge. At least it saved a trawl through the register of births, deaths and marriages.

Logging on to her computer she saw that Cooper had already sent her Thornbury's reports. Even though she was itching to read them she had to deal with the fallout from O'Connor's extra-curricular activities. Das still wasn't convinced that Kate hadn't been involved despite their earlier conversation and she was insisting on being kept up to date on a regular basis which, judging by the email, meant at least twice a day. A quick 'nothing further to report', and Kate finally felt free to open Cooper's message.

'Coffee!' Hollis announced, backing through the door with a tray of cardboard cups. 'I didn't know if Matt would be back but I'm happy to drink his if he's not.' He passed a cappuccino to Cooper and a latte to Kate before taking his own coffee and plonking himself down at his desk and looking around expectantly.

'Eleanor Houghton was Eleanor Eldridge before she got married,' Kate said. 'See what you can find out about her, especially anything from the eighties. There's a lot of online stuff about Greenham and it'll all need wading through.'

Hollis looked disappointed. He wasn't fond of spending hours in front of the computer – none of them were, apart from Cooper – he'd rather be out in the field. Kate knew he wouldn't complain though; and that he'd do a thorough job.

'Start with any news reports. Then have a look at anything recent – looking back to that time. Sam, I want you to do the same with Anastasia Cohen. Barratt's trying to find a next of kin but, until he does, assume she was there. I don't know if Cohen's her married name but I'm sure you can find out. Her boss says she's recently divorced if that helps. Oh, and see if you can link her to the nickname Taz. Matt's auntie remembers a young girl by that name, and it could easily have been her using a nickname.'

Jobs allocated, Kate finally opened Cooper's email message. There were five reports in all, each one had a reference number which seemed to refer to a date. The first. OT140383 was from March 1983 and was a scan of a typed document. The print was blurry in places where the ink ribbon had dumped too much black on the page, but every word was legible. It appeared that Olivia Thornbury was using the alias Sarah Burton and had told the women that she met that she'd been a social worker, but she'd given up her job to help with the protest. Thornbury commented that she'd managed to gain the trust of a small group of women and had established friendships with two others from outside the group. These two women seemed to be the focus of her report as they were involved in organising the previous demonstration which had resulted in a number of arrests. She labelled these women as militant in their beliefs and actions, but she only had their first names which was of little use to her superiors.

The second report was much more interesting. Dated later in 1983 it contained an account of the 'Teddy Bears' Picnic' protest and the fallout from the arrest of one of the organisers. It seemed that the thinking behind placing an undercover officer amongst the women was to destabilise at least one group and sow dissent in the hope that they would either abandon the protest or turn against each other and fracture the unity of the camp. DC Thornbury's report expressed concern that some of the women suspected a 'mole' and that her position had been compromised. There was a rumour that the police had been 'tipped off' about the plan to breach the fence and there was an air of suspicion turning group against group. She didn't say so, but Kate got the impression that Thornbury may have started the rumour.

A comment in the last paragraph stood out:

```
One of the women is the wife of the
radical artist and socialist, Lincoln
Sullivan. I recommend investigating his
patrons and sponsors with regard to
funding protests at the camp.
```

Julia *had* been there.

'Cooper, Hollis?'

Both DCs looked up from their computer screens.

'Julia Sullivan was definitely at Greenham at the same time as Olivia Thornbury. We've got a confirmed link.'

'Nice one,' Cooper said with a big grin. 'And I've found out that Cohen is Anastasia's maiden name. I'm on her Facebook page at the minute but everybody there seems to call her Anna. No sign of Taz.'

Kate wondered if the nickname was a red herring. It had just been a hunch. Anas*tas*ia – it seemed to make sense but there had been tens of thousands of women at the peace camp over the years and Taz could have been a diminutive form of any number of names.

'Okay, keep at it.' She took a sip of her now lukewarm coffee and opened the next report. This one detailed the effect of some of the tactics the police were using against the women and it seemed especially insidious to have one of their own on the inside to suggest ways to further intimidate and undermine. It appeared that the policy of following random women for hours on end was especially effective as was raiding their encampments at night and evicting them. Thornbury went on to detail encounters between hardened protesters and women who wanted to leave, even suggesting that there was a culture of indoctrination and the leavers were regarded as traitors.

This theme was developed in the penultimate report where Thornbury seemed to have become involved with a group of younger women who were 'fixated' on 'overthrowing the establishment by any means necessary'. She was especially concerned about one, a teenager who was trying to decide whether to leave the camp to go to university or to 'stay and fight'. There were accounts of conversations between this girl and some older protesters and then:

```
The girl, Taz, has decided to leave and
take up her place at Newcastle University
to study law. It seems that the
indoctrination doesn't work on everybody.
```

Something about the tone suggested that Liv Thornbury may have had a hand in the girl's decision.

'Sam, where did Anastasia Cohen study law?'

Kate heard Cooper typing rapidly.

'Newcastle, according to her Facebook page.'

Still too much of a coincidence? Kate didn't think so.

The final report was from early 1984 and it had a strikingly different feel. Kate couldn't help but wonder how the person who'd transcribed Thornbury's words would have interpreted her state of mind as she phoned in this account. It seemed that the young DC was becoming increasingly paranoid about being found out and punished by the women at the camp. She seemed to be showing some empathy to their cause and some genuine concern for some of her 'friends and family'. It wasn't uncommon for undercover officers to become so immersed in their fake identity that they started to lose touch with who they really were and lost focus on their brief. Was it possible that Liv's promotion after she left Greenham hadn't been a reward but a bribe? The police force had been an entirely different beast at the time and Kate knew that officers had been placed in stressful situations without proper psychological assessment. Had Thornbury cracked? Or at least come close?

She read on. There was a list of names further down the page; women Thornbury suspected of knowing she was a police officer. All first names and, among them, *Eleanor*.

31

As Cooper and Hollis continued their internet searches, Kate pushed back her chair and grabbed a pen and paper. Often she thought more clearly when she could write her ideas down and look for patterns and discrepancies. With her team she'd usually do this on the whiteboard in the incident room, but she didn't want to distract the other two from their work.

First, she jotted down the names of the four victims and the dates that she believed them to have been at Greenham Common. The most likely period of overlap seemed to be from winter 1983 to the end of 1984 – almost the whole of Thornbury's assignment. Not overly helpful. She noted down the ages of the victims – all different – from Anna in her mid-fifties to Eleanor Houghton in her early seventies. Again, no pattern. The only common factor was that they lived in South Yorkshire but it was a big area and the distance between Liv Thornbury's house and Julia Sullivan's was nearly thirty miles – not what Kate would regard as local to each other.

They weren't from the same socio-economic group, two were married to men, one was a lesbian and one was divorced. The lack of a clear pattern suggested that there was nothing random about these murders. The victims hadn't been targeted because they were the same age, or body type or used the same shop or car wash. The murders were personal. But why? Kate looked again at the names and the dates and arrows she'd written around them. They may as well have been Egyptian hieroglyphs for all the sense they made.

She glanced up as Barratt pushed open the door, looking as frustrated as she felt. 'No luck with either of the Sullivans,' he announced, slumping down into his seat. 'I've been to Lincoln Sullivan's studio and Sadie's house twice. Eleanor Houghton's nephew didn't know if his aunt was at Greenham and didn't appreciate being woken in the early hours. I've also managed to have a chat with Anna Cohen's ex-husband, but he couldn't tell me much about her life before they met. He said he wouldn't be surprised if she'd been at Greenham as she had some fairly 'out-there' views.'

'That doesn't tally with her most recent case,' Cooper said, peering at him from over the top of her monitor. 'She defended a man accused of beating his wife. Got him off. Not very sisterly.'

'But if he was innocent…' Barratt began.

'He probably was,' Cooper said. 'That time. I've had a look at his record, and he'd been questioned twice before about injuries to his wife. Both times she refused to make a statement.'

'Any press reports?' Kate asked, an idea forming in her mind.

'A few, local papers.'

Julia Sullivan had also been featured in reports in the local press, as had Olivia Thornbury. And Eleanor Houghton had been married to a prominent businessman who was often in the local papers – not always for positive reasons. Whilst not being 'high profile', these women were far from anonymous. Was that how the killer had found them? Perhaps seeing Liv Thornbury's photograph in a local paper had sparked a memory and prompted the killer to research other people associated with their time at Greenham. If that was the case, could they work out who was next? If they scoured every local news report for women in the right age bracket and then tried to find out if they'd been at Greenham, Kate would have probably been comfortably retired before they found a suitable candidate. There had to be a better way.

She opened her email again, seeking inspiration and saw two new messages. The first was a preliminary forensics report on Anna Cohen and her possessions. Nothing to get excited about. No fingerprints other than Cohen's own, no DNA and nothing from her clothing.

'Bloody invisible,' Kate muttered to herself.

'What?' Hollis asked, leaning back and stretching his improbably long arms above his head.

'Just talking to myself,' Kate admitted. 'This killer's bloody invisible. Nothing from the forensics on Anna Cohen. I've got the report from Julia Sullivan's house as well. Fancy a tenner bet that it's the same?'

Hollis shook his head. 'Too rich for my blood. Fifty pence?'

Kate smiled at his response as she clicked on the second message which contained a detailed report of the findings at Julia Sullivan's property. Kate scanned it, expecting to find the same lack of evidence as at the Houghton house, handles wiped clean, carpets vacuumed, dishes washed.

'Shit,' she said aloud.

'Problem?' Hollis asked as Barratt and Cooper meer-katted up from behind their monitors.

'Dunno,' Kate said, reading to the bottom of the message. 'Just got full forensics back from Julia Sullivan's house.'

'Wiped clean?' Barratt guessed. 'Bugger-all in terms of evidence?'

Kate ignored him. 'Dan, when did Lincoln Sullivan say he'd last been at the house?'

'April.'

'Damn.'

The report revealed three sets of fingerprints. Those of Julia, Lincoln and Sadie Sullivan. All three had valid reasons for their fingerprints being in the house even if they hadn't been there for two months or longer.

'This makes no sense,' Kate said. Hollis left his desk and moved to stand behind her, reading over her shoulder.

'So, no sign of anybody else having been in the house?' he said. 'That's just like at the Houghtons'.'

'No, it's not,' Kate said. 'At the Houghtons' bungalow we had clear evidence that the killer had wiped down surfaces, put things in the dishwasher, even vacuumed the fucking carpets.'

Out of the corner of her eye she saw Hollis take half a step back, obviously shocked by her outburst.

'Sorry,' she said. 'But it's so frustrating. Why did they clear up at the Houghtons' but not here? How could they leave no trace without doing some sort of cleaning?'

'Gloves?' Hollis suggested. 'If Julia was in the bath then the killer could have walked upstairs with minimal contact with door handles and surfaces.'

Kate had thought about gloves. It made a kind of sense except for one detail. 'There was no sign of a break-in,' she said. 'We'd been working on the assumption that Julia let her killer into the house. Wouldn't she have noticed if she'd been wearing latex gloves, or any gloves? And why would she get in the bath if she had a visitor? There were no signs of a struggle either in the house or on her body.'

'She?'

'I'm currently thinking the killer is another woman from Greenham. It makes sense.'

Hollis's eyes drifted off as he considered this probability. 'Why? Couldn't it have been another police officer – they were mostly men? Or an irate husband who blames the Greenham women for corrupting his wife or daughter or sister?'

Hollis was right but she felt that the reasons he'd suggested were a little tenuous. There was also the question of trust. Liv Thornbury and Julia Sullivan had been alone when they met their killer – would they have been as likely to trust a man as a woman? Why would Julia allow a strange man into her home? And why would Olivia Thornbury have met a man in a remote place in the early hours of the morning unless he was somebody who she didn't perceive as a threat, somebody she knew? And the Houghtons. Would they have let a strange man into their house? They were both elderly and vulnerable but she got the impression that Peter Houghton was shrewd and wouldn't have easily been conned.

As she was about to share her thoughts with the team, a detail from the report caught her eye. There were no fingerprints on the shard of mirror that had been used to make the incisions in Julia's wrists and neck. Had the killer slipped gloves on to break the mirror and then attack Julia Sullivan after drugging her and placing her in the bath?

'There is another scenario that makes sense,' Cooper said. 'Why wipe everything down if there's a valid reason for your prints to be in the house? It's very time-consuming. Why not just wipe the murder weapon?'

'You think Lincoln or Sadie could have done this?'

Cooper shrugged. 'Neither of them has an alibi. Lincoln was estranged from his wife because of her extreme politics and Sadie admits that she wasn't happy about her mother's views.'

'But they'd have realised the change was due to her head injury, surely and been lenient with her?'

Hollis shook his head. 'Both of them seem to blame her

religious conversion for her views. Neither Sadie nor Lincoln mentioned the head injury.'

Was it possible that Julia Sullivan's daughter and husband didn't know the extent of the damage caused by her car crash? Kate found it hard to believe, but the woman *could* have kept medical details from her family if she'd thought she had a good reason for doing so.

'How old would Sadie have been in 1983 or 4?'

'Eight or nine,' Cooper said. 'Old enough to remember her mother disappearing for weeks on end. Old enough to harbour resentment towards the women who kept her away.'

'Or does her husband blame the women in some way?' Hollis added.

'We need to speak to both of them again. Where the hell *are* they?'

'I don't know where they are now, but I know where Lincoln Sullivan will be tomorrow morning,' Cooper said. 'There's a gathering of local dignitaries at the National Coal Mining Museum in Wakefield to witness the unveiling of his painting. I read about it on his website earlier. It's some sort of preview event. He's expected to be there.'

'Well, he won't be expecting *us* to be there. Let's give him a surprise.'

32

O'Connor was sweating. It was nearly 11pm and every pore seemed to be oozing moisture. He glanced around at his colleagues who, thankfully, all seemed to be experiencing the same symptom. He didn't want them to think he was anxious or uncomfortable. It was the bloody trees. They seemed to have trapped the heat of the day and were now sending it down in waves to warm the ground and the unfortunate officers sheltering beneath them. He almost expected to start sprouting fungi on his face and stab vest, emerging from the forest like some hairy, ancient Rip Van Winkle when he finally made the arrest.

Everything had happened so fast. Border Force had pulled the records of all Sims's drivers who were routed through Port of Tyne and had found two with convictions for minor offences. One had been fined for common assault and the other had been caught driving without due care and attention. Privately, O'Connor wondered if these had been used as leverage by Sims when he was recruiting drivers for his new scheme, offering them jobs when other companies probably wouldn't have. That would have to wait until after this evening's operation – then there'd be plenty of time to interview the key players. Northumbria Police had put together a team to intercept the lorry in Kielder Forest and had agreed to allow O'Connor to make the arrest so the case could be passed back to South Yorkshire Police. Even DCI Das had been supportive and allowed O'Connor to take part in the operation despite his involvement with the murder case that his team was currently investigating.

His Airwave radio crackled into life. 'Target has turned off just before Bellingham, heading to Kielder. Comms muted.'

The lorry was obviously following the same route as before – it may even have been the same driver, but O'Connor was doubtful. He'd have thought Sims allowed time between each trip to swap drivers regularly. He slipped the radio into the pocket on the shoulder of his vest in case one of the lights flashed and alerted the lorry driver to their presence, then shifted position to get a clearer view of the dark mouth of the car park's entrance.

He checked his watch, covering the glow from the digital display with a cupped palm. Ten minutes, he reckoned. Ten minutes and a white lorry should be appearing in front of them. Unless this driver had chosen a different route. Or a different car park. Shit, how stupid would O'Connor look if nobody turned up? Or if a group of illegal immigrants was found wandering round another pulling-in place?

He didn't dare to check his watch again and had no sense of how much time had passed since he'd last risked a glance. Three minutes? Five? Ten?

The absolute silence of the night was broken by the distant sound of a vehicle engine. O'Connor tensed his muscles and held his breath, keeping perfectly still. The sound came closer, moving at speed until it was next to their hiding place then it sped past, Dopplering into the distance.

'Shit,' he mumbled under his breath.

Another engine, this one deeper, rumbling like something prehistoric was emerging from the oppressive forest. Closer. Lights arcing across the gravel. A white lorry pulled slowly into the dark clearing like a liner pulling up to a silent quay. Light spilled out of the cab as the driver's door opened, splashing the ground a sulphurous yellow.

Everything seemed to be happening in slow motion. The driver climbed down and went to the back. He seemed to take an age to unfold the lifting platform and open the doors. Then he disappeared briefly before reappearing burdened with a pile of boxes. Three more trips into the black interior and then another figure appeared.

'Police!' a shout went up and then there was movement everywhere. O'Connor fixed on the driver and ran towards him while his colleagues approached the other man. Exactly as planned. But then a dark figure cut across O'Connor's path and he stumbled briefly before continuing forwards.

'Fuck!' There was no sign of the driver. Men swarmed the platform at the rear of the lorry, pulling and dragging three shapes which looked like bundles of clothes but could only have been the stowaways from the hidden section of the lorry's interior.

'Where's the driver?' he yelled, scanning the scene. Four heads turned to him, but it was obvious nobody knew.

'Where did he go?' O'Connor repeated, turning to look at the wall of black trees. His colleagues had formed a huddle with their captives a few yards from the lorry; nobody seemed to be looking for the driver.

A metallic slam had O'Connor spinning back round to the lorry. The bastard had climbed back into the cab and was trying to start the engine. The vehicle roared into life and the white reversing lights turned the scrum of men into a monochrome freeze-frame as the lorry turned.

'No you don't!' O'Connor shouted, running to the entrance to the car park to block the driver's exit route. He stood, arms outstretched, as the driver stopped.

'Police!' he shouted. 'Stop.'

The lorry seemed to pause, listening as he stood facing it down, David against Goliath, squinting against the full beam of the vehicle's headlights. Then it roared and the suddenly the lights got closer and brighter. O'Connor was aware of people shouting. He heard his name.

Then there was only darkness.

33

'This looks like the entrance to a nature reserve or a 1970s holiday camp,' Hollis said as he led the way to the glass doors of the National Coal Mining Museum.

'What do you know about the seventies?' Kate asked. 'When were you born? 1997?'

Hollis shook his head in disgust. She knew his real year of birth and it seemed he wasn't going to rise to the bait, not this morning. He had a point though. The green-and-white single-storey building definitely looked like something from another era – Kate thought youth centre circa 1985 – but it was probably the least interesting part of the site.

Despite having been brought up in a mining community, Kate had never been in a coal mine. Her own father and most of her friends' dads had worked down the pit and she suspected some of the boys she went to school with ended up there, at least for a couple of years, before they were all closed, but it wasn't women's work. She knew of a cousin of a friend who worked in the colliery offices and her own grandmother was rumoured to have been a cleaner at the pithead baths but she'd died when Kate was two so she'd never known if there was any truth to the story. She'd been to Beamish Museum in County Durham with her son, Ben, when he was at junior school, but he hadn't been interested in the mining village or the replica pit; he wanted to get on and off the trams and spend an hour in the sweet shop. Kate had tried to explain what his granddad had done for a living, but she might as well have been talking about the Romans or the Vikings for all Ben had understood about his family history.

When the Mining Museum had first opened, she'd been tempted to visit – to try to fully understand what the struggles of the men had been for, to experience the hardships second-hand but, somehow, she'd never got round to it. She knew that there were activities and exhibitions inside that might interest her, but she'd always felt odd going to places like this without a child or two in tow. Not that kids would be overly interested in reading about the role of women in the miners' strike of the 1980s or looking at paintings depicting mining through the ages – two of the attractions that appealed to Kate. The big draw for children was the 'authentic' pit experience – going underground in the cage-like lift and visiting the coal face in the company of an ex-miner. She suspected the adventure playground came a close second.

As she pushed open the door to the reception area a sea of heads turned in her direction, facial expressions ranging from quizzical to the open annoyance of Lincoln Sullivan who was facing the door, addressing the crowd. Kate nodded in his direction and went to stand at the rear of the gathering, folding her arms and leaning against a square concrete pillar – directly in Sullivan's eyeline. Hollis mimicked her posture in a position close to the door. She knew they were being far from subtle but there was nothing to be gained from pouncing on Sullivan in private and she wanted to see if their presence put him off his stride or made him obviously nervous.

Dressed in his trademark faded jeans and oversized black T-shirt, Sullivan looked out of place amongst the suits and tidy hairstyles of the people who'd turned up to see the painting unveiled. The artist drew his eyes away from Kate's, ran a hand through his tousled grey hair and resumed his speech.

'I'm often asked whether I'm a real Yorkshireman,' he said with what might have passed for a self-deprecating grin on a less formidable man. 'It's the name. Lincoln seems to suggest southern and middle class to a lot of people. Or American – we know how fond they are of using surnames as first names.'

A murmur of recognition buzzed around the audience like the low hum of electric current.

'So, I'll tell you the truth,' he continued. 'I'm Irish. Not born and bred but four generations removed. My great-great-grandmother was a huge fan of the US president who welcomed those fleeing the famine and encouraged them to fight in the war against slavery. It's claimed that he kissed the Irish flag as thanks for services rendered and in recognition of his recognition.' Sullivan paused, clearly expecting a response to his wordplay. When none was forthcoming, he went on, 'My ancestor insisted that her son call his first male heir Lincoln. That tradition has been passed down through the family – fortunately, I've produced a single daughter so it looks like it might grind to a halt with me.'

A ripple of polite laughter greeted this last remark and Kate tuned out when Sullivan went on to describe his inspiration and his process. She didn't know what he'd said to the assembled crowd before they'd arrived but there was no mention of his late wife. It seemed that, for Lincoln Sullivan, it was business as usual.

The artist stepped to one side to allow a well-dressed woman in her forties to take centre stage. She introduced herself as director of the museum, thanked Sullivan and then did a brief warm-up to the big reveal. The event was overly theatrical and Kate had to avoid Hollis's eyes a couple of times – this was just the sort of thing that could make the DC behave like a bored schoolboy.

The cloth covering the painting was removed in a grand sweep of white cotton and the painting that Kate had admired in Sullivan's studio suddenly dominated the space. Appreciative sighs and knowing mutters swept through the assembled guests as, en masse, they moved forward for a closer look.

Kate seized an opportunity to get closer to Lincoln Sullivan and tugged at his sleeve. 'A word?'

Huge eyebrows drew together in a fierce scowl as the artist frowned down at her. 'Now?'

'It can't wait.' Kate fought the urge to apologise for the interruption as she followed Sullivan to a small office behind the reception desk.

'What's this about?' he demanded, glancing at Hollis who had entered the room and shut the door firmly behind him.

'We need to talk to you again about your wife's murder,' Kate said. 'We have new evidence, and it suggests you may have further questions to answer about the night she died.'

Sullivan perched on the edge of the office desk, leaning forwards, glaring at Kate. 'What evidence?'

Kate took a breath. She knew the forensics were not conclusive and there was nothing that would stand up in court but, she believed, if she could wrong-foot Sullivan she might just trick him into making an error.

'When was your wife at Greenham Common?' she asked.

Sullivan's eyes widened and he sat back, looking at Hollis as if for support. 'What the hell has that got to do...?'

'We think her murder may be linked to her activities at the peace camp,' Kate continued, deliberately vague. 'Could you answer the question please?'

Sullivan shook his mane of grey hair as if in disbelief. 'She started going in 1982. There was a chain letter going round calling for women to attend some sort of protest and she joined in with that. Then she went back at every opportunity for a couple of years.'

'Every opportunity? So she went back often?'

'Yes. She sometimes spent weeks there.'

'Did she tell you anything about her experiences? Name any friends she made?'

'Probably. But it's a hell of a long time ago. The world's changed a lot since then. Why would I be able to remember the names of a handful of women that my wife knew?'

He was getting riled, Kate could tell, but he didn't seem defensive. If anything, he was puzzled by her approach. Time to change tack. 'And you were last in your wife's house when?'

Sullivan just stared at her as if he was trying to make sense of the question. When he replied, Kate noticed a subtle shift in his tone. He was suspicious and guarded.

'I don't recall what I *told* you,' he said. 'But I left the house on April 14th and haven't set foot in it since. And, for the record, it's not my wife's house; mine is the only name on the mortgage.'

'You definitely haven't been back?'

Sullivan made no comment or gesture to confirm or deny his statement. Instead, he started to scrub at the palm of one hand with the thumbnail of the other. Kate could see flecks of white paint drifting to the carpet like dandruff as the artist picked at the skin. He was obviously trying to create the impression that he was totally at ease as he looked away from his hands and back at her face.

'I don't think we're any further forward, are we, Detective Inspector Fletcher? I have no idea why you're asking about my wife's involvement with the Greenham protests or why you seem to think I might have lied about the date I left our marital home.'

Kate considered her next move. Her abrupt change of topic hadn't fazed Sullivan in the slightest – he was either very confident that she could prove nothing, or he was wholly innocent of any involvement in Julia's death.

'Okay.' She sighed. 'Forensics from the house found only three sets of fingerprints. You and Sadie gave our officer your fingerprints for elimination purposes and your wife's, your daughter's and yours were the only ones found. In a case that we believe to be connected to this one, the surfaces in the house were wiped clean. I'm having trouble understanding why this didn't happen in your house. Unless the killer knew that his or her prints would already be there for legitimate reasons.'

Sullivan threw back his head and laughed. '*That's* all you've got? Bloody hell. So now you think the killer is either me or Sadie? And I suppose, like myself, my daughter has no alibi?'

Kate stayed silent.

'Could the killer have worn gloves? Could he have spent so much time cleaning up after his last murder that he wanted to save time with this one? Has that occurred to the great minds of South Yorkshire Police?'

'It's possible,' Kate conceded as Hollis shifted uncomfortably. Sullivan had them on the back foot. 'But it seems unlikely that the killer left no trace evidence at all without cleaning up after himself, or herself. And there was nothing to suggest that any cleaning had been done. So far there isn't a fibre or a hair that shouldn't have been there.'

'If you think I killed my ex-wife then please, give me a motive,' Sullivan demanded.

'She was an embarrassment,' Kate said. 'You said yourself her views and opinions were odious to you.'

'Which is why I left. Why did I kill the other one? Because of his or her views? Christ, do you know how many politicians I loathe? How sick I am of self-serving chancers who pretend to want to improve the lot of the poorest in society while lining their own pockets? I think an automatic rifle would be a much more efficient weapon for wiping out people whose views I find odious.'

'One of the other victims was at Greenham Common at the same time as your wife,' Kate said. 'And we suspect there's a link with a third murder.'

Sullivan raised his hands, palms up in an exaggerated shrug. 'And? What possible reason could I have for killing people my wife may have known over thirty years ago?'

'Oh, come on,' Kate said, frustrated with his attitude. 'She abandoned you on a regular basis to hang out with women that the media labelled as "loony lesbians" and "feminist fascists". How did that feel? How did it look to your macho miner chums?'

The artist looked at her almost sympathetically and slowly shook his head. 'How old are you, DI Fletcher? Old enough to remember the eighties?'

'I remember,' Kate said. 'I was a teenager.'

'So you'd understand if I told you that those of us on the left didn't see ourselves as a radical group. We weren't revolutionaries plotting the downfall of governments, we just wanted everybody to be treated fairly. For poor communities not to be made poorer by the decimating of their industries.'

'My dad was a miner,' Kate said. 'I know what happened.'

'Then you'll understand when I tell you that I *supported* my wife's cause. We all wanted a better world for our children and, if it took Julia away for weeks on end, it was a price worth paying.'

'Even if it left you at home trying to get your career started while raising a daughter?'

Sullivan tilted his head and frowned. 'What are you talking about?'

'Sadie. You couldn't have been happy having a young child under your feet when you were courting the great and the good of the political left.'

'Oh, DI Fletcher.' Sullivan sighed. 'Once again you don't have the full facts. You can't arrest me on assumptions and speculation.'

'What speculation?'

'Sadie wasn't at home with me. Her mother took her on every trip to Greenham Common. *Every* one.'

34

Three missed calls from Das. Kate stared at the screen of her phone trying to prioritise. They needed to find Sadie Sullivan immediately. How was it possible for the woman to have disappeared? She also wanted to get an update on Anastasia Cohen's condition. If the woman *was* Taz she might hold the key to the whole case but, until she was in a position to talk to them, she was an unknown, and potentially vulnerable if her attempted murderer knew that she was still alive. But she didn't dare ignore the DCI.

'Kate,' Das snapped after a single ring. 'Where the hell have you been?'

'Sorry ma'am, I've been interviewing Lincoln Sullivan, he's–'

Das cut her off. 'Listen, is Hollis with you?'

'Yes, he's–'

'There's been an incident,' Das said. Kate immediately suspected another murder until Das's next words made it impossible to think clearly.

'O'Connor was hit by a lorry last night. He was at the Kielder rendezvous site with officers from Northumbria. I don't have all the details, but it seems the driver they were trying to arrest turned the vehicle on Steve and rammed him.'

'Was he in a car?' Kate managed to ask, imagining mangled metal, glass and blood.

Silence. Then, 'He was on foot, Kate. The lorry hit him head on.'

'Is he... did he?' She couldn't form the question that she didn't want to ask.

'He's alive. Multiple fractures to his legs and pelvis. There's damage to his spine as well. It's far too early for the medical staff to make any sort of prognosis. I spoke to his ex-wife this morning. She's taken the kids up to see him. He's in the Royal Victoria Infirmary in Newcastle.'

The words weren't making sense. She didn't know that O'Connor had children. As far as she knew he was single and didn't want to be tied down. How could he not have told her about his family? How...?

She realised her mind was skirting around the important information, not allowing her to focus on the extent of O'Connor's injuries and what they might mean for his future. It was easier to be outraged that he hadn't trusted her, easier to be angry with him.

Hollis was leaning against the side of the car looking at her with obvious concern. She signalled for him to get into the driver's seat so he wasn't watching her, making her self-conscious.

'Did they arrest the driver of the lorry?' Kate asked. The only thing that could make this any worse was if the perpetrator had managed to escape.

'He's been arrested and charged with trafficking offences and attempted murder. He's not going anywhere, Kate – they got him.' Her tone was calm, placatory and Kate allowed herself to breathe properly.

'Okay. Er, I need to find Sadie Sullivan as a matter of urgency and then–'

'No. Come into the office, Kate. Barratt and Cooper are here. I think you need to talk to your team.'

'Have you told them what's happened?'

'Not yet. I thought it best if it came from you but I'm happy to brief them before you get here if it'll help.'

Das was offering to make it easier but Kate couldn't accept. They were a team and they deserved to hear about this from her so they could move forward together.

'I'll do it,' she said. 'I'm with Dan and I can tell from his face that he knows something's wrong. I'll have to fill him in on the drive back to Doncaster. I'll be there in about half an hour.'

'What did Sullivan say?' Barratt asked as soon as Kate sat down at the large desk. 'Anything to suggest it's him?'

Kate shook her head. 'Not now, Matt. I need to talk to you and Sam.' She looked over at Hollis who seemed to be finding the grain in the wooden surface of the desktop fascinating. He'd been virtually silent since she'd told him about O'Connor, and she could see that the weight of knowledge that the other two didn't share was getting to him.

'Steve was hurt last night during the Northumberland case.'

Sam glared at her as though she were to blame. 'Hurt how? Is it serious?'

'Very.' It took a few seconds to relay the information that Das had shared but, for Kate, it felt like time had slowed, that she was speaking through liquid and the words were taking an age to form.

'But they got the bastard that did it?' Barratt sat with

clenched fists, staring at her as though he wanted to hit something.

'Yes. He's in custody in Hexham. He's been charged with attempted murder.'

Barratt exhaled noisily. 'Well, that's good.'

'Can we visit?' Cooper asked. 'Is he able to talk to anybody?'

'I don't know. His ex-wife and kids know he's been injured. Presumably they'll be allowed in but that might be it as far as visitors go.'

'His...?' Barratt looked from Kate to Cooper to Hollis. Kate was surprised. If anybody knew about O'Connor's home life she would have expected it to be Matt as they'd spent a lot of time together on quite a few cases.

'I didn't know either. Looks like Steve kept his private life very private.'

They sat in silence for a few seconds.

'Look,' Kate said eventually, 'this is a really shitty thing to have happened and I know we all feel awful, but there's nothing we can do for Steve at the moment. Das has promised to keep me updated and I'll make you lot the same promise. When he's allowed visitors, I'll make sure one of us goes up to Newcastle – and it doesn't have to be me. For now, I think we should all do what we do best and get on with solving these murders.'

As pep talks went it was pretty pathetic, Kate knew that, but she couldn't think of anything else to say. She felt empty, lifeless and totally lethargic but she also knew that work was the best way for her to cope with her anger and grief. She hoped the others felt the same.

'I've got news,' Cooper said. 'I've found Anastasia Cohen's car on CCTV on the night she was pushed off the bridge. I've been tracking back from where she was found, and I picked something up outside Rossington.'

'That's great,' Kate said, hearing the overenthusiastic tone in her reaction and immediately feeling disloyal to O'Connor.

'It gets better.' Cooper offered her a weak smile. 'It's going the wrong way and it's after the event.'

'Show us.'

Cooper connected her laptop to the whiteboard and turned on the projector. She tapped a few keys and a black-and-white image appeared on the screen behind Kate. A timestamp in the top right corner gave the date and time. It was less than twenty minutes after Anastasia Cohen's fall had brought the northbound M18 to a standstill.

'The white Audi is Anastasia's car. We don't know where it ended up but I'm hoping I can use ANPR cameras to track it now I have definite location and time.'

She hit 'play' and the car sped past the camera. Then she rewound and played the clip in slow motion.

Kate leaned closer, squinting at the windscreen of the car. 'It's impossible to see who's driving,' she snapped, frustrated.

'We know it's not the owner,' Cooper said. 'I'm hoping, if I can find it on more cameras, we might just catch a glimpse of the driver.'

'It's looking like Sadie Sullivan is a distinct possibility,' Kate said and gave them a brief account of her conversation with Lincoln.

'I'm not convinced,' Barratt said, leaning back in his chair and running a finger round his collar. Kate was pleased to see she wasn't the only one struggling with the heat. 'I could understand if she'd killed her mother first and then murdered the others to throw up a smokescreen but why start with Liv Thornbury?'

'I'm assuming that Sadie knew Liv at Greenham and has been either nursing a grudge or she's seen her in the local press, identified her and killed her for something that happened thirty years ago. Thornbury was undercover. If Sadie realised that, she may have felt betrayed or let down in some way.'

Cooper shook her head. 'But she was a kid. How old would she have been? Seven? Eight? What could these women possibly have done to her to merit murder? One of the victims is her own mother – that I can understand, it suggests a deeply personal motive but not the others.'

Barratt was nodding in agreement. It was a valid point. All children held grudges, felt slights as though they were punches, but few went on to murder the people who'd upset them. Had Sadie been abused in some way? It seemed unlikely – most accounts of the atmosphere at Greenham suggested it was nurturing and welcoming rather than abusive.

'Her father says she was there most of her holidays, until she started secondary school. Maybe she resented her mum for dragging her down there. It was hardly likely to be fun for a kid,' Hollis said. 'And she blames the others for making her mum keep going back?' His voice tailed off, he was clearly unconvinced by his own suggestion.

'I still think we need to take a closer look at Lincoln Sullivan. And those weird church people. What's their connection?' Barratt asked.

Kate didn't have the answers but she was still convinced that Cora Greaves had influenced Julia when she was at her most vulnerable in the hospital and persuaded her to keep information from her family.

She was about to put this theory to the others when her phone pinged. A text. She read the contents quickly.

'Sam. Looks like somebody's saved you a long and tedious job. Anastasia Cohen's car has turned up in a back alley off the industrial estate on York Road. Apparently, it was abandoned down the side of one of the units and it was spotted this morning when the bins were emptied.'

Hollis was staring at her, mouth agape.

'What?' she snapped.

'That's less than a quarter of a mile from Lincoln Sullivan's studio.'

35

Somebody had taken a crowbar or a baseball bat to Anastasia Cohen's Audi A3. The windscreen was shattered and the roof and bonnet were badly dented. There was little room in the alleyway where the car had been abandoned but whoever had damaged the car had obviously managed to get a few good swings at the bodywork. The driver and passenger doors were partly open and three of the tyres were flat.

'Looks like somebody set a fire in the rear seat but it didn't catch,' an overall-clad Martin Davies said. 'Lucky for us really. We should be able to lift prints from the interior as the mouldings inside the door are plastic and so is the steering wheel. Good surfaces.'

'Are the mirrors broken?' Kate asked.

The man pushed his hood down and frowned at her. His dark skin was damp with sweat and his bald head shone in the afternoon sun. He looked annoyed by her interruption, but Kate suspected it was more likely due to having to work in such an enclosed space in the heat.

'Everything's broken. Looks like it's been joyridden.'

Kate tried to imagine the sequence of events. The killer

dumped Anastasia off the bridge, drove off in her car, was picked up by CCTV near Rossington a few minutes later and then what? The best way to get rid of an unwanted vehicle was to leave it in a rough area with the keys in. She texted Cooper.

Try CCTV and ANPR around Denholm flats.

It was the most likely place to try to get rid of a car and would be obvious to somebody who knew the area. Once the car had been spotted it would have been driven around for a while and then burnt out – or so the thieves thought. Luckily, the last part of the plan hadn't worked.

'Can I have a look?' Kate asked.

The SOCO shrugged and pointed to one of the white vans parked nearby. 'Get suited up.'

White coveralls rustling, Kate followed step plates to the vehicle and peered through the open passenger door. She could smell something acrid and realised it was the failed fire on the back seat. Burnt vinyl and foam caught the back of her throat. 'No personal effects?'

'Nothing. Glove compartment was empty and all the side pockets in the doors.'

Kate pointed at the console between the two front seats. It was raised and padded on top with a nearly hidden catch below the padding. 'In there?'

The man tilted his head to get a better look. 'Not checked. Hang on.' He leaned in and, with a gloved hand, released the latch. The top lifted to reveal a cavity.

'All yours.' He stepped back allowing Kate a closer look. The compartment contained a lead to charge a phone and a USB stick.

'Bag those,' Kate said. She observed as he bagged and tagged both items, initialled the bag and passed it to her. She checked her watch and added her initials and the date and time.

'I'll log these on my way out,' she said, unzipping her overalls and shrugging one arm out, desperate to be rid of the cloying fabric which seemed to have trapped every degree of heat she'd given off and amplified it tenfold.

'I want the contents of that USB emailed to me as soon as possible,' Kate said as she handed the bag over to a uniformed officer with a clipboard and slipped off her shoe covers. He nodded, made a note and took the bag from her.

'Anything?' Hollis asked as she approached the car.

'Nope. Car's trashed. Looks like somebody tried to set fire to it but it didn't take. Found a USB stick and a phone charger but everything else has been cleared out. There's not even a tissue or a chewing gum wrapper.'

You think our killer did this?' Hollis looked sceptical.

'Unlikely. It looks like it was dumped for joyriders to find and have a bit of fun.'

'Denholm?'

'Probably. And half the CCTV cameras there have been smashed or taken down.'

Hollis stuck his hands in his jacket pockets and sighed. 'I thought we might finally have something on one of the Sullivans. It seemed like far too much of a coincidence for Anna's car to turn up so close to Lincoln's studio.'

Kate nodded, feeling as despondent as Hollis looked. 'And yet that's what I think it is. Just a stupid bloody coincidence.'

'Worth having another word with Sullivan? See if he knows where Sadie is?'

'I doubt it.' Kate sighed. 'It might look like harassment. We've got no legitimate reason for a visit and only one question to ask.'

She was about to open the car door when her attention was caught by a shout from the direction of the abandoned Audi.

She turned to see the bulky shape of Martin Davies jogging towards her like an out-of-season snowman. He was holding up an evidence bag and waving it at her. 'DI Fletcher!'

Panting, Davies thrust the bag towards her. 'Just found this trapped in the headrest of the driver's seat.'

Kate held the bag up to the light and could just make out a strand of hair. It was impossible to be sure, but it looked quite long. Anastasia Cohen's hair was short and greying.

'Root?' she asked – the root of a hair being crucial to obtaining a full DNA profile of the owner.

Davies smiled and nodded.

Kate grinned back. This was a huge piece of evidence. Lincoln and Sadie Sullivan had both given a DNA sample after the discovery of Julia's body.

36

Sam Cooper was smiling as she pushed open the door to the briefing room and deposited her laptop and a tray of coffees on the desk.

'Please tell me you've found something,' Kate said. It had been two days since she'd seen Anastasia Cohen's ruined car and one day since she'd received by email the contents of the USB stick found in that car. At first glance it had contained dozens of music files but Cooper had asked for the chance to see if she could find anything else and Kate had turned over all the information. An alert had gone out across South Yorkshire Police for officers to be on the lookout for Sadie Sullivan and Kate was considering extending it to neighbouring forces; possibly even going national before the end of the week. The woman seemed to have dropped off the face of the Earth. There was no sign of her at her house and her agent claimed not to have heard from her for nearly two weeks. He was especially annoyed because they were about to launch Sadie's new book and he needed her to sign off on some of the publicity. He'd never known her to be late for anything so to disappear was completely out of character.

'I've found something,' Cooper said. 'In fact, I've found a couple of somethings.'

Barratt and Hollis grabbed two of the coffee mugs and Sam passed one to Kate before using the remote to turn on the whiteboard.

'Before we start,' Kate said. 'I need to give you all an update on Steve.' She'd spoken to his consultant the night before and some of the news was positive. O'Connor had been revived from his induced coma, he was aware of his surroundings and could remember details from the night he was assaulted. The bad news was that he hadn't regained feeling in his lower extremities and the consultant didn't sound very hopeful.

The three remaining members of the team took in the news in silence.

'Okay Sam,' Kate prompted when the DC made no attempt to start her report. 'Kick us off.'

Cooper nodded. 'Firstly, I've been doing some digging into the death threats on Julia Sullivan's Twitter feed. Especially the one threatening to cut her throat. I wasn't optimistic but a friend of a friend helped me out and I've found out who the account belongs to.'

Kate kept quiet, knowing that Cooper preferred to reveal information in her own time. She also knew better than to ask about the 'friend of a friend'. Sam had a lot of friends who were good at finding things out.

'The email connected to the account is registered to a company in the United States. It's a publisher – small press, mainly religious stuff – but the registered managing director is Manning Johns. Mr Johns is also head of the Church of the Right Hand in the US.'

'That makes no sense,' Barratt said. 'Why would somebody from her own church be harassing Julia Sullivan?'

Kate remembered what she'd discovered on the forum a few

days ago. 'To make her afraid,' she said. 'Then Cora and Alistair Greaves could swoop in and comfort her. It's the way they operate. They isolate members from other means of support, friends, family, and then suck them further in. An up-and-coming politician could have been very useful to their cause in the UK.'

The information was interesting, but it didn't help with the murder investigation. It seemed that Julia Sullivan had been a victim even before she'd died and, had she lived, it was impossible to say how far the exploitation might have gone.

'Nice work, Sam,' Kate said. 'I'll flag it up as a hate crime and pass it on.'

Cooper nodded but Kate could see she was disappointed. She probably wanted to take it further herself, but cybercrime wasn't in their remit and focusing on this would only distract from the murder investigation.

'You said you had "a couple of somethings". What's next?'

'I had a look at the files from the USB stick and you were right,' she said to Kate. 'All the files are music albums. It seems Anna's taste is varied rather than niche. There's some eighties stuff – Duran Duran and the Thompson Twins – and a lot of recent artists. She seems to like Ed Sheeran, Adele and – no judgement – One Direction.'

Kate smiled as Barratt snorted a mouthful of coffee through his nose. 'Christ, she's in her fifties! Not really the target audience for boy bands.' He glanced at her, his face reddening. 'Not that there's anything wrong with being in your fifties, it's just...'

'Leave it, Matt, you'll only dig yourself in deeper,' Hollis said.

Cooper tapped on the desk as she watched their interaction – an impatient teacher waiting for the naughtiest boys in the class to settle down. 'But,' she said loudly, bringing their focus back to what she was trying to say. 'In two of the folders I found jpegs mixed in with the MP3 files. At first glance I thought they were cover art for the albums but they're not.'

She displayed a document on the screen. 'This is a screen grab of an email dated a few days ago. It's from somebody calling themselves "Titch" and the address is "titch_1983". Familiar?'

'Same email address as the one used to contact Liv Thornbury,' Kate said.

'This appears to be the second email, look.' She zoomed in on the text.

```
Hi again, Taz. I wonder if my last email
got to you — perhaps you don't remember
me so I thought another photo might bring
back more memories. I loved my time at
Greenham Common and remember you very
fondly. You taught me so much and I often
think of your stories and explanations.
You were my hero. Good times, eh? It
would be great to catch up sometime.
   Love, Titch
```

'It says "last email" so there was at least one before this. After a bit of digging, I found it in Adele's 25 album. It had an image with it.' The photograph was shockingly familiar. 'It's similar to the one on Thornbury's laptop.'

'Is Anna Cohen in the picture?'

Cooper highlighted three of the faces of younger women. 'She could be one of these but the photograph's grainy when I blow it up so it's hard to tell. There isn't a child in the image so no sign of Sadie Sullivan.'

Kate looked at the black-and-white photograph. Were all these women in danger or was it only a select few? Was there another victim out there already, waiting to be found and identified? 'I take it you've not found any replies to these emails?'

Cooper shook her head. 'No. I don't know why she kept these jpegs unless she wasn't convinced titch_1983 was above board. Which then suggests to me that she intended to meet this person and saved the emails as insurance.'

'Anything else?' Kate asked. They could spend hours speculating but it wouldn't get them any closer to finding Sadie Sullivan.

'There's this.' Cooper projected a still from a CCTV camera onto the whiteboard. 'It's the nearest working traffic cam to Denholm flats.' The footage played in slow motion and Sam stopped it after a few seconds.

'This is Anna Cohen's Audi. Heading towards the flats. And this...' she fast-forwarded, 'is the same car two hours later heading in the opposite direction. Look at the difference.'

The car was moving much faster as it left the Denholm flats area and swerved slightly before almost over-correcting as it approached the camera.

'It was stolen. We can't see the driver in either shot.'

She loaded another snippet of CCTV footage. 'This is from much earlier in the evening.'

It showed a section of road with a sign in the distance. A white Audi drove away from the camera, slowed down and turned left just after the sign.

'Where's this?' Hollis asked, leaning forwards.

'The car's just turned into the car park of the Dog and Gun. Twelve miles from where Anna was found but only a fifteen-minute walk from Denholm flats. If Sadie drove Anna's car from the motorway bridge and dumped it, she wouldn't have had far to go to pick up her own car from the pub.'

'She doesn't have a car,' Kate said. 'At least, that's what she told us. And it's a hell of a walk from Denholm flats to Sadie's house. It's on the other side of town, an hour at least.'

'Maybe she took her bike,' Hollis suggested. 'Left it at the pub and then went back for it. It would have been dark when she cycled home but she might have kept to lit roads. She might show up on a traffic cam somewhere if we can trace the most direct route from the pub to her house.'

It was a good idea. In the absence of Sadie Sullivan, the best they could do was to build the case against her.

'Good thinking. Have a look, Sam. Hollis and I will see if the landlord of the Dog and Gun remembers anything. Matt, I want you to find out who Sadie's friends are. Ask her father, ask her agent. Has she got a holiday home somewhere? Might she be holed up with an ex?'

Barratt sighed, obviously sharing her frustrations. 'I'll give it a go.'

'Anything else, Sam?'

Cooper grinned. She'd obviously been saving the best until last. 'I spoke to Sadie's agent,' she began. 'He's really pissed off with her because she's got a new book out and he needs her to do some promo stuff. He wouldn't tell me much about it, but he did send me this.'

She tapped the keyboard of her laptop and showed them a picture of a book cover. It was bright and colourful like the framed ones Kate had seen in Sadie's kitchen, but it wasn't the images that caught Kate's attention – it was the title.

'Oh, shit,' she breathed as Hollis read it out.

'The Monster in the Mirror.'

37

The Dog and Gun was part of a national chain of carveries advertising cheap meals and cheaper drinks. Built from red brick, it sat in a large car park like a blood splatter on concrete – its various extensions and wings reaching out towards the road and the hedge which separated it from a housing estate.

'Bet it's a bloody maze inside,' Hollis said, his top lip curling with distaste. Kate knew he wasn't a fan of what he called 'plastic pubs', preferring smaller, older establishments preferably with underground bars or industrial history.

'Not up to your exacting standards?' she teased. Hollis ignored her and marched towards the only door visible from where he'd parked the car. She followed him into a cavernous area with islands of tables and chairs dotted around on a scuffed, deep-green carpet. In one corner she could see the manic flashing lights of an array of slot machines and ahead was a long, dark-wood bar which ran the width of the room.

'Come on, I'm buying,' she said, nudging Dan to one side. She ordered a Coke for herself while Dan chose an orange juice and lemonade. Both asked for plenty of ice to combat the heat, which was stifling, despite the openness and space of the room.

'Is the bar manager around?' Kate asked as the glasses were placed on a brass tray in front of her.

'That would be me,' said the woman serving her. Kate had assumed she was a student doing a summer job or even a sixth former on a year out. The woman barely looked old enough to be serving drinks legally. Dressed in a lilac tie-dyed vest and baggy natural linen trousers, she looked more festival-ready than work-ready and the image was completed with the addition of vivid blue streaks in her blonde hair and a silver sleeper in her left nostril.

'I'm Lou,' she said as Kate and Hollis showed her their warrant cards. 'I'm the weekday bar manager.'

'Do you work evenings during the week?' Kate asked.

Lou snorted. 'I start at ten, have a couple of hours break in the afternoon and then work six until closing. The pay's shit but it's not a career choice. I finished my degree last year and I'm working out what to do next. This pays the bills and I get every weekend off.'

There was something a little over-earnest in her tone which suggested that she was trying to convince herself rather than Kate and Dan.

'So you'd have been here last Tuesday evening?' Kate asked

'Yep.'

'Was it busy? I'd have thought Tuesdays would be fairly quiet.'

The woman smiled. 'That's obviously what the bods at head office thought so they have a Tuesday Treat. Two meals for the price of one and a half-price drink. We were rammed, same as every Tuesday night.'

Kate wondered if Sadie had realised this, made it part of her plan. It would have been easy to pass unnoticed in a large crowd of people. There were alcoves and annexes off the main room where she and Anna could have sat away from the families and couples enjoying the discounted meals and drinks on offer. Scrolling to a picture of Sadie, Kate passed her phone over the bar. 'Do you remember seeing this woman in the past few days?'

Lou looked at it closely, giving the photograph serious consideration. 'Nope. Sorry.'

Kate took the phone back. 'How about this one?' She showed the woman a picture of Anna Cohen taken from her company's website.

'Hmm. Well dressed, looked like she was here for a business meeting rather than a cheap meal.'

'You remember her?'

'Think so. She stood out a bit. Asked for a wine list. We had a bit of a laugh about it because we don't do much beyond a basic red and a paint-stripper white.' She looked at the screen again. 'I'm sure it was her. Come to think of it, she *was* with somebody – another woman. Dark hair. The other one didn't come to the bar. The first one got her a soft drink. I remember thinking how sensible that was. This one switched to soft drinks after a glass of wine.'

'Sensible?'

'There was a bike helmet on the table. I assumed one of them had cycled here and the other one was driving. You'd be surprised how many people think they can have about four pints and still be under the limit.'

'Trust me, I wouldn't,' Kate said. She'd attended more than her share of road-traffic accidents while working as a uniformed officer in Cumbria and knew how people tended to overestimate their capacity for alcohol.

'Did they stay long? Have a meal?'

'I don't know. I just remember the first drinks order and the bike helmet. They were sitting over there.' She pointed to a table in a corner near the door. 'They weren't in my eyeline and it was a busy shift.'

'So you don't know when they left?'

'Sorry. But we have CCTV in the car park. I can call the company and get them to release the footage from Tuesday night.'

Kate nodded. 'That would be a great help.' She took a sip of her Coke and smiled at Lou.

'Oh, you mean now?' The woman looked surprised. 'I hadn't realised it was urgent. I'll have to find their details.' She disappeared through a doorway behind the bar.

'Looks like we're right about Sadie,' Hollis said, leaning on the bar. 'I just hope we can prove it.'

'We've possibly got DNA from the car,' Kate reminded him.

'She might say Anna allowed her to drive the car because she was incapacitated,' Hollis said, his tone morose. 'Or it came from Anna's clothing after they hugged goodnight and she was never in the car.'

'Bloody hell, you're Mr Negative today,' Kate said. 'Come on, everything's stacking up against her. Once we find her, we can check her email and phone records and link her conclusively to Liv and Eleanor.'

Hollis sighed and shook his head. 'She's clever, Kate. I don't think it'll be that easy.'

Lou breezed back with her phone in her hand. 'I just need an email address and they'll send the files today,' she said, reaching down to grab a pen and a pad of Post-it notes from under the bar. She slid them across to Kate and she scribbled Cooper's email address. 'Ask them to send it there,' she said. 'She's a colleague working on this case.'

Lou read out the address twice to whoever she was speaking to at the security company and then hung up. 'Anything else?'

Kate thanked her for her time, drained her drink and led

Hollis back to the car. They'd just set off back to Doncaster Central when her phone rang.

'Cooper. That was quick. Have you got the files?'

'What files?'

'You're supposed to be getting some CCTV files from the security company that covers the Dog and Gun.'

'Er… not yet. That's not why I'm ringing. I've had an idea about where Sadie might be.'

1984

I don't know how to face a week here without Taz. When we arrived, I ran round to where her bender had been last time and she'd gone. Just disappeared. It was like there was a Taz-shaped hole in the world and nothing else could ever fit into it. Mum says I'm being daft, that I knew Taz was leaving to go to university, but she doesn't understand. This place isn't right without her and I thought she wasn't really going to go. I thought university was just an idea, a story. This place needs her. I need her.

The police are different. They used to come in groups, gangs, and shout at us but now they seem to keep their distance a lot more. They still shout sometimes but now they spend more time pacing round the perimeter like tigers trapped in cages – but they're outside the cage, we all are. Or maybe we're the zoo animals and they just wander round and look at us like we're some exotic species that's interesting but might bite if they get too close.

The women are different as well. I wonder if they got some of their energy from fighting with the policemen (and they *are* all men) and without it they can't recharge their batteries properly. It's a funny atmosphere, like in the summer holidays when I can't be bothered to do anything and the air's all still and dense, so I just sit in the garden, not waiting exactly but not doing anything else.

Quite a lot of them have gone home. There are gaps around the perimeter and clusters round the gates as if the gates are magnets and the woman are iron filings. Or perhaps they're huddling together for warmth and protection. Sarah's still here but she's different – like a shadow of herself. She tries to be normal but she reminds me of my nan's old cat. Every time I thought it was sleeping and tried to creep up on it, it would jump up and shoot across the room. Sarah's like that now. She talks the same and takes part in the things going on around the camp, but the slightest thing makes her jump a mile. The other day we were sitting around and the women were talking about the miners' strike. One of them noticed a policeman coming towards us and Sarah leapt to her feet and ran away. She seems more scared of them now they leave us alone. I wonder if she wants to go home – back to her family and her life.

I thought a lot about that last visit and Taz's reaction when some of the women were leaving. She called them traitors but, now she's gone, is she a traitor as well? Did she say the same about me and Mum when we had to go home, or were we all right because we'd promised to come back? It's all very confusing.

There are still stories in the evenings. We sit round the fires, blankets draped round our shoulders like witches' capes and the women talk about their homes, or their jobs – the ones they used to have – or their husbands and boyfriends. Some of them have girlfriends – I didn't know that was allowed but Taz explained that it's just like having a boyfriend except she's a girl. They do all the same things. She winked when she told me that and I felt a bit odd and squirmy in my tummy.

Sometimes the stories are about the future – what it will be like when the missiles are gone and everybody's safe. Sometimes the women talk about getting rid of the government, the people who run the country, and putting women in charge. They say it'll be better, but there's a woman in charge now and they all hate her. I think it's because she tries to be like a man, all hard and tough, but she has to do that to keep everybody in order – doesn't she?

I sometimes think the women hate everything in the world. I could make a list: the government, the missiles, America, the soldiers, pollution, litter, factories, banks. There are a lot more things, but these are the ones I understand. They want to get rid of them all. Sometimes, when somebody has passed round a bottle of wine or whisky, one of them tells me that she's doing all of this for me. I want to tell her to stop. Or to do it for herself. I don't want that responsibility. It's not fair.

38

'Matt's spoken to one of Sadie's ex-boyfriends. He doesn't know of a second home, but they did spend a lot of time in Northumberland and south-west Scotland. Walking, camping, that sort of thing.'

'Sam, we can't check every campsite in those areas, it would take weeks and cost a fortune.'

Sam sighed and Kate got the feeling that the DC was trying to resist saying 'Duh!'.

'One of the things that's been bugging me about the Liv Thornbury case is the timing. If Sadie doesn't have a car, how could she have met Thornbury so early in the day? She could have stayed at a pub or a B & B but she'd have to have been up with the lark to get to Burbage Edge so early. What if she camped nearby? She could have got a train to Sheffield and cycled out to the Peak. If it's somewhere she feels safe...'

'She might be there,' Kate finished. 'But staying on a campsite isn't much less anonymous than a B & B. I'm sure they'd ask for details.'

'What if it wasn't an official site. Liv's climbing friends might know of somewhere that climbers use regularly.

Somewhere close to the edges. Let's talk to somebody from the club.'

'They might not be very keen to tell us about unofficial camping spots. It's illegal unless you get the landowner's permission.'

Hollis snorted. 'I'm sure plenty of climbers discreetly pitch a tent late at night for an early climb. We can say we're doing follow-up questions after looking at Matt and Steve's interviews – ask whether they saw Liv with anybody on her early-morning walks, or if there'd been any new faces in the climbing community.'

It was a long shot, but they had little else at this point.

Broomhill Climbing Club used an indoor climbing wall near Sheffield University's main accommodation blocks. Kate had rung Barratt's contact from when he and O'Connor had interviewed Liv's climbing friends and arranged a meeting within the hour with Tyler Dixon who ran the club that Liv Thornbury had attended. He'd been at the wall instructing and agreed to fit them in during his lunch hour. A short, wiry man in his thirties, Dixon seemed to be a bundle of barely contained energy as he showed them into the café area of the facility. It was just a corner of the building that had been carpeted and had a few tables and chairs. A short counter stood in front of the window with an array of sandwiches, tray bakes and bags of crisps. A kettle stood on a separate table with trays full of mugs, boxes of tea bags and a jar of coffee. Kate looked at the refreshments and declined Dixon's offer of a drink. His tight-fitting red T-shirt was soaked with sweat and his short blond hair stood up in spikes as he removed a safety helmet.

'What's this about?' he asked. 'Your colleague said on the

phone that it has something to do with Liv's suicide. I've already given a statement. We all have.'

'We're still investigating Liv's death,' Kate confirmed. 'It turns out it has similarities to two others and it now seems unlikely that she killed herself.'

Dixon sank onto a hard plastic chair, his expression unreadable.

'You okay?' Kate asked.

He nodded. 'Just a bit stunned. I couldn't believe Liv would do something like that, but she'd left a note. I went to her funeral, had a good cry with Sylvia and then sort of moved on. Much as I miss Liv, I had to accept what she'd done and respect it. Now I don't know what to think. It did seem weird that the police had started asking questions but I thought it might just be something routine.' He ran a shaking hand over the stubble on his chin and cheeks.

Hollis went to the counter and came back with a glass of water. 'Drink this, mate,' he said, sitting down opposite the climber. Dixon gulped it greedily.

'We need to know who might have spent time with Liv in the weeks before she died. Her partner said she had to give up climbing due to arthritis, but she was still going out into the Peak, walking around the edges.'

'She was still doing a bit of climbing as well,' Dixon said, wiping his mouth. 'Sylvia didn't know. Not difficult pitches and nothing overly technical. She said she needed to wean herself off, that she couldn't just go cold turkey.'

'She was getting up early and going for walks as well. Did she mention those?'

Dixon's eyes suddenly drifted to a group of children getting ready to climb. Kate could see he was working out how to answer.

'She was meeting somebody,' he said eventually. 'I don't

know who she was, and I don't think there was anything seedy about it, but I also don't think she'd told Sylvia.'

Hollis was making notes. He glanced up. 'You didn't mention this before. Did you ever meet this person?'

Dixon shook his head. 'I didn't see much point. Liv's dead and I only saw this woman from a distance. It didn't seem worth causing Sylvia any upset. I'd been camping near the edge to get an early-morning climb in and I saw Liv walking the track below the rocks with a woman. She seemed to be tallish and had dark hair but that's all I saw. I was too far away to see her face.'

'Camping?' Kate asked. 'At a site?'

'Er...'

'We're not interested in prosecuting you for trespassing,' Kate said. 'We need to know if there's a regular spot where climbers might camp.'

Dixon nodded. 'Okay. There's a clearing in the heather that some of us use in the summer. It's well known. Climbers from all over the area pitch up to get an early start.'

Kate could feel her heart rate accelerating. This was promising. 'On the morning you saw Liv with the woman was there anybody else camping?'

Dixon closed his eyes and pinched the bridge of his nose. 'I honestly can't remember.'

'And you didn't see this woman camping there?'

'Again, I can't remember. The deal is that you arrive late and leave early and never build a fire or use a barbecue. A few times when I got there, there were a couple of other tents, weekends mostly, but you don't always see who's in them.'

Kate passed her phone over the table. 'Could this be the woman?'

Dixon studied the photograph of Sadie Sullivan for a few seconds and then shook his head. 'I really can't say. She was too far away.'

A child screamed, either in pleasure or fear, Kate couldn't tell. Dixon looked over and smiled. 'It's great to see them so enthusiastic. I wish my parents had taken me climbing when I was a kid – it's so good for building confidence.'

'Tyler, could you show us where this campsite is?'

'Show you? Like, take you there?' He seemed confused, as though Kate's request was bizarre.

'If you don't have time, you could show us on a map.'

He brightened at Hollis's suggestion. 'Hang on.'

He disappeared, leaving Kate and Hollis to watch the children trying to follow the directions of their instructors. Most seemed to be coping well with the stretches and pulls as they crawled up the wall like Spiderman, but one was just swinging in his harness, giggling. Kate smiled at his obvious delight at being so high up.

'Daft bugger,' said Hollis.

'You're just jealous,' Kate said. 'You'd be terrified to do that.'

'True,' Hollis agreed. 'Must be nice to have that fearlessness. I wonder what age it all changes. When do we start to be scared of everything? Especially responsibility.'

'Whoa!' Kate said, leaning back in her chair. 'That's way too deep. Watch the little kiddies enjoying themselves and please, try not to think.'

Tyler Dixon returned waving a sheet of A4 paper. 'Here we go,' he said, placing it on the table between Kate and Hollis. 'You both okay with OS maps?'

Hollis nodded but Kate could only manage a non-committal grunt.

'This is Burbage Rocks,' Dixon was saying, pointing to a place on the map where the orange contours gathered together like a tiny musical stave. 'There's parking at the end here near the bridge, if you go out of town on Ringinglow Road you can't miss it. The place we usually camp is on this flat area.' He drew a circle in black pen about an inch away from a green dotted line which Kate seemed to remember meant a footpath.

'It looks like it's all heather but if you walk straight back from the rocks as soon as you see a big block of gritstone that looks like a mushroom you should find it. It's a flat patch of grass about fifty feet wide.'

Kate folded the map in half and thanked Dixon for his time.

'Did you get all that?' she asked as they walked back to the car. 'I assume you can read a map.'

'Not a clue. I failed my geography GCSE twice,' Hollis said.

'Great.' Kate sighed. 'Where's Bear Grylls when you need him?'

39

The sun was hot and high as Hollis squeezed the pool car between an old Land Rover and a small SUV. The tiny parking area was busy and the grass around the bridge dotted with couples and young families enjoying treats from the ice-cream van parked on the opposite side of the road.

'Wasn't expecting so many people,' Kate said. 'School holidays don't start for another few weeks.'

'Maybe that's why,' Hollis replied, scanning the knots of people. 'I bet these are all getting their fix of the Peak before it gets overrun for the summer.'

They set off, following Kate's memory of Dixon's instructions and the dotted line on the map extract. The peaty path was as solid as concrete and the heather and grass whispered scratchily in a faint breeze.

'You can see why Dixon made the point about fires,' she said. 'One loose spark and the whole area would go up.'

They trudged on, Kate's feet feeling hot and tight in her 'sensible' work shoes. *Not as sensible as a pair of walking boots*, she thought ruefully, stumbling over yet another thick heather root that was trying to throw a tripwire across her path. She looked across the lower ground to the west trying to make out the villages of the Hope Valley but the air was hazy and she could barely see the church in Hathersage. To her left the ground rose up slightly to the edge of the city and she realised with a jolt that they were probably less than two miles from Liv Thornbury's house. Liv and Sylvia may have been able to make out Burbage Rocks from the top floor of their house on a clear day.

'Does that rock look like a mushroom?' Hollis asked, stopping suddenly, and tilting his head to one side.

'Only if you've eaten some first,' Kate said, squinting at the chunk of rock.

'No. It does. Look, it's narrow there.' He pointed. 'Then it's thicker at the top.'

Kate looked more closely. He had a point. 'Is there a path heading away from the edge,' she asked, scanning the ground at her feet.

'There's something here,' Hollis said, pointing to a faint trail a few paces ahead of where they were standing.

He was right, there was a slash of dark peat cutting through the vibrant green, only wide enough for one person. Kate led the way slowly, the roots even more lethal than on the edge.

'Watch your footing,' she said, hearing Hollis stumbling behind her.

He mumbled something that sounded like a string of swear words before almost crashing into her back. 'Sorry, not used to this,' he panted.

Kate scanned the flat area ahead of them. The path was starting to fade as the heather gave way to springy turf interspersed with clumps of bracken. Four more paces and she was standing in a clear area of short grass with a few stones scattered around.

'Here, look,' Hollis said, pointing to a patch of ground near the edge of the clearing. Kate walked closer trying to make out what he was pointing at.

'This patch of grass has been flattened,' Hollis said. 'When I used to go camping as a kid, before my dad bought the caravan, he used to make me walk the pitch looking for loose pegs or rubbish we'd left behind. The tent always left a pale, flat patch if we'd been there for a couple of nights.'

Kate squatted down and ran her hand across the grass. He was right, it had been flattened by something, probably a tent, but it didn't help them.

'Much as I'm in awe of your bushcraft knowledge,' Kate said. 'I don't see how this helps. There's nothing to suggest Sadie was here. I was hoping there'd be somebody camping here who might have seen her.'

'Well you're out of luck,' a voice said from behind them. Kate turned to see a tall, well-built man dressed in combat trousers and a navy-blue polo shirt with the national park logo on the breast pocket. He was glaring at them with startling green eyes, nestled beneath wiry eyebrows which matched his heavy grey beard.

'We're police officers,' Kate said, holding out her warrant card.

The man crossed his arms and stared, clearly unimpressed.

'We were hoping to find somebody here. We think she may have been camping for the past couple of nights.'

'Well, she's obviously gone,' the man said. 'And good riddance.'

'Can I ask your name?'

'Len Whitehall. I'm a ranger and I'm sick of bloody kids coming out here to party. They have no idea how to behave. There's been more than a dozen tents down by the bridge some weekends and the sodding fires... They think they've put them out but it's all peat round here and it can be smouldering underneath for days. I have to keep checking that nothing's caught even if there's been nobody here for a week.'

'What about climbers?' Kate asked before he could continue his tirade. 'Many of them about?'

The man looked across the clearing as though checking that everything was in its proper place. 'We get a few. They tend to pitch up here, well away from the road. They're not the problem. They arrive late and pack up early. And they don't set bloody fires. I tend to turn a blind eye if it's only one or two. I still come up and check though – you never know.'

'So you're up here quite often?'

'Most days in the summer.'

Kate took out her phone, scrolled to a picture of Liv Thornbury and showed it to him. 'Do you recognise her?'

Whitehall drew in breath sharply. 'I should. I was there when the police got her down from the rocks. After she'd hanged herself.'

'We're investigating her death,' Kate said.

'That was weeks ago. And I thought it was suicide.'

Kate showed him her phone again. 'What about this woman?'

Whitehall stared at the photograph of Sadie. 'I'm not sure,' he said. 'She could be one of the climbing crowd. There's one or two women who camp on their own. There was a lass here last night, pitched up at eightish. I was on my way home and saw the tent from the track over there – wouldn't have seen it from the road. I'd been out in the Land Rover checking a patch of fence that had come down. The only person around was a woman down at the bridge – no car so I assumed she was hiking and had stopped for the night.'

'Did you speak to her?'

'No. Left her to it. She was filling a kettle with water from the stream, so I thought she probably had a stove and knew what she was doing. Besides, I couldn't see any smoke coming from up here.'

'And it wasn't this woman?' Kate showed him the photograph again.

'Could have been,' he said with a shrug. 'I didn't get a close look. She had long hair, tied back. Hard to see what colour because she was in the shadow next to the bridge.'

Kate thanked him and trudged back to the car leaving the ranger kicking over the stones and scuffing through the ashes to make sure there was no danger from the remains of the campfires.

'It's like she's disappeared into thin air,' Kate snapped as Hollis used the remote to unlock the car. 'If it *was* her last night then we've missed her by a few hours. It's so bloody–'

Her phone rang, interrupting her complaint. 'DI Fletcher? This is Staff Nurse Helen Ford, I was told to contact you if there was any change in Anastasia Cohen's condition.'

Kate released the breath she'd been holding since she'd heard the word 'nurse', fearing the worst for O'Connor. 'Go on.'

'Anastasia has regained consciousness. I haven't been able to contact her ex-husband, but her sister's on her way.'

'Her sister?'

'She came to visit after the accident. Left her mobile number and instructions to call if anything changed–'

Kate didn't hear anything else the woman said. 'We need to get to the DRI!' she shouted at Hollis. 'I know where Sadie Sullivan is.'

40

Kate spent part of the drive to Doncaster desperately trying to organise protection for Anna Cohen. She spoke to Helen Ford and told her that she wasn't to allow any visitors access to the unit until the police arrived. She'd also asked for Anna's "sister's" number but when she dialled it there was no answer – she suspected another burner phone. She just hoped they weren't too late and that somebody could stop Sadie before she gained access to Anna's room.

Doncaster Royal Infirmary was a bleak, sprawling mass of concrete and tiny windows. Kate knew where the intensive therapy unit was but she needed the fastest route to the ward where Anastasia Cohen was being treated. She checked online and found a map of the hospital.

'East car park,' she told Hollis. 'Don't worry about finding a space, just dump me as close to the doors as you can get. And then get parked. I'll text you when I know what's happening.'

She hadn't asked for the ward to be guarded because it was already secure. Entrance to the ITU was strictly controlled because of the risk of infection to the patients who were constantly monitored. But if Anna was conscious, that protocol would probably be relaxed.

As soon as Hollis stopped the car, Kate leapt out and plunged into the lobby of the eastern wing of the hospital. Last time she'd been here she'd approached from a different corridor and she was momentarily confused by the signs and the different coloured lines on the floor. She stopped and took a second to get her bearings then shot through a set of double doors and up a flight of stairs to the ICU.

'Anna Cohen,' she gasped as she reached the reception desk. 'Which room?'

The nurse on duty took a step back and glanced from left to right as though looking for backup.

'I'm a police officer,' Kate said, fumbling her ID out of her jacket pocket. 'I've spoken to Helen Ford this morning. One of my colleagues should already be here.'

The woman looked at her blankly. 'There's only nursing staff here. No police. Anastasia's in room six.' She pointed to the left and Kate nodded her thanks. They hadn't moved Anna yet which might mean that she was still under close observation.

'She hasn't had any visitors today?'

The nurse tapped her tablet. 'Hang on, let me check. I've just come on shift. No. Nobody's been in to see her today. She regained consciousness nearly four hours ago. Family was informed. She's still disorientated and suffering some amnesia due to the trauma. The specialist is optimistic that it may only be temporary.'

Kate hunched over, hands on her knees and sucked in as much breath as she could manage. She should have let Hollis do the running and she should have driven the car. 'I really am getting too old for this,' she mumbled.

'Sorry?'

She straightened up and smiled at the nurse. 'I said I'm

getting too old for running up flights of stairs. I left my much younger colleague parking the car.'

'Looks like he's here now,' the woman said, nodding towards the door. Kate turned to see a uniformed officer she didn't recognise.

'Where've you been?' Kate snapped. 'I asked for somebody to be here over an hour ago.'

The man blushed a deep and unflattering pink which clashed with his strawberry-blond hair and pale-grey eyes. 'Sorry, ma'am. I only got the call half an hour ago and parking's–'

Kate held up a hand to shut him up. 'Oh well, you're here now. And don't call me ma'am, I'm DI Fletcher.'

The blush deepened as he nodded.

'Name?'

'Redgrave.'

'Right, Redgrave. Stay here and don't let anybody in who doesn't work here or isn't one of us.'

She turned to the nurse. 'Am I okay to see Anna Cohen?'

The nurse nodded. 'Five minutes. As I said, she doesn't remember anything about what happened to her.'

She might, thought Kate, *with a bit of gentle prompting.*

Anna Cohen was lying in bed and looked much as she had when Kate had first visited, eyes closed, breathing regular. A doctor was doing something with one of the IV lines, her back to Kate.

'Is she awake?' Kate asked. 'I need to ask her some questions.'

The doctor turned at the sound of her voice and Kate froze.

She was looking straight into the eyes of Sadie Sullivan.

41

'Does this look like her?' Cooper asked, tilting her monitor so Barratt could see the still image from the CCTV footage.

'Who?'

Sam sighed. She knew Matt had been busy trying to trace Sadie's contacts, but he should have known who she was talking about.

'Sadie Sullivan. Is this her?'

Barratt stood up and moved closer for a better look. He reached out to tap Sam's keyboard but she slapped his hand away. Nobody touched her computers without an invitation.

'Zoom in,' Barratt instructed.

The black-and-white image showed a dark-haired woman wheeling a bike through a crowd of people.

'Where's this?' he asked.

'Zebra crossing between Sheffield railway and bus stations. I know Kate and Dan think she might have headed out to the Peak and I thought, if she had her bike, she would have probably used the train to get to Sheffield. The bike looks like it's got panniers on the back. Perfect for camping.'

'Could be her. When's it from?'

'The day after Anna Cohen was pushed off the bridge. We know she has an electric bike. If she's got a decent battery, she'd have no trouble getting to Burbage Rocks and back – probably three times over if she's fit and doesn't use the assistance.'

Barratt was staring at her, eyes wide. 'How do you know shit like that?'

Sam rolled her eyes at him. 'Internet.' She was about to give him a lecture on the joys of disappearing down a rabbit hole of fascinating information when her email icon flashed across the screen. Three quick taps and she was staring at more files of CCTV footage.

'Where's that?' Barratt asked. 'It looks like it's later in the day.'

'Car park of the Dog and Gun. Kate asked the company to send over footage from the night we think Sadie met Anna. Hang on.'

She played the footage at four times normal speed, narrowing her eyes so she could concentrate on the cars slowing down to park.

'There!' She spotted Anna Cohen's Audi. 'Thank you, Anna.' The woman had parked within view of the camera. Sam watched as she got out, hitched her handbag higher on her shoulder and walked out of shot, presumably to the pub entrance. Her shadow grew longer as she left the camera's field of vision and then it disappeared. Sam checked the timestamp. Just after half past eight. Assuming they'd stayed in the pub long enough to have at least two or three drinks, she fast-forwarded two hours. The car was still there. Sam sped up the footage slightly and watched as the clock in the corner got to eleven, then ten past.

'Here's Anna,' she breathed. 'Oh, and here's her friend.' She pressed pause and turned to Barratt. The image on the screen clearly showed Sadie Sullivan sitting in the passenger seat of Anna Cohen's car.

'Sadie Sullivan got in the car with Anna! Look what she's carrying. A bloody bike helmet. She must have left her bike at the pub and come back for it. Maybe she convinced Anna to give her a lift home and lied about the route.'

Barratt leaned closer, grinning. 'This is fantastic! We've got her. She was the last person to see Anna Cohen alive – this'll take some wriggling out of. Can we see if she comes back on foot later, or see if she leaves the car park on her bike?'

Sam thought for a second, calculating the possible time frame she'd need. She sped forward, watching as Sadie closed the passenger side door and the car left the car park. At around the time when Anna had fallen off the bridge she slowed the footage slightly. 'Let's see...'

They watched the empty car park as the minutes ticked towards 2am, then 3am.

'What's that?'

A shadow cast by the security lights in the car park. A black shape on lighter tarmac. It looked like a person, but it was hard to be sure of the detail. They watched as it disappeared and then reappeared but in a slightly different form. There was something else, an extension to the blackness of the shadow. A tiny spark of light off something metal.

'What the hell's that?' Barratt asked.

Sam grabbed a still and enlarged it slowly until it lost definition in a mess of grey pixels.

'Hang on.' She uploaded it into her image-enhancing software. 'Shit. Can you see that?'

Barratt turned to her with a huge grin. 'It's the handlebar of a bike. Looks like somebody was pushing it using the centre post. It's her. It's got to be. She left with Anna then came back for her bike. It's enough to arrest her, it *has* to be. We should let Kate know. And keep looking at the Sheffield footage. If she got there by train she might have gone back to the station. If we can find out what time she left Sheffield we might be able to trace her movements. Work out which train she took.'

Sam grabbed her phone and scrolled to Kate's number. She turned to grin at Barratt as she put the device to her ear, listening impatiently to the ringtone before the voicemail kicked in.

'No answer.'

She tried again intending to leave a message. This time the phone was engaged.

'Kate. It's Sam. Give me a call. I've found something interesting on the CCTV from the pub.'

The phone rang just as she put it back down on her desk. Hollis.

'Dan. I was just trying to get in touch with Kate.'

'Me too. She's not answering. We're at the DRI. Sadie might have been posing as Anna's sister to gain access to her. Kate went up to ICU to make sure she's not managed to get in to visit Anna, but I've not heard from her since. I'll see if I can find a number for the ward.'

He hung up but not before Sam had identified the emotion in his voice. Dan Hollis was on the verge of panic. Something was very wrong.

42

Kate couldn't breathe. The woman they'd been looking for was smiling at her as though she was happy to see a beloved family member.

'DI Fletcher. What a shame you're too late to help Taz. Or should I call her Anna? I hate to leave a job half finished.'

Sadie had something in her hand that glinted in the bright sunlight cutting through the window blinds. Kate couldn't make out what it was, until Sadie took a step towards her and she realised it was a hypodermic syringe. Automatically ducking out of the way as Sadie took another step towards her with the syringe held out like a weapon, Kate lunged towards the bed, her instincts screaming at her to check on the pathetic figure beneath the sheets. It was a trick. Sadie had bargained on Kate's training kicking in, urging her to protect life and Kate had done exactly what was expected of her.

'Shit!' Kate hissed as the other woman barged past her and out into the corridor. She couldn't tell if Anna Cohen was alive but there was nothing she could do either way. She followed Sadie out into the corridor shouting to the startled nurse.

'Check on Anna Cohen! She might have been injected with something!'

The corridor outside the ITU was around fifty yards long with doors leading off on either side but Sadie had obviously decided that flight was a better option then hiding. Kate saw her crash through the doors to the stairway and turn left. Up.

Aware that her phone was ringing, Kate hit the double doors at speed, using them to slow her momentum long enough for her to turn up the first flight of stairs. Chest heaving, she used the bannister to steady herself as she turned a corner and realised that there wasn't another floor above her. The only way out was onto the roof of the building. Four floors above the car park.

Her phone was ringing again but she ignored it, slowing as she approached a grey metal door that stood slightly ajar. If Sadie was waiting to ambush her on the other side, there was nothing she could do to prevent herself being pushed back down the stairs. *If* Sadie was waiting. What the hell was the woman thinking running out onto the roof?

Struggling to catch her breath, Kate fumbled her phone from her pocket, dialled Hollis's number and turned down the sound. He'd be able to hear her but, if he spoke, Kate, and more importantly Sadie, wouldn't hear him.

'Dan. I won't be able to hear you,' she explained, hoping he was listening and not trying to talk over her. 'Sadie Sullivan's here. She's on the roof and I'm following. Text Barratt or Cooper for backup but keep this line open. I need you to be able to hear what's going on and to respond. I have no idea what she'll do.' She removed her suit jacket, screwed it up and tossed it down to the landing before slipping her phone into the top pocket of her blouse and taking a step closer to the door.

There was a gap of about three inches between the metal and the frame, but all Kate could see was a thin strip of roof covered in thick felt. No sign of Sadie. She could wait until others arrived. She hoped her mention of the roof meant that Dan had told Barratt or Cooper to alert the fire brigade and ambulance as well as the police. Was that Sadie's plan? To jump?

Kate took another step. She couldn't accept that. Sadie Sullivan needed to be caught and to face justice. There was only one way that was going to happen.

The door opened soundlessly, and Kate stepped out into the full heat of the afternoon sun. No sign of Sadie. Where the hell *was* she?

Off to her left was a high metal dome with a grille in one side that Kate assumed was a vent of some kind. It was easily big enough for a grown woman to hide behind. Taking a deep breath, Kate tiptoed closer and then, in one fluid movement, stepped round to the other side.

No ambush. Instead, Kate saw that Sadie was sitting on the raised lip that ran all the way round the section of roof they were on. It was about two feet high and built from concrete topped with a row of red bricks. There was no safety rail, no barriers, nothing to stop a determined person from tumbling off. All Sadie had to do was lean backwards.

'Sadie!' Kate shouted. 'Come down. It's finished.'

The woman gave Kate a lazy smile. 'Not yet, it isn't. I'm still here. This was always the plan, didn't you see that?'

There was a sense of symmetry to the idea of Sadie killing herself after the methods she'd chosen for murder, but it all felt a little theatrical. Kate wasn't convinced.

'You don't need to do this,' she said, holding her hands out at waist height in what she hoped was a non-threatening gesture of openness. 'We can talk.'

The other woman laughed. 'What about? Nice day, isn't it? Got any holidays planned?'

'You don't really want to do this.' Kate took a step closer.

She'd done some training in negotiation, but her mind was blank – she had no strategy beyond somehow stopping Sadie from falling to her death.

'Of course I do.'

'Why?' Kate asked.

'Why?'

'Why did you kill those women? And Peter Houghton? What was it all about?'

Sadie sighed and rested both palms on the wall, either side of her lap. A light breeze flicked a few strands of hair onto her face and she tossed her head to dislodge them.

'They deserved it,' she said simply.

'Why?'

'They were liars. Except Houghton. He was just... what's the phrase... collateral damage? Wrong place, wrong time.'

Kate tried to remember what she'd pieced together about what Sadie might have experienced at Greenham. How had these people been dishonest? What had they told her?

'Do you know what it was like, growing up with that kind of pressure?' Sadie asked. 'I questioned everything I did, everything I thought, everything I bought. I was never good enough, never deserving, never worthy of the future that those women wanted for me.'

Kate kept quiet. She could see that Sadie was lost in memories, trying to tell her story in a way that would make sense. She took a step closer as Sadie's eyes drifted across the Doncaster skyline.

'I've been here before,' Sadie said, shifting position slightly so she could look straight at Kate. If she noticed that the distance between them had narrowed she didn't show any sign of concern. 'Well, not here exactly, not *this* roof. Everything I've done to those women I tried to do to myself when I couldn't live up to their expectations. When I felt like I was being ungrateful for what they'd done.'

Kate's thoughts were spinning as she tried to make some sort of sense of Sadie's words. She'd tried to kill herself because of the actions of her victims. What on Earth had happened to her?

'I was supposed to be different, to help make everything better but I couldn't. I just wanted to tell stories and I turned out to be bloody good at it. I'm successful, people love my work but all I feel is guilt. You've seen my home. When I buy myself something nice, I feel like I'm doing something wrong. What has it done to the environment? Was it made in a sweatshop? Is it ethical to have a big house all to myself? I can hear all their voices talking about communities and sisterhood and solidarity and I know I've let them down. I feel like I need to be punished. And I've tried. I've cut myself, I've deliberately stayed in abusive relationships, I've stood on bridges and ledges and clifftops. Because of those women. But *they* let *me* down. They made me feel like this when they've all done much worse things than me. They all lied and let everybody down.'

Sadie's fists clenched as she took a deep breath.

'Liv was the worst,' she said. 'She became one of us, part of us and all the time she was a spy. She was a police officer trying to stop us, to betray us. How did she live with herself?'

Kate took another half step while Sadie looked down at the roof.

'She didn't even try to deny it. Said it had been her job back then.'

'She was a decent person,' Kate said quietly. 'She did a lot for others, minorities, equal rights for women and the LGBTQ community. She was an advocate for diversity within the police force.'

Sadie shook her head defiantly. 'She was a liar! Like Eleanor. All that shit about building a better world, looking after the environment and then she went and married Peter Houghton. Sold out completely.'

Kate knew she needed to try again – to give Sadie something to think about. 'She still cared for people,' she said. 'Eleanor was active in her local church. A neighbour told me that she was scared of her husband but underneath she was kind. She tried to help.'

Had she seen a flicker of doubt on Sadie's face or was it just another strand of hair caught by the breeze?

'And Anna... Taz... she worked so hard defending people who couldn't defend themselves. You probably only heard about the high-profile case but that wasn't what she usually did. She protected women from abuse. We spoke to her ex-husband and she hated having to take on the case that was in the papers.' This wasn't strictly true, but Kate needed to buy time and if that meant embellishing the few facts she had, then she was prepared to add a few details.

'Doesn't matter,' Sadie said, shuffling along the wall slightly, her eyes fixed on Kate. 'They all lied. They all changed. Even my own mother. The woman who took me there in the first place. She became a different person.'

Another half step.

Kate's breathing had slowed to a normal rate and she could hear traffic on the road that ran past the hospital. A plane flew low, probably just having taken off from Robin Hood Airport and she heard the warning beep of a heavy vehicle reversing somewhere below.

'Sadie, your mother was ill. She sustained a massive head injury in the car accident. That's what changed her.'

'No. We'd have known if she'd been hurt badly enough to change her personality. She just turned against everything she'd believed in. She was a liar.'

'She didn't want you and your father to know. While she was

in hospital, she was preyed upon by some unscrupulous people who convinced her that they knew her better than you both did. They helped her to change by keeping her apart from you and Lincoln. She was vulnerable. It wasn't her fault. Sadie, she was still your mother.'

The other woman took a deep breath and shook her head. 'No,' she said simply.

Kate took another step. Three or four more and she'd be able to reach out and grab the white coat that Sadie had worn to disguise her identity.

'It's true, Sadie. None of these women deserved to die. They were good people, people who cared and were cared about.'

Another step.

Sadie looked up and gave her a weak smile. And then she leaned backwards. Kate ran forward, lunged and grabbed something. A wrist? An ankle? She didn't know but it was warm and solid. She clung tightly even as she felt herself being dragged over the edge.

'Dan, she's gone over the side of the roof. I'm holding on but I–'

And then she was falling.

43

'What happened to your beard?'

O'Connor smiled weakly. The lack of facial hair made him look younger, more vulnerable.

'They shaved it off. Hygiene. Apparently, beards are breeding grounds for germs. I might not grow it back.'

Another face came into view on the screen of Kate's tablet. Cooper.

'We've told him to grow it back. Nobody needs to see that ugly mug.'

Kate laughed and winced. Her arm was still in a sling to allow her broken clavicle to recover and the two broken ribs were incredibly sore even after five weeks of her being almost immobile. She tried to hide her pain though; O'Connor was in a much worse state and had a much longer and harder road ahead of him. He'd have all the support he needed through the Police Federation but she knew that much of his resolve came from the knowledge that he'd been injured doing the right thing and that his instincts had been rock solid. Houghton Haulage had been thoroughly searched and Tony Sims was facing some very serious charges.

Shifting her back against the pillow, Kate tried to find a more comfortable position. She still wasn't sure how Sadie Sullivan had landed on top of her, but she knew that, if they'd fallen all the way off the roof she wouldn't have been here, enjoying the banter of the others. Dan had quite literally saved her life. He'd followed her instructions, worked out what was happening and called for help. The fire service had managed to get an elevating platform in place below where Sadie had been sitting with her back to them. The drop had still been brutal because they'd not had time to get the platform in position properly. Kate and Sadie had fallen fifteen feet but both women had survived and, much to her annoyance, Kate had the worst of the injuries.

Sadie had been charged with the four murders and the attempted murder of Anastasia Cohen who was still in recovery. Kate had interrupted Sadie before she could inject the lawyer with whatever she'd had in the syringe, but the woman was still facing months of agonising therapy.

Kate's broken bones had meant that she hadn't been able to help with the house move – which was a blessing. Nick had sorted everything, including hiring movers to finish her packing and overseeing the final stages of the sale of her flat.

Now, leaning back on her bed... their bed... looking out over the fields, she knew that he'd been right. It was time that she and Nick made their relationship more solid, more permanent.

She smiled at the group on the tablet. Barratt had made a joke and Cooper was slapping him on the arm. Hollis was holding his phone so she could see them all, gathered on O'Connor's hospital bed. He'd been moved to Doncaster to be nearer his children and his ex-wife, and his colleagues made regular visits. They kept the mood light, never talking in detail about Steve's injuries, never offering false assurances about the possibility of him being able to walk again, but not treating him with kid gloves.

They knew what worked. They knew how to be with each other – and with her. Despite her doubts about her age and her capabilities, Kate knew she couldn't give this up yet.

They were a team.

THE END

ACKNOWLEDGEMENTS

I'd had an image in my head for more than a year before I began to write this book. It was something I wanted to use as the basis for a Kate Fletcher novel, but I had no idea how it would fit into a narrative. On one of our long walks along the River Eden during the first lockdown of 2020 my partner, Viv, was telling me about an article she'd read about walking on Greenham Common. I stopped, grabbed my phone and started to type. Within a few minutes I had my plot mapped out. I owe her a huge debt of gratitude for giving me this story.

Thanks, as always, to the great team at Bloodhound – especially Tara and Clare. I always feel like I'm in safe hands as soon as a manuscript is accepted.

A huge thank you to everybody who has bought my books over the years and to anyone who has left a review or sent me a message of support. Hearing that somebody has enjoyed one of my novels never gets old.

A NOTE FROM THE PUBLISHER

Thank you for reading this book. If you enjoyed it please do consider leaving a review on Amazon to help others find it too.

We hate typos. All of our books have been rigorously edited and proofread, but sometimes mistakes do slip through. If you have spotted a typo, please do let us know and we can get it amended within hours.

info@bloodhoundbooks.com

9 781913 942830